The
Atonement

Books by Beverly Lewis

The Atonement
The Photograph
The Love Letters
The River

HOME TO HICKORY HOLLOW

The Fiddler • *The Bridesmaid*
The Guardian
The Secret Keeper • *The Last Bride*

THE ROSE TRILOGY

The Thorn • *The Judgment*
The Mercy

ABRAM'S DAUGHTERS

The Covenant • *The Betrayal*
The Sacrifice
The Prodigal • *The Revelation*

THE HERITAGE OF LANCASTER COUNTY

The Shunning • *The Confession*
The Reckoning

ANNIE'S PEOPLE

The Preacher's Daughter
The Englisher • *The Brethren*

THE COURTSHIP OF NELLIE FISHER

The Parting • *The Forbidden*
The Longing

SEASONS OF GRACE

The Secret • *The Missing* • *The Telling*

The Postcard • *The Crossroad*

The Redemption of Sarah Cain
Sanctuary (with David Lewis)
Child of Mine (with David Lewis)
The Sunroom • *October Song*

Amish Prayers
The Beverly Lewis Amish Heritage Cookbook

www.beverlylewis.com

The
Atonement

BEVERLY
LEWIS

BETHANYHOUSE

a division of Baker Publishing Group
Minneapolis, Minnesota

Published by Bethany House Publishers
11400 Hampshire Avenue South
Bloomington, Minnesota 55438
www.bethanyhouse.com

Bethany House Publishers is a division of
Baker Publishing Group, Grand Rapids, Michigan

Printed in the United States of America

Library of Congress Cataloging-in-Publication Data

Names: Lewis, Beverly, author.
Title: The atonement / Beverly Lewis.
Description: Minneapolis, Minnesota : Bethany House, a division of Baker Publishing
    Group, [2016]
Identifiers: LCCN 2015038000| ISBN 9780764216572 (hardcover : acid-free paper) |
    ISBN 9780764212482 (softcover) | ISBN 9780764216602 (large print : softcover)
Subjects: LCSH: Amish—Pennsylvania—Lancaster County—Fiction. | Man-woman
    relationships—Fiction. | GSAFD: Christian fiction. | Love stories.
Classification: LCC PS3562.E9383 A95 2016 | DDC 813/.54—dc23
LC record available at http://lccn.loc.gov/2015038000

Scripture quotations are from the King James Version of the Bible.

This story is a work of fiction. With the exception of recognized historical figures and events, all characters and events are the product of the author's imagination. Any resemblance to any person, living or dead, is purely coincidental.

Cover design by Dan Thornberg, Design Source Creative Services
Art direction by Paul Higdon

16 17 18 19 20 21 22   7 6 5 4 3 2 1

In loving memory of
Herbert Jones,
pastor, missionary, encourager . . .
and my dear daddy.

November 28, 1925—January 9, 2014

Hope is faith holding out its hand in the dark.
—George Iles

Prologue

FILL UP THE EMPTY PLACES in your heart. . . .

These were the words I'd written in the first of several journals back when I came up with the idea of doing charitable work. Looking at it now, my initial plan had been rather impulsive, like a New Year's resolution. But the more I sought out new places to offer assistance, the more I craved doing so. *Jah* indeed, the more I helped others, the less helpless I felt myself.

So here I was, three years later, still continuing my weekly volunteering: reading to hospice patients, serving food to the homeless, and organizing donations with other Amish workers to raise money for the Mennonite Central Committee. I also managed to squeeze in my housekeeper-nanny job for Martie, my married sister, and still keep up with daily chores at home. It could be a hectic pace, but I was determined to fill every inch of my emptiness with activity, the kind that made a difference for others.

But it wasn't easy. Sometimes, my sisters nitpicked about my time away. Like Lettie and her fraternal twin, Faye, did just this morning in the autumn sunshine as we worked together to toss hay to the mules. As if to dare me, Lettie looked me in the eye. "Don't forget about *Aendi* Edna's canning bee tomorrow, Lucy. You promised to go."

I groaned audibly. *The work frolic?*

Lettie looked crestfallen as she took a swipe at the hay. "So you forgot again."

Faye gave a weak smile. "Between your chores and everything else, you don't have much time left for us."

"We're together *now*," I pointed out.

Faye looked sad. "Remember when we used to get up before dawn and go walkin' to the meadow overlook to watch the sun come up? Now ya rush off right after breakfast for parts unknown."

Despite the cloud of tension, we kept working silently. After a while, I tried to clear the air with a joke I'd read in *The Budget*.

Faye forced a little laugh, and Lettie looked pained.

"You don't even have time for a beau, do ya?" Lettie said out of the blue.

Faye stopped working, as if waiting for me to respond.

Lettie pressed further. "Not even Tobe Glick?"

Tobe again . . .

It was time to go inside and help *Mamm*. "We'll finish this later," I said.

On our way toward the house, with Faye and Lettie trudging quietly behind me, I could feel the westerly breeze picking up, carrying the scent of newly harvested corn. Yet despite the whispering wind, I could still hear my sisters' pleas.

───※───

Early the next morning, I hurried up Witmer Road to Ray and my sister Martie's place, just past a large Amish farm with a sign warning *Private Drive, No Through Street* posted near the end of its long lane. Multiple power lines scraped the pure blue sky above the familiar dairy, though of course none ran toward the house.

Ray and Martie lived on a lush rise of land not far from *Dat's* farm, their fields spreading out below the barn and house like an immense quilt. Younger than me by two years, Martie had tied the knot at just nineteen and already had two little boys: Jesse and Josh. Several times a week, I gave Martie a hand by redding up or cooking or caring for her towheaded sons, doing whatever was needed.

On this particular day, as I came upon the tree-rimmed meadow on the left, I noticed an older *Englischer* gentleman on the foot-bridge, where Mill Creek's banks met the golden cowslips. The well-dressed graying man looked somewhat *schwach*—feeble—as he leaned on a three-pronged cane while the creek gurgled past.

Slowing my pace, I stared . . . then let out a sigh. I'd seen this man on the footbridge on other occasions, always around this time of year. Perhaps even on the same day, September twelfth, though I wasn't certain.

Today, however, the man was alone, without his wife or lady friend who'd always accompanied him before.

The first time I'd spotted them, maybe ten years ago, they were holding hands and facing each other on the little bridge. I was struck by their affectionate gestures—the way the man sometimes slipped a strand of the woman's light brown hair behind her ear, or touched her cheek, even leaned his head against hers. Such a tender way they'd had with each other, and in public, no less.

Over the years, I'd wondered about the older couple. Perhaps the man had been widowed and found love a second time—most couples married for decades showed nary a speck of affection.

When I'd seen them last year, the woman had been weeping, yet bravely trying to smile. The man had taken a white hand-kerchief from his trouser pocket and patted her tears.

Englischers, I remember thinking. *Their emotions on display* . . .

Even so, it had been hard not to stare, caught up in the wistful *what-ifs* of my own life.

The picturesque footbridge *was* an exceptionally tranquil spot. Maybe that brought out feelings of nostalgia for the couple. Or was it something more?

Momentarily, I thought of going to meet the man simply to offer him a smile—willing to make a fool of myself—but he was clearly deep in thought and, if I wasn't mistaken, muttering to himself. Then I noticed his white SUV parked nearby and decided to keep on walking.

Although it was none of my business, I had asked around about the mysterious couple, but no one seemed to know anything, which wasn't surprising.

Still, I couldn't help wondering, *Where is the woman? Why did he come without her?*

Up the road, I could see Tobe Glick coming this way in his two-wheeled cart, his hand shooting high in the air when he spotted me. "*Guder Mariye,* Lucy Flaud. *Wie bischt?*"

I smiled back and wondered if my friend had ever noticed the older couple on his trips past this area. When Tobe slowed his cart, I asked him.

He squinted into the sunshine, straw hat pushed down over his blond bangs. "*Nee,* can't say I have."

"It seems strange." I added that I'd seen the man and a woman a number of times. "But only around this time of year."

"Might be some sort of anniversary," Tobe suggested. "Would ya like me to go an' ask? You're dyin' to know."

"*Ach,* Tobe."

"Well, ain't ya?"

Puh! He knew me well.

"Never mind," I said right quick. "See you at Preachin'."

"I'll be countin' the hours, Lucy." He winked mischievously.

"By the way, we all miss seein' you at Singings. It's been the longest time."

I laughed a little, and he grinned. Our private joke—Tobe had been hounding me about returning for several years. "You know I've outgrown youth gatherings." Truly, nearly all the fellows my age in our church district were already married and starting their families. And I was reminded of my single status each and every Sunday, when I was required to walk in with the younger teens and others who weren't married.

"Well, I'm not exactly a Yingling, but I still enjoy attending." Tobe paused a moment. "Even though it'd be more fun if you started goin' again."

One year younger than me, Tobe was twenty-four and still unmarried, oddly enough. Despite his attendance at Singings, he didn't seem all that earnest about his search for a life mate. Most Amish girls in East Lampeter Township thought he was too picky, but that didn't stop them from competing for his attention. He was handsome and very hardworking, yet there was more to his appeal. Tobe was a kind young man with a reputation for integrity—had a good sense of humor, too.

"Gut seein' you, Tobe." Tears were welling up. I had to get going.

"You too, Lucy." He clicked his cheek and the mare obeyed, pulling the carriage forward.

I kept my face forward. What's the matter with me?

Forcing my thoughts again to the older man on the footbridge, as well as to the missing woman, I knew I would never celebrate any sort of romantic anniversary—not in my best of dreams.

CHAPTER 1

CHRISTIAN FLAUD STEPPED OUT of the dark blue passenger van and paid his driver. Considering how glum he felt, he would have preferred to walk the three-mile stretch to the white clapboard meetinghouse. But his wife had urged him to call for a driver, following the strenuous day filling silo. After all, he was sixty-four now and not the young man he'd once been. In fact, Christian had almost nixed the idea of going, but for some time now, his friend Harvey Schmidt had been talking about the newly offered grief support group, unique to this community church. The small-group approach was an effective way to handle one's sorrow—or so Harvey said, having attended the launch of the Thursday-night program some months back. Christian, however, wasn't exactly mourning a typical loss, and Harvey wouldn't be there to sit with.

Sighing, Christian made his way across the parking lot toward the modest church building, taking note of the large pots of orange and gold mums on either side of the main door and regretting anew his past mistakes. Peering up at the quaint white bell tower, he recalled the last time he had been here. It was summertime, and he had been seventeen and in the middle of the worst running-around season—"*es Schlimmscht Rumschpringe*," his father had called it. His younger sister Emma had even scorned his given name. "*Christian, indeed!*"

At the time, he had stepped outside the Old Order church of his upbringing. But even so, it was with some degree of reluctance that he'd agreed to meet his then girlfriend, Minerva Miller, at the unassuming meetinghouse. Despite being raised with strict boundaries like Christian, Minerva had left their church for the Beachy Amish, but her path out of the Old Order was problematic. And the community meetinghouse, where a nightly revival was being held, had been their secret compromise one sultry July evening more than forty years ago.

Christian glanced at the line of gnarled oak trees at the far end of the paved lot, tempted by another memory. There, with the moon twinkling through the tree branches, he'd had the nerve to reach for her slender hand. *Minnie*, he'd affectionately nicknamed the beguiling brunette then. The recollection was dusty with the years, and he knew better than to let himself reminisce a second longer.

No need to relive that defiant chapter.

Still, it was odd the sort of memories a place could trigger. Like Christian, Minnie had long since married, and his short friendship with her had nothing to do with attending the grief group tonight.

This approach to getting help was so foreign to his way of thinking. "Help I should've gotten before now," he whispered as he neared the church door.

Inside, the entryway was profuse with flourishing plants— scarlet wax begonias and purple coneflowers, and a tall weeping fig tree, similar to some he'd seen in Saint Paul, Minnesota, at the Como Park Conservatory he and Sarah had visited last year. Christian wandered over to one side of the vestibule, to a large corkboard displaying notices and announcements and some tear-off pizza coupons for an upcoming youth outing. He was reaching to look more closely at a business card advertising a Shetland pony for sale when he heard footsteps behind him.

A clean-shaven, tall blond fellow wearing a blue-and-gold tie greeted him. "Welcome, I'm Dale Wyeth." The young man looked Christian over, apparently curious about his Plain attire. "Are you here for the grief support group?"

Nodding, Christian removed his best straw hat and accepted the firm handshake, glad he'd worn his Sunday trousers.

Dale Wyeth blinked awkwardly. "We'll be meeting downstairs. I'll show you the way."

Amused, Christian followed him to the basement room.

Downstairs, a handful of men and women were milling about, some already seated. He spied a vacant chair at the far end of the room and, amidst stares, hurried to sit down.

What have I gotten myself into?

During the preliminary remarks, the middle-aged leader, Linden Hess—a cordial man in short sleeves and blue jeans who introduced himself as one of the staff pastors—shared briefly that his eight-year-old daughter had died two years ago.

Christian inhaled deeply, shaken by the admission. *Eight years old.*

Dale volunteered to distribute the syllabus to the dozen or so folk in attendance as Linden emphasized the need to talk about one's grief with at least one other person as an important first step toward healing.

Christian shook hands with the couple sitting beside him—they had lost their young son to leukemia a mere three weeks earlier. There was such a depth of sorrow in their eyes that Christian wondered if he, too, carried his private pain on his countenance. *For all to see.*

When the minister began to read from Ecclesiastes 3, Christian's shoulders stiffened. He forced himself to listen, even though he had read the first four verses many times in the past few years: "'To every thing there is a season, and a time to every purpose under the heaven: A time to be born, and a time to die . . .'"

Christian looked straight ahead. Why did it feel like he was the only one sitting in the room across from the minister? The warmth from his neck crept quickly beneath his beard.

"Grief comes in like the waves of the sea, and sometimes it's deeper than expected—takes us off guard," Linden said, beginning the session titled "Shattered Dreams."

"Remember, grief is unique to each person . . . and at times it may be so distracting that you feel like you're trudging blindly through the day." He glanced about the room, asking for any comments or questions from the group.

One woman raised her hand and explained how unclear her thoughts had become since her sister's passing.

A dapper-looking gentleman in a red cardigan sweater, a three-pronged cane by his chair, admitted how hard it was to sleep through the night in recent days. "I keep reliving my wife's diagnosis." He covered his eyes with his handkerchief, and another man went to sit next to him. "I'm in the process of losing her . . . daily," the older man said.

Linden nodded sympathetically before continuing, his voice low as he glanced now and then at the man slowly regaining his composure. "Personally, I couldn't believe how unpredictable my grief was, and for the longest time. And even though we all know that death is a natural part of life, I never realized the debilitating pain it would bring."

Christian's heart went out to the older man, still wiping his eyes at the far side of the room. It was all Christian could do to stay put in his chair and not try to console him. *I can't imagine losing my precious Sarah thataway. . . .*

Later, Dale Wyeth and Christian were partnered for the sharing time that followed the session.

"Tomorrow it'll be one month since my father passed," Dale began. "I looked after him for a full year before the end came."

"Did he live with ya, then?" asked Christian, feeling uncomfortable engaging in such personal talk.

"My place was too small to accommodate my parents, so Mom and I took turns caring for Dad in their home." Dale's chin twitched. "They had no long-term care insurance. I did everything I could to help . . . and to give my mother a break."

The People had always assisted their ailing and elderly, even building *Dawdi Hauses* onto the main house to provide for aging relatives. But while Christian didn't put all fancy folk in the same box, he hadn't expected such a revelation from a Yankee. Dale's compassionate attitude struck him as atypical. "That's quite admirable."

"Well, I loved my dad—thought the world of him." Dale bowed his head briefly. "I still do."

Christian fell silent, remembering his own father, no longer living.

"Dad worked long hours at his hardware store to take care of Mom, and my sister and me, growing up." Dale glanced away for a moment. "It was the least I could do."

"*Nee*, 'twas the *best*."

Dale studied him, light brown eyes intent.

"I understand . . . lost my own father three years ago." Christian was taken aback by the connection he felt with Dale. He'd rarely talked of *Daed*'s death to anyone.

"I'm very sorry," Dale offered.

"My Daed lived a long and fruitful life. But losin' him . . . well, it's a grief that's been mighty hard to shake."

More plainspoken sharing came from the young man. "I'll

never forget the prayer Dad offered for our family before he closed his eyes for the final time." Dale's voice was thick with emotion. "It made me want to step up my prayer life; he valued it so."

Christian listened as Dale spoke freely of his family and the fact that he'd inherited his father's hardware store. "A fair number of Amish frequent it."

After the benediction, Dale stayed around, seemingly interested in continuing their conversation. "I realize this has nothing to do with the meeting here," he said, pushing his hands into his trouser pockets. "Frankly, I've been curious for a few years now about how I might live more simply, less dependent on the grid. The current solar storm activity and other natural events make me realize just how easily disrupted modern life can be."

Christian frowned. "Really, now?"

"I'd like to be more self-sufficient."

"Well, ain't something most *Englischers* would consider doin'."

Dale laughed. "If you knew me, you'd know I'm not like most 'Englischers,' as you call them."

"I'm just sayin' you might find it harder than you think."

Dale nodded thoughtfully. "No doubt." He hunched forward as if to share a deep confidence. "I've always had a do-it-yourself streak and have been doing a lot of reading about this. Besides, it's not too hard to imagine that we English could wake up one morning with no way to sustain the life we've become accustomed to . . . at least temporarily."

Christian ran his fingers through his long beard, suddenly leery. Dale sounded like some of those survivalists who spent decades preparing for the end of the world. "Not even your cell phone would work, if it came to that," Christian told him. "But I daresay all of that rests in God's hands."

"Definitely," Dale replied. "I believe that wholeheartedly, but I don't think it's wrong to prepare a backup plan. I think of it as getting closer to the way the Lord may have intended for us to live."

Christian noted the sincerity in the young man's reply, but he'd known a few folk who'd dabbled in the Old Ways and fell short, quickly becoming disillusioned and finding their way back to their familiar modern environment. Even so, Christian enjoyed his conversation with Dale and appreciated his respectful manner.

They said good-bye and parted ways. *An unusual fellow,* Christian thought as he waited for his ride. He certainly hadn't expected to meet anyone like Dale tonight.

Lucy leaned on the kitchen table to read her Bible in *Deitsch,* the room lit by the gas lamp overhead. She was pressing onward through yet another chapter when she saw her father enter through the back entrance. He bent low to straighten the large rag rug in the mud room, talking to himself as he removed his straw hat and shoes. Recently, she'd noticed the dark circles under his gray-blue eyes.

"Is your Mamm around?" Dat asked as Lucy rose to offer him something to drink or nibble on. After all, he'd left right after supper, where he'd merely picked at the roast beef and potatoes on his plate.

"She's upstairs early." Lucy motioned toward the stairs. "But I made a snack for ya."

He looked surprised, his eyes softening, and she felt obliged to explain. "Mamm asked me to."

"Oh, of course."

She opened the fridge and removed the tuna and Swiss cheese sandwich with sliced dill pickles, made the way her mother had instructed. She put it on a small plate.

"Lucy, listen." He made his way to the counter and rested

against it, his hands on his anguished face. "I did a peculiar thing tonight."

"Dat, you look tired." She moved the plate nearer to him.

He nodded. "*Jah*, but I can't go up just yet. But you go on if ya want."

Heading for the stairs, she paused and glanced back to see him still standing there, his expression unsettling. "You all right, Dat?"

He looked at her, opened his mouth. "I, uh, went to a class for grieving folk," he said.

She looked at him, stunned.

With a frown, he fixed his gaze on her, then bowed his head for a time. "You're long past it, ain't ya, Lucy?"

Her heart constricted, the old defenses kicking in. Without a word, she moved back to the kitchen, opened the cupboard, and took out a tumbler. "I'll make ya some chocolate milk. It's your favorite."

"No need to." He started toward the fridge, waving his hand nonchalantly. "I can mix it up myself."

She stepped ahead of him. "Go an' sit at the table, Dat. I'll bring it over to ya."

He lingered for a moment, tugging on his chest-length graying beard. Then he made his way across the kitchen, and the wooden chair made a sharp scraping sound as he pulled it out to sit with a moan. "*Denki*, Lucy . . . a *gut* and kind daughter you are."

She observed her father, obviously wanting her company. Yet she couldn't bring herself to join him.

"If you don't need anything more, I'm feelin' tired," she said softly. And with that, Lucy made her way up the stairs.

CHAPTER 2

CHRISTIAN STARED ABSENTLY at the green-and-white-checked oilcloth, still nibbling on his tuna sandwich long after Lucy had gone. Lettie and Faye had briefly wandered into the kitchen for some oatmeal cookies, offering him one. Presently, they stood over by the counter to chatter between themselves. *They have each other,* he'd thought many times over the years.

He raised his arms to stretch, hoping Sarah might still be awake when he headed upstairs. She alone was his solace. Lettie and Faye were dear sisters; that was apparent. Lucy, for her part, had always seemed more bonded to Martie. Christian felt sure the twins would marry within a few years, and at one time he might have thought the same about Lucy. She'd had such a winning way about her during her early courting-age years. *Back when we were close.* He sighed.

He recalled when Lucy was just four, and he had taught her to ride his brother Caleb's pony. Her coy little smile was all it took to lift his spirits on a difficult day . . . the way she'd peek around the corner of the stable at him. "*Kumm do,* little Lucy!"

he would call, and she'd run barefoot straight to him and leap into his arms.

One night during her *Rumschpringe*, Lucy had insisted on staying with him far into the wee hours, holding the lantern when one of the cows was birthing. *Always at my side*, Christian remembered, *before Travis Goodwin came along.*

The honey-colored wood planks shone in the light of the gas lamp. Sarah and the twins had scrubbed away the dirt that morning after breakfast, and he reminded himself yet again how blessed they all were. Lucy, as usual, had been off somewhere, probably volunteering. Neither he nor Sarah could complain, since she and the twins pulled their weight with domestic chores, making Sarah's load less heavy. *Once they marry, Sarah will want us to move next door to the* Dawdi Haus. He pondered how that might work when his mother was already settled over there. Perhaps they'd have to build another addition onto the main house like his older brother had just last year.

Christian was glad to sit there and fold his hands at the table he'd made for sweet Sarah decades ago. *The most beautiful bride ever.* He remembered his first glimpse of her that long-ago November morning as she took her place on the first row of benches, there in her father's farmhouse, a picture of loveliness and virtue in her newly made royal blue dress and sheer white apron. His bride for life, handpicked by the Lord God above.

Christian rose from the table, drifting out to the white wraparound porch, where the hickory rockers still sat even this late in the season. Last fall, he'd created a meandering walkway through Sarah's flower beds with large, flat fieldstones as a surprise for her while she was over in Williamsport visiting a cousin. He'd filled in the gaps with low-growing moss to make it extra nice. Well, Sarah could hardly believe it when she returned, calling it the prettiest garden path she'd ever seen.

Smiling at the memory, he drew in the night air. The grief

meeting was something he really didn't want to think about . . . there'd been such a burden of sorrow in that room. The porch seemed to sigh under the weight of his thoughts.

Christian looked south toward the dark fields, and in the distance, the windows of farmhouses flickered gold. Crickets pulsed in rhythmic chorus, and one of the barn toms wandered over and rubbed up against his leg, meowing loudly. "It's nearly bedtime, Ol' Thomas," he said with a glance down.

He thought of Dale Wyeth, his assigned partner for the duration of the sessions, and looked forward to seeing him again next Thursday at the group. *For certain, the world would be a better place if everyone yearned for a less complicated life.*

Upstairs, Christian reached for the flashlight he and Sarah kept on a low shelf near the bed and made his way to the bureau for his pajamas. After pulling them on, he found Sarah asleep, her waist-length hair spilling over one shoulder. She had taken to putting her graying light brown locks into a thick ponytail at night, and he rather liked it.

In the dimness, Sarah moved in her sleep. "Just now home?" she murmured.

"*Nee,* was downstairs sittin' a spell." He moved to her bedside and perched there, reaching to stroke her soft face.

She raised her head slightly. "Wanna light the lamp?"

He leaned over and kissed her cheek. "Just rest, love . . . we'll talk in the mornin'." Switching off the flashlight, he wished he felt up to telling Sarah about the surprising things he'd learned this strange yet enlightening night. *Especially that grief can last for years,* he thought. *All the same, where does my grief fit with the group?*

Christian shook his head. "Maybe nowhere at all . . ." he whispered.

"Gonna stay up all hours?" Lucy asked, standing in the doorway of her twin sisters' shared room. They had been whispering and attempted to squelch their merriment the moment Lucy made her presence known.

"We might," Lettie giggled, her wheat-colored hair in a loose braid.

Lettie would much rather be married than still living at home. Faye, on the other hand, seemed content to wait patiently for God to bring the right fellow around.

"Where'd Dat take himself off to so quickly after supper?" Lettie asked from where she sat on the small loveseat, facing Faye on the edge of the bed. The moonlight poured in through the windows, the green shades still up.

"If Dat didn't say, then maybe it wasn't important," Faye suggested gently as she brushed her long blond hair. "Sometimes he looks ever so sad when he doesn't know he's bein' observed," she added.

"Could be he still misses *Dawdi*." Lucy stepped toward the window to peer out at the landscape below. The moon's white light made everything dreamlike.

"Say," Lettie spoke up, "Rebekah Glick heard that Tobe and you were talkin' out on the road."

Lucy sighed. "You and Tobe's sister have too much time on your hands."

Lettie giggled. "Well, *you* two should stop pretending you don't like each other and get hitched before you're too old to have kids."

Lucy shook her head.

"*Ach!*" blurted Lettie. "Surely you find him ever so likable, don't ya? Everyone else does!"

Lucy took a breath. The twins were staring at her, eyes wide, questioning in the girls' usual spirited way. A moment passed before Lucy smiled, and her sisters seemed to relax.

"Well?" Lettie asked.

Lucy crossed her arms. "Fine. If you're really so curious—"

"We are!" Lettie and Faye cried nearly in unison.

"Tobe's a nice enough fella, but—"

"You're not interested," Lettie said. "Isn't that what you *always* say?"

"But what if he's the only one left?" Faye interjected before Lucy could answer.

Lettie rose from the loveseat and headed for bed. "Have ya thought 'bout that, Lucy?" She pulled the quilt up to her chin.

Lucy tried to keep her composure. "If Tobe's the only one left, then that's how it'll be, I 'spect." She moved away from the window, toward the footboard and leaned on it, looking down at her sisters there in bed.

"Could you outen the light for us?" Lettie asked.

"If you're ready to sleep . . . I'll spare ya havin' to get up again."

The twins agreed they needed a good night's rest—they were planning to get up extra early to help Dat with shearing sheep over at their closest-in-age brother's place. James's farm was within walking distance down Witmer Road, since Dat had parceled the last bit of land off to his youngest son.

"You'll be servin' food to the homeless again tomorrow, I 'spect," Faye said, smiling sweetly. "Like each Friday noon."

Lucy nodded. "I've come to know those poor people," she said, going to put out the lamp. "I'll see yous in the mornin'."

"I realize I grumble sometimes 'bout missin' ya," Faye said. "Still, I love that ya care so for others."

"And I love you," Lucy said.

"*Gut Nacht*," Lettie murmured softly. "Maybe *we* should dress in tatters. We might see ya more often."

Lucy smiled as she left the room. *Lettie, Lettie*, she thought.

Her sisters began talking again, and she paused in the hallway.

"I think she *does* like him but won't say," Lettie said, revisiting the discussion about Tobe.

"*Jah*," Faye replied. "You might be right."

"What's more, I think Lucy knows where Dat went tonight," Lettie said.

"Does it matter?" Faye replied.

Lettie was silent for a moment. Then she said in a loud whisper, "Why does everything have to be a mystery round here?"

Lucy didn't need to hear more and slipped off to the end of the hallway, where she opened the door to the third floor and made her way up the steep stairs. For some years, she had enjoyed the privacy of this spacious bedroom, complete with a sunroom at one end. Mamm had seen to that when it was decided, Lucy recalled now.

On a night like this one, with a splendid moon, she had the benefit of the silvery light spreading across the hardwood floor and the large multicolored rag rug beside the bed. Like the twins, she, too, had a loveseat made by Dat and upholstered in leaf-green by Dawdi Flaud before his passing. It was set near the hope chest under one window. And by the windowsill, five African violet plants blossomed—pinks and purples, her favorites.

She made her way to the double bed and lay down on the green-and-yellow Bars quilt. She ran her hand over the pattern, a quilt she and Dat's Mamm had made together. A widow for three years, *Mammi* Flaud lived in the connecting *Dawdi Haus*, something for which Lucy was grateful. Her elderly grandmother had a way of tempering nearly everything with her lighthearted and positive outlook on life.

Like Tobe . . .

Despite feeling all in, Lucy rose to get her knitting—a surprise she was making for a homeless teen mother. While she finished off the final rows, she thought of Lettie and Faye in the bedroom below. Sometimes she envied their close sisterly bond. What *would* it be like to have a twin? Naturally, she had great affection for all three of her sisters, and she was thankful for Mamm's kindhearted way with Lettie and Faye. *Our mother knows how to manage those two . . . keep things private.*

Staring into the darkness outside, Lucy recalled the twins' endless curiosity about Tobe, always so sure they were on to something.

"Surely you find him ever so likable, don't ya?" Lettie had blurted.

Jah, Lucy thought wistfully. *Ever so . . .*

Restless in the wee hours, Christian realized he'd left his papers from the grief support meeting in the hired driver's van. Clad in his hand-sewn blue pajamas and long tan bathrobe, he rose from the bed and walked downstairs to the front room. He was amazed by how light it remained outside. The pompous grandfather clock, bequeathed to Sarah by her maternal grandmother, chimed twice, the sound so strident in the stillness that Christian recoiled as he stood at the front window.

He contemplated the course outline, wishing he had kept it in his care. At this quiet hour, he felt the need to reread its pages.

Moving from the window, he wandered to the kitchen, lit the lamp, and noticed Lucy's Bible still lying on the table. He wasn't in the habit of looking at his daughters' personal things, but he found himself opening the Pennsylvania Dutch translation and saw what Lucy had written inside the front cover: *I don't want to do what's wrong, really, but I seem to do it anyway.* Then she'd copied the eighteenth verse of Romans chapter seven word for word: *"For I know that in me (that is, in my flesh,) dwelleth no good thing: for to will is present with me; but how to perform that which is good I find not."*

Christian closed the Bible reverently and sat on the wooden bench that ran the length of the table. "Dear, dear Lucy," he said tenderly. "We're *both* stuck in the past, but one of us denies it," he whispered.

Leaning his head into his hands, he wondered what to do about next Thursday's meeting at the community church. Should he return?

He considered asking Lucy along, wondering how she might respond. It was probably out of the question, since she wasn't the same daughter to him—altogether unlike the youngster with adoration shining from her eyes, proud of her big, strong Dat.

She's lost faith in me, he thought. Besides that, somehow or other, Lucy had managed to free herself from the heartache. Either that or she'd shoved the pain away, where it couldn't gnaw at her heart.

Like I've tried to do . . .

CHAPTER 3

ON THE RIDE INTO TOWN the next morning, Lucy considered the verse she'd read earlier in her devotional book. *Verily I say unto you, Inasmuch as ye have done it unto one of the least of these my brethren, ye have done it unto me.*

She stared out the window, clutching the large bag filled with items she'd gathered over the past week and her finished knit surprise as her driver pulled into the parking lot for the local Salvation Army. Ken Rohrer, Laurita Robinson, and Jan Scott—regular English volunteers—were already loading up the soup truck for the noontime run. The vehicle was on its last legs, she'd been told, with a shaky transmission, and Ken liked to joke that it resembled a silver Winnebago. During the winter, the heater barely kept their hands warm enough to serve food through the opening in the side, and in the deep of summer, the air conditioning frequently went out, leaving them with only two small rotating fans as defense against the pounding sun. Inside, with hot food in close quarters, Lucy and the other servers perspired until their clothes were damp, but no one complained.

Today, however, the weather was ideal, and Lucy paid her

driver, reminding him when to pick her up that afternoon. She rushed over to the food truck to see what was left to be done. From inside, Laurita called, "Roast beef today!"

Smiling, Lucy climbed the back steps of the truck, placed her sack with two scarves and a warm blanket inside, and then perused the shelves and drawers, taking note. They were short on sugar packets, plastic forks, and napkins, and they needed another large serving spoon.

"Ken's getting the coffee," Laurita said, rushing out. "I'll check on the donations."

"*Gut*, I'll get the rest," Lucy replied, hoping there was enough sugar this time.

Once the truck was ready to go, Lucy settled in with Laurita and Jan on the side seats while Ken drove across town to the designated vacant lot where typically up to a hundred hungry and homeless folk would be waiting.

I hope there are no fistfights today, thought Lucy, sighing. The last run, she'd actually abandoned her serving station, rushing out with Ken and another guy to get between two angry and clearly intoxicated men. Fortunately they were able to get them calmed down without anyone having to call 9-1-1.

As they rode to the site, Lucy thought of Kiana and her little boy, Van, with whom she'd become acquainted early last spring. During her pregnancy, the slight, dark-eyed teenager had been kicked out of the house by her widower father after refusing to tell her boyfriend, who'd later found out anyway and wanted nothing to do with the baby once he was born. The poor girl had gone from one friend's house to another until her options had dried up. She'd been forced to choose the only viable alternative for herself and little Van—a homeless shelter.

Kiana had shared her heartbreaking story early on in the friendship with Lucy, who could scarcely wait to see the young mother and her two-and-a-half-year-old boy each week.

But a couple of weeks had passed, and Kiana and Van hadn't come to the Friday meal. *Where can they be?* Lucy wondered as the food truck pulled into the parking lot. The people began to form a line, but Kiana and Van were nowhere in sight.

Lifting her long dress a bit, Lucy got out of the truck to open the back door, where Jan passed the folding table down to her, followed by the coffee and water canisters, cups and condiments, and trash can. Once the drinks were set up next to the truck, Lucy opened the side serving window.

While Ken, Laurita, and Jan passed food down to the line, Lucy handled the drinks outside, her favorite duty. Most of the women who volunteered preferred to serve food. It seemed safer, more protected and insulated somewhat from the pain and suffering, but Lucy jumped at the opportunity to mingle with people, many of whom she'd come to know by first name.

"Lucy, my Amish angel," Old Chip said with a toothless grin as he meandered up to the refreshment table, holding his plate. "Roast beef? How do *we* rate?"

Lucy smiled and poured his coffee the way he liked it, handing him several packets of powdered cream. "Enjoy it while it lasts," she said, glad he was one of the first in line.

Wearing ragged jeans and an oil-stained long-sleeved shirt, Chip laughed. "What's for eats tomorrow?"

"Maybe your favorite—mystery meat loaf."

Once a high-level engineer, Chip had fallen into alcoholism and as a result lost his wife, family, and home. Now living on the streets and suffering the early signs of dementia, Chip grimaced good-naturedly at Lucy's remark. He gingerly carried his plate and coffee as he made his way to the curb, where he sat with a dozen or more other men.

"Have ya seen Kiana and her son?" Lucy asked the man next in line. Stout "Stan the Man," as he called himself, was cradling his plate with its generous helping of mashed potatoes and gravy.

"I'm not sure I know who you mean," Stan said as he grabbed the coffee Lucy offered.

"You know, straight brown hair, loud neon shirts, a little boy 'bout so big." Lucy indicated Van's height with her free hand.

Stan smiled with recognition. "Can't say I've seen them. Not in a while anyway. Any Kool-Aid today?"

She shook her head. "We rarely have it," she told him, deciding not to pursue her question with the others waiting. She kept an eye out for Kiana, hoping she'd still come. At one point during a lull before folk started returning for seconds, Lucy wandered over to catch a glimpse of the end of the line. But Kiana just wasn't there.

Maybe it was a good sign—Lucy certainly hoped so. Lucy had fretted, as well, back in June when Kiana hadn't shown up. But the following Friday, Kiana had returned and made a point of explaining that someone from a church near their shelter had come with a bus to take them, along with others in need, to a potluck meal in the church annex. *"It was wonderful,"* Kiana had told her, eyes sparkling. *"Like a Thanksgiving feast."*

Lucy couldn't blame her. Sometimes the soup kitchen meals were tasty, like today; other times they were hardly edible. It largely depended on donations, and the time and materials available to the cooks for food preparation. *Nothing like the meals Mamm makes!*

Lucy considered Kiana's circumstances yet again and wondered how a father could put his daughter out on the street.

She noticed Ken just beyond the food table, gesturing to Lucy's right. Turning, she gazed across the lot and spotted Kiana in her long black skirt, her little boy in her arms. Lucy's heart leaped up.

They're here!

Kiana and Van joined the very back of the line, and Lucy filled a number of cups ahead of time with cold water and coffee, hoping it would be enough to last a few minutes while she went to greet the young woman with dark hair and expressive eyes.

"Hey, Lucy." Kiana grinned when she saw her.

"I've been wonderin' if yous would come."

Van smiled up at her, his blue shirt stained with food, perhaps, and there were holes along the hemline of his little gray hoodie.

Lucy patted his head, and he giggled, leaning closer to his mother.

"It's gonna get cold soon, so I brought you a few things," Lucy said. "Don't leave before I get my sack to you, all right?"

Later, after Lucy returned to her post to pour more cups of coffee, she watched Kiana sit on the ground to eat, talking occasionally to her son. *What must her life be like, living this way . . . not knowing what her future holds?*

When it was time for mother and son to head back to the shelter, Lucy brought her sack from the truck and gave it to Kiana. Little Van hurried over and got another bowl of applesauce and one more chocolate chip cookie.

Peering eagerly inside, Kiana pulled out two small blankets and woolen scarves. Last of all, there were two pairs of knitted mittens—one for an adult and the other for a small child. "Did you make these?" she asked, eyes wide.

Lucy shrugged. "Didn't take long, really."

Kiana paused, studying Lucy. "You're so nice to us."

"I worry 'bout ya," Lucy said with a glance back at the other workers. "And I understand your situation better than ya know."

Tears filled Kiana's eyes. "Thank you," she whispered and gripped the bag, her son clinging to her skirt. Her fingernails were long, some split and dirty.

"Will I see ya here next Friday?"

Kiana nodded and blinked away more tears.

With a lump in her throat, Lucy went back to take her place

once again. Yet all the while, her eyes followed Kiana and Van as they plodded across the wide grassy lot.

How do they survive?

She began to pray silently. *O Lord, please keep them safe, along with all the others . . . the middle-aged man who calls himself Spider, and young Kat, who reminds Spider to wear his old sweater—remember her, God? And help stooped-over Nannie Rose, and Mort and Allen, and Dean and his sister Dawn.*

Lucy felt at a loss to recall each of their names. Besides, the familiar sense of futility was returning, suffocating her words. That same horrid feeling that had taken away all hope after she'd pleaded with God, night after night . . . with nothing to show for it. *Absolutely nothing.*

But Lucy wasn't the type to give up or give in. Not even when it felt like her heavenly Father had quit on *her*, even if praying felt like talking to a closed barn door. No, the Almighty surely couldn't ignore *everyone* she prayed for, could He? And if God answered only one of her countless prayers for those who suffered, it would be worthwhile to continue.

"Even if heaven's silent," she whispered, "I won't quit knockin.'"

CHAPTER 4

MARTHA FLAUD ZOOK—mostly known as Martie—sat with her little ones on the sunny side of the front porch Tuesday morning. She enjoyed a chance for a breather in one of the old brown wicker chairs she'd found at a yard sale over on Hobson Road. Of all things, she'd spotted a similar wicker table recently at an estate sale. She was still tickled about the purchases and the large rag rug she'd made for the outdoor room. The rug's cheery variegated colors stretched across much of the area where she presently sat watching chickadees fly back and forth between the two maple trees across the well-kept lawn. Earlier, she'd sprinkled dry porridge oats on the ground for the sparrows while awaiting Lucy's arrival. Due to her husband's appointment with the feed salesman, they'd had an extra-early breakfast.

Her older son, Jesse, pushed a toy pickup truck along the railing, puffing out his lips as he made accelerating sounds. The blue toy was something he'd seen and pleaded for at Country Crafters in the Bird-in-Hand Farmers Market last Saturday, though she'd encouraged him to choose a toy horse and buggy instead. Startled now by the boisterous screech of Jesse's imaginary brakes, the miniature birds flew far away.

Jesse was now trying to balance the toy so it wouldn't fall on his eighteen-month-old brother, Josh, who was toddling near. Martie smiled, delighting in the pretty morning while she wrote in her small lined notepad, jotting down ideas for her weekly column for *The Budget*. Martie enjoyed working as an Amish scribe for the well-known Plain publication, sharing bits of community news and happenings. She also relished reading other Amish newspapers, such as *The Diary* and *Plain Interests*, the latter being the source of the recipe she'd snatched up for an applesauce made with her favorite blend of McIntosh and Summer Rambo apples.

As she often did, Martie had decided to begin the week's column with a statement about the weather. *We've had cooler nights lately and were recently blessed with a steady soaker for a good half day. For those who planted late fall crops, the gardens still are not quite done, but canning season is coming to an end at last,* she wrote.

Continuing, Martie included news of her ninety-four-year-old Mennonite neighbor's recent passing, a woman well-known to the Amish in East Lampeter. Anna Esbenshade's funeral was scheduled for this coming Saturday morning, and many Plain folk would be present. Martie also added tidbits about recent travels, such as her older cousin and husband's trip to Altamont, Tennessee, where they'd spent two days with their son and family, getting a peek at their newest grandson. "They surely wish the new baby and his family lived closer to Lancaster County," she whispered to herself.

> *My aunt Edna Lapp attended a circle letter gathering in Indiana for a day of food, fun, and fellowship—timed perfectly to mark all the writers' September birthdays.*
>
> *Of course there have been other goings-on nearer home. Last Saturday, Mimi Yoder invited the young people over to play*

*volleyball. Since Mimi had just turned sixty-five the day before,
she was given a sunshine box with cards and handmade presents
from the womenfolk in the neighborhood that same evening.*

Martie put down her pen and looked up to see who was coming
this way. It was Eppie Stoltzfus driving her gray family buggy at
a good clip, slowing as she waved. Eighty-five-year-old Eppie was
clad in black, and Martie wondered what her persistent neighbor
had on her mind today. And where on earth was she going all
dressed up?

Typically Eppie would have stopped by to share the latest gossip, but today her carriage kept going, much to Martie's relief. She
was determined not to write the tittle-tattle the woman seemed
so anxious to share. *"Such interesting reading for* The Budget, *ya
know?"* Eppie would say, brown eyes alight. Her most recent visit
had to do with a letter from an elderly aunt in upstate New York
whose Amish grandson had admitted to attending meetings at
the local chapter of Alcoholics Anonymous. *"Think of that!"*
Eppie had said, talking a blue streak about it yesterday when she'd
dropped by with a loaf of zucchini bread . . . and to feed Martie
all of this business. Martie, however, didn't think this type of
secondhand news was right for any column, so she'd stayed mum,
knowing that would not stop Eppie from trying again.

"Vroom!" Jesse hollered, getting too rambunctious with his
truck. His thick blond bangs flew about as he carried on.

"Now, son." Martie shook a finger at him.

Jesse made his truck explode with noise all the louder.

Little Josh startled, and Martie reached for him. He was chubby
and sturdy for his age, but he teetered forward into her arms, his
lower lip quivering.

"Kumm here to *Mamma,"* she soothed.

Ray had briefly questioned Jesse's peculiar choice of toy at
breakfast that morning, where Jesse had set the cherished truck

on the bench next to him while he ate his scrambled eggs and toast. Martie had brushed it off as something harmless. She'd wanted to please her son by purchasing it, yet she was walking a thin line with her husband as a result. "Oh, Ray, he's not even three," she reasoned. "Surely he'll tire of it soon."

To her relief, Ray had agreed—the toy was very small, after all. Martha did wonder where Jesse had come up with the idea of having a truck to play with, considering they were Old Order Amish. There certainly weren't any motorized vehicles on their farm.

"*Wie geht's, Schweschder?*" Lucy came bounding up the dirt lane to the side steps and onto the porch. She wore a pretty green dress and matching apron, her light brown hair done up neatly in a bun at the base of her neck. Her blue-green eyes sparkled as she went to hug Jesse, but she frowned at the sight of his truck. "*Ach*, where'd *this* come from?"

Martie waved off the question. "Well, you're right on time, ain't ya?"

"Would've been here sooner, but Eppie Stoltzfus spotted me walkin'—wanted to give me a lift, like usual. But I preferred to walk. Naturally, she wanted me to tell you somethin'."

Martie groaned.

"She wants to know why you didn't use her story 'bout that terrible saw . . . the one she says must've had it in for two different Amish carpenters."

Shaking her head, Martie asked, "Which one was this?" *Eppie has so many stories. . . .*

"A couple months ago, her neighbor got his hand caught in a saw, and then his own son did the same thing a few hours later on the selfsame day."

"I must've blocked it out of my memory." Martie grimaced. "Doubt the readers want the gory details Eppie's so eager to share."

"She has the most hair-raisin' gossip, ain't?"

Martie had to laugh.

Lucy was nodding. "I tried to steer the conversation to something else, like you do around Eppie. But she seemed real determined to tell me this directly. 'It's never too late to add it, even though it's after the fact,' she told me."

Martie glanced at Jesse, who'd perked up as if listening, but just as quickly he returned to playing with his truck.

Leaning over, Lucy kissed Josh's warm, plump cheek. "Just wanted you to know why I wasn't here sooner. Oh, and I need to run over to market later and pick up a few things for Mamm."

"You'll walk clear to Bird-in-Hand?" Martie lifted Josh onto her lap, and he leaned against her bosom, tugging on her apron bodice.

"Oh, I'll get a lift from someone, I 'spect, sooner or later."

"With Eppie, maybe?"

They laughed once more, till Martie noticed Lucy staring at the bright blue truck again.

"Ain't nothin' to worry 'bout," Martie said softly, nodding toward the truck as she turned Josh around to face his Aendi.

Lucy tousled Jesse's hair. "You're growin' ever so fast!"

Martie moved Josh onto her knee. "It's been awful hard to wean this one," she muttered. "He's such a Mamma's boy."

Lucy smiled and led Jesse from the porch into the house. Martie followed with Josh and set him in his high chair at the table with some small wooden blocks. She went to the fridge and poured a bit of milk into a sippy cup and set it down in front of her younger son, who winced but eventually reached for it and sucked away.

"Oh, don't let me forget to give you some extra linens and things I found in my closet upstairs. I have a-plenty." Martie paused, hoping enough time had passed. "Maybe you could use them for your hope chest," she added.

"*Denki*, but I really don't need anything more," Lucy said.

"Mamm's worried I'll be a *Maidel,* ya know. Like that would be an awful thing."

"Aw, Lucy." Martie was sorry for bringing it up and said so.

Lucy changed the subject right quick, moving to the counter. "It's *gut* of you to core and quarter the apples already." She placed them in a large kettle and slowly added the cider, then put the lid on to wait for it to simmer. "Looks like we're not puttin' up near as much as the twins and I helped *Mammi* Flaud do a few days ago."

"You don't know how blessed you are to have her just a few steps away." Martie felt she ought to say it. "I miss seein' Mammi as often as when I was still next door."

"You're busy with your boys, though. So I'm sure she understands. Things change when you get married and start your family." Suddenly Lucy looked glum.

"You all right?" Martie paused from washing the pint jars in the sink.

"Just thinkin', is all."

Lucy turned back to the gas range to stir the cooking apples. "Do ya need anything at market?"

"*Denki,* I did my shopping already."

"You're *schmaert* to buy store-boughten items way ahead. Learned that from Mamm, no doubt."

Martie listened, curious as to what was really going through Lucy's mind. This sister had always been a riddle and a half, funny and smart and thoughtful, yet sometimes so troubled. *And for good reason,* she thought. And yet, so much could have been avoided if Lucy had ignored her heart and done the right thing. *Jah,* Lucy was one of a kind in the Flaud family, with her constant activity, which annoyed Lettie and Faye to no end. But Martie guessed the twins still knew little about Lucy's deeds that terrible year, other than that she'd dated an outsider.

They never knew she was engaged and planning a fancy wedding. . . .

"When have ya seen our brothers last?" Martie asked as she stood the sterilized canning jars on end on the drain board.

Lucy turned quickly. "Not sure." She smiled faintly. "Does Preachin' count?"

Martie overlooked that, tempted to say something about Lucy's busy life, but held her peace.

"Here, let me dry off the pints," Lucy offered as the boys behind them began to giggle.

Martie went over to them at the table, hoping to see some block building, but what she saw made her join in the amusement. Jesse had several blocks balanced on top of his truck like miniature cargo. "You think that little truck can hold all those blocks, do ya?"

Jesse giggled again as Josh tried to knock them off the bed of the pickup, and Martie just let them be.

Later, when the apples were soft, Lucy helped Martie press them through a sieve and discard the skins, returning the pulp to a pan and adding sugar.

When they were finished with the sauce and Martie was cleaning up, she glanced at Lucy, who was staring out the window with the oddest expression. She looked lost, even pained.

"*Ach*, what is it?" asked Martie.

"I enjoy our times together so much," Lucy said simply before turning back to her work.

It gave Martie pause. *After all this time, she's still suffering.*

CHAPTER 5

THAT AFTERNOON LUCY SET OUT walking toward the Bird-in-Hand Farmers Market, past Hannah's Quilts and Crafts at the corner of Witmer Road and the Old Philadelphia Pike. She was careful not to lose her balance on the visibly deep ruts in the road caused by horses' hooves. The weather had turned warmer than in recent days, so much so that Lucy actually considered walking all the way, but when Danny and Rose Anna Yoder, a young couple from her church district, waved her down and offered a ride, Lucy gladly hopped aboard.

She noticed the seat had been newly upholstered and wondered how long it would be before Dat might have theirs redone. Mamm had been making enough hints here lately to get Dat's attention, especially after one of the little grandsons had wiggled his finger into a small hole where the fabric had been accidentally cut, making the opening bigger.

"Ain't surprised to see you out and about," Danny Yoder remarked, angling forward to look her way.

Lucy smiled. "I'm runnin' errands for Mamm."

"Off to market?" Danny asked, already wearing his black felt hat, which surprised her because it wasn't officially autumn.

"*Jah*, and if ya don't mind, you can just drop me off wherever it's convenient," Lucy said.

"Heard you've been helpin' over at the Mennonite Central Committee," Rose Anna said offhandedly.

"Oh, I like to whenever I can."

"My mother was talkin' with me the other day," Rose Anna went on, "and she wondered if any of you girls might help her sew up some trousers for my little brothers. I would, but Danny's been encouraging me to open my quilt shop behind the house. That's sure got my hands full."

Danny grinned at her. "Better go ahead and tell Lucy you're ready to open your doors next week."

Rose Anna pushed against him playfully. "*Ach*, you."

"What? Ain't a secret, is it?" Danny chuckled. "I say just let the word out."

"Are ya havin' a grand opening like some womenfolk do?" asked Lucy, curious why Rose Anna was being bashful about the shop.

"Ain't makin' much of a fuss." Rose Anna blushed.

"But I wish she would," Danny said, evidently interested in drumming up some extra income, like many Amish around the county. Farming didn't provide the income it once had, what with land so scarce and farms so small.

"Well, I'm sure you'll attract lots of customers," Lucy said, smiling. "And what a *gut* time of year to get your feet wet in retail, considering the fall tourist season's in full swing."

Rose Anna nodded and folded her hands in her lap. "That's what my parents have been sayin', too."

"I'll be sure to spread the news around."

"Oh, would ya?" Rose Anna beamed.

Lucy said she would. "And since I can't speak for my sisters or for Mamm, I'll just say that I'm too busy myself to help with the trouser sewin' you asked about. Real sorry."

"I understand. But would ya mind askin' at home, maybe?"

A little surprised, Lucy wondered why Rose Anna was seemingly putting her interest in opening the quilt shop ahead of her own little brothers. Still, she guessed she couldn't fault her for knowing her limits.

"*Jah*, I'll check with Lettie and Faye. They'll let you know at Preachin', okay?" For sure and for certain, Lucy knew firsthand how easy it was to keep overextending, till pretty soon you met yourself coming and going.

***

At market, Lucy moved from table to table, gathering up Mamm's requests first. Then she compared prices for cider spice bags and hot mulled cider, as well as fruit butters, so she could tell Martie, who was interested in eventually setting up a small store at the back of her house with similar items, once the boys were older.

Later, while waiting in line for soft pretzels—a treat for her twin sisters—Lucy spotted the well-groomed gentleman she'd seen on the footbridge last week. He was perfectly coordinated in a cream-colored cardigan sweater and chocolate brown trousers, and it looked like he was buying a quart of canned peaches from Rhoda Blank, one of her mother's friends. The man balanced his three-pronged cane on the floor as he fetched his billfold.

Thinking now was her golden opportunity, Lucy waved when he glanced her way. "Hullo," she said. "You don't know me, but I've seen you before a number of times at the small bridge on Witmer Road."

The man nodded his head, studying her. His warm, open face was lined with wrinkles. "I have to say you look familiar to me, as well." He picked up his purchase and moved toward her, leaning heavily on his cane.

"I pass by there on my way to my sister's place a few times a week, rain or shine."

His hazel eyes brightened. Then he glanced at his bag of peaches. "I bought something for my wife." He tapped the bag. "She has a real taste for anything peachy."

Lucy wasn't sure if she should introduce herself, because he hadn't offered to shake her hand like Amish menfolk typically did, even when meeting *Englischers*. So she made more small talk. "Oh, she'll enjoy Rhoda's peaches." She bobbed her head toward their friend's market booth.

"Yes, absolutely." His eyes glistened. "We often come to market together. Well, we did before she fell ill. . . ." His frail voice trailed off.

Lucy waited for him to say more, but suddenly it was her turn next in line for soft pretzels, and the older man seemed to take notice. "Well, enjoy the rest of your day, young lady," he said, dipping his head and moving on.

I should have asked his name, Lucy thought sadly.

On the walk toward home, Lucy could think only of the man whose sick wife had a hankering for peaches. He appeared to be close in age to Lucy's maternal grandfather, who lived southwest of Quarryville with her mother's eldest brother and family. "What a kindly old man," she thought, hugging the shoulder along the busy road.

The whine of leaf blowers came from the grounds of a nearby church on the Old Philadelphia Pike, and she slowed, out of breath, wishing she'd arranged for someone to pick up her and her purchases.

Later, when she passed Ray and Martie's steep lane, she wondered how the rest of her sister's day was going. Here lately, Martie had seemed a bit sluggish, having gained some extra pounds because she was less active in the vegetable garden and whatnot. *The boys are too small to be left unsupervised.*

⁓⁓⁓

Once she arrived home, Lucy found Lettie and Faye busy chopping vegetables with Mamm. Lucy set down the few things she'd bought for Mamm and removed the soft pretzels for her twin sisters, placing them on the table on a paper towel while the girls' backs were turned.

Leaving to gather eggs, Lucy smiled at the thought of Lettie and Faye's surprise, even though she wouldn't get to see their happy expressions this time. She thought back to Kiana and Van's delight at the gifts she'd given last Friday. At times, she stopped in her tracks when she thought of all the many homeless people in the area. *And around the world. So many need help.*

Tomorrow, Lucy would spend the majority of the day at the local hospice, where she often read to elderly patients. *If Lettie and Faye understood the joy of volunteering, surely they wouldn't begrudge my time away.*

CHAPTER 6

BEFORE BREAKFAST THE NEXT MORNING, Lucy remembered to ask her twin sisters about sewing trousers for Rose Anna Yoder's brothers. "She's busy preparing for the opening of her new quilt shop," Lucy said, removing a jar of strawberry jam from the pantry and setting it on the table.

"Did she ask you first?" Lettie said as she scrambled eggs at the gas range.

"Actually she did, but I thought either of you might have more time," Lucy said, immediately regretting how insensitive that sounded.

Lettie flashed a look over her shoulder at Lucy. "You must think your time's more important than ours."

"*Ach, Schweschder,*" Faye whispered, slicing the homemade bread she'd made yesterday for toast.

"Speak gently, girls," Mamm cautioned, her light brown eyes flashing as she carried a carton of orange juice to the table.

"I hesitate to say this, Mamm, but I'm honestly startin' to think Lucy's becoming a bit high-minded," Lettie said, demonstrating that mornings were not her best time of day. "I mean, what's she tryin' to prove?"

Lucy expected their mother to shake her head in disgust, but she sat down on the long bench and simply sighed. "Goodness, Lettie. Would ya mind sayin' what ya mean?"

Lucy cringed.

Lowering the heat setting under the eggs, Lettie then turned to face them. "Does it seem strange to anyone else that our older sister flits from one place to another all week long? *Ach,* she scarcely has time for her responsibilities here at home." Lettie paused. "Am I mistaken?"

Faye flinched, and Lucy exhaled under her breath. *Not again, Lettie.*

"Well, here's my question to ya, Lettie: Are you angry and upset . . . or hurt?" Mamm asked gently, and Lucy knew their mother was anxious to clear the air.

Lettie's expression remained defiant, but her voice hinted at tears. "Maybe all of the above."

Despite her frustration with Lettie's frequent complaining, it pained Lucy to see her this way.

"Doesn't it seem to you that Lucy thinks it's all right to ask Faye and me to do something she supposedly has no time for?" Lettie's face was pink.

"Surely ya don't think Lucy's passin' the buck." Mamm looked solemn.

"That's exactly what she's doin'. What's more, we rarely see her anymore." Lettie's shoulders rose and fell. "Been that way for years now."

Faye stood frozen beside the toaster, eyes downcast.

"What do *you* say to this, daughter?" Mamm asked Lucy.

"I don't purposely stay away from home," Lucy answered softly.

Mamm looked back at Lettie. "Your sister's old enough to

make her choices 'bout where she works or spends her time, just as you and Faye are."

"And we choose to stay an' help *you*, Mamm," Lettie replied.

Mamm frowned. "I recommend you apologize to Lucy right here, right now."

Lucy pressed her lips together and observed poor Faye, still standing near the toaster, looking terribly chagrined. *Faye's trying to mind her own business, bless her heart.*

But Lettie shook her head. "For pity's sake, Lucy's runnin' around like a chicken with its head chopped off!" With that, she left the kitchen.

The back door slapped against the frame as Lettie flew out of the house. "Oh, Mamm," Lucy said. "I'm so sorry . . . I hope—"

Mamm waved her hand. "Ain't your place to apologize."

Faye immediately took Lettie's place at the stove, and Lucy hurried to fill the juice glasses before Dat arrived any moment now. He wouldn't appreciate being stalled in his work because breakfast was behind schedule.

"I don't think Lettie slept well last night," Faye said sadly. "She's really not herself."

Lucy inhaled deeply. "It's prob'ly a *gut* thing I'll be gone much of the day, then."

Not necessarily agreeing, their mother looked weary as she rose to help get the food on the table.

Lucy considered various ways to smooth things over. She had forgotten promising Lettie a short walk. As for Rose Anna's request, she'd just have to find someone else to do the sewing, especially if Faye took her twin's side on this. But right now Lucy was more concerned about finishing breakfast so she could get to the hospice center on time.

"I'll do the sewin' for Rose Anna's little brothers," Faye suddenly offered, dishing up the eggs.

Mamm smiled. "*Denki*, Faye. Ever so kind."

Lucy nodded. "Be sure to let Rose Anna know on Sunday, *jah?*"

Faye said she would, and Mamm glanced toward the back door, a worried look on her face.

Surely by tonight, Lettie will feel better, Lucy hoped.

⁓⸻⸙⸻⁓

Christian pushed the barn door shut and started across the rolling yard toward the driveway. He glanced at the sky, trying to determine when the next rains might come. The air was rich with the fresh smells of soil and silage, and he thanked the Lord God for this beautiful new day. *Wilt Thou bless everything our hands find to do today, for Thy honor and Thy glory?* he prayed.

Just then, the back screen door opened, and Lettie burst forth, her cheeks bright red. She dashed toward the stable, gray skirt flying. "What's gotten into her?" He hurried his steps, his stomach rumbling. *Sarah will surely know.*

Earlier this morning, while reading his devotional book and having his first cup of coffee, Christian had pondered how to go about asking Lucy to accompany him to the grief support group tomorrow evening. But as before, he had come up short. He wasn't worried about being refused—that would likely happen. He was concerned about further meddling with their daughter's heart, breaking open a wound that refused to heal. It wasn't that Lucy was rude or disrespectful. But the vacant way she sometimes looked at him broke his heart.

I have only myself to fault. . . .

Reflecting on the day's reading, he recalled one particular passage about how nothing ever came into one's life unless the Sovereign Lord willed it. "I can hang my hat on that," Christian said, reaching the house. He removed his straw hat inside the mud room, then placed it on its wooden peg. He could hear Lucy talking with Faye in the kitchen amidst the clatter of utensils as he scrubbed his dirty hands in the deep sink for that purpose.

With everything in him, he hoped God might bring peace to his eldest daughter's soul.

But how, O Lord? What else can I do?

⁂

In her hurry to get going, Lucy had failed to take along her sack lunch, something she realized much too late. *I can eat later,* she thought, caught up now in reading aloud a short story from *Guideposts* at the bedside of elderly Wendell Keene. Over the past few weeks, Wendell had shared many of his life experiences, including the fact that, throughout his years, he had used his own money to plan other people's funerals—people without families, often destitute. Lucy had never heard of this sort of thing. *How sad that a person could die and have no family to offer respects!* For this and other reasons, she felt a unique bond with terminally ill Wendell.

The soft-spoken man's granddaughter and husband were the only family Lucy had met thus far, though during only one visit, as they lived in Illinois and the husband couldn't readily get off work—or so Wendell had excused them to Lucy. Surprisingly, soon after he'd arrived at the center, Wendell had declared Lucy to be one of his family. She'd smiled, humored that he was so accepting of a young Plain woman like her.

Closing the magazine after the story, Lucy couldn't help but see Wendell's tears in the crevices of his wrinkled cheeks.

"You must be tired, Miss Lucy." He gave a faint smile.

She shook her head. "I can keep reading, if you'd like."

His eyes were moist as he glanced toward the window, then back at her. "You must have better things to do than to keep an old geezer like me company."

Lettie's recent remarks came to mind. "There's nowhere else I'd rather be."

The man struggled to breathe, then started to cough. The

backs of his hands were marked with crusted brown age spots, and it crossed Lucy's mind that someday Mammi Flaud's little pink hands might look like this, too.

Wendell motioned for Lucy to lean closer. He drew a shaky breath. "When you're here reading or just sitting near, I feel peaceful . . . less afraid." He opened his palm. "There's something real special about you."

Lucy smiled, embarrassed.

"I know something about your culture," he revealed. "Most Plain girls your age are married and having a family, but you . . . you're here. Why is that?"

She gave a good-natured shrug. "Just haven't met the right fella, I s'pose."

Wendell frowned. "Well, you must be running from the boys."

"My family probably thinks the same thing."

Wendell folded his gnarled hands. "I wonder if you might consider reciting the Lord's Prayer for me?"

She nodded. "I only know how to say it in *Deitsch*, if that's all right."

"No doubt the Lord will understand." He chuckled and she enjoyed the sound, never having seen the man so jovial.

Slowly, she began to recite the words. When she finished, Wendell's face was wet with tears again.

"I studied German for two years in college, eons ago," he told her. "If I'm not mistaken, I picked up the words for *heaven* and *father*."

She was moved by his pleasure.

"I also attended church when I was a teenager . . . even into my adult years. Not so much in a long while, however." He paused, his breath labored. "These days I try to pray, but the words are like dust."

Lucy felt ill at ease. He was describing how she felt every day, though it didn't seem that Wendell was admitting to being angry with God. Truth be told, she couldn't imagine such a meek man feeling that way toward the Almighty, yet he seemed so discouraged.

His eyes, dim as they were, sought hers.

She patted his arm. "All of us feel lost at times."

He nodded. "Some of us more than others, I presume."

"You need your rest."

Wendell closed his eyes and chuckled again, more softly this time, whispering, "Rest has escaped me for many years, Miss Lucy."

She swallowed, feeling helpless and uncomfortable. Oh, if only her parents were here at this moment, one of them would have an appropriate response on the very tip of the tongue.

That night in bed, Lucy watched the moon slide slowly across the dark sky and thought of Wendell and the anguished look on his face. *"Rest has escaped me,"* he'd said.

If only she'd had the presence of mind to remember the Bible verse she'd heard so often before. *Come unto me, all ye that labour and are heavy laden, and I will give you rest.* How well she knew the verse, but embracing its meaning was another thing yet. *Besides,* she thought, *who really has time to rest?*

Getting out of bed, she went to sit on the chair beside her desk, praying Wendell wouldn't die before someone might offer him renewed hope. She wondered what Tobe might have said to help. She'd observed him with folk who needed support, offering solace and advice.

Jah, she thought. *Tobe would have known what to say.*

"But what would he say to *me* if he knew the truth?" she murmured into her hands, leaning on the desk.

Alas, that was something she could not afford to find out.

CHAPTER 7

THURSDAY EVENING WAS CHILLIER than the past few nights, and Christian lingered at the table, having another cup of coffee and a second helping of angel food cake. "Mighty tasty and light," he complimented Sarah, who sat to his right, waiting till he finished to clear the rest of the table.

"My Mamm always says it's like eating sugary air," Sarah said with a smile.

Faye sat patiently, too, and asked if he wanted anything else to eat while Lettie forked up the last crumbs on her dessert plate. Lucy looked lost in thought. *Restless as she's become.* Christian felt unsure about asking her to the meeting tonight. In fact, he wasn't certain he wanted to make the effort to go himself. Even so, he'd tracked down last week's handout from the driver, and had his own writing tablet and pen nearby to take out to the carriage, once he'd hitched up.

"You could've called for a driver again, love," Sarah suggested softly. "Go easy on yourself."

"*Jah*, I know."

"I'll help ya, Dat," Lucy offered without looking at him. Rising from the bench, she went to the sink and ran the water, washing her hands. "I'll groom Sunshine for ya right quick, too."

Ever helpful Lucy, he thought.

"All right, then." Smiling at Sarah, he pushed his dessert plate back and his chair, too.

Sarah followed him out to the mud room, where she kissed his cheek. "I'll wait up for ya this time. Sorry 'bout last week."

He reached for his best straw hat. "You were tired, dear. No need to apologize."

"I hope it's beneficial, 'specially considerin' it's an evening meeting."

"I've thought the same thing 'bout the later hour." He mentioned that the majority of those present last week were working folk.

"Havin' the extra cup of coffee was *schmaert*."

He liked Sarah's doting, having her near. "Well, I best be goin'," he said, glancing around the corner to see where Lettie and Faye were before bending down to kiss her soft lips.

Sarah smiled sweetly, and his heart was full.

Outdoors, he and Lucy made short work of hitching Sunshine to the enclosed family carriage. Glancing at Lucy a time or two, Christian decided to ask straight out. "Are ya busy this evening?"

Avoiding his gaze, she paused, and he realized he was holding his breath. *O Lord above, is she considering it?*

"It's not for me, Dat," she said at last.

He sighed inwardly. It had been so long since they'd even ridden anywhere together alone—father and daughter.

Lucy looked down at her black apron and brushed it off with her hands. "Besides, I'm not dressed for public."

"Well, it wouldn't take ya that long to change, *jah*? I'll wait."

Ol' Thomas came scampering over and meowed loudly at her feet. "Hullo, boy." Lucy leaned down to pick up the enormous gray tom and carried him back into the stable.

Christian waited a good five minutes or longer, but Lucy did not return. Quietly, he reached for the driving lines and encouraged Sunny forward, around the barnyard and out to the road.

Just as last week, Dale Wyeth was the greeter, standing in the church lobby as though waiting for Christian to arrive. Sunshine's harness had gotten loose somehow on the way there, and Christian was quick to express regret for showing up a few minutes late.

Downstairs, they took their seats in the second row—Christian was relieved to be more sheltered there. The older man with the red sweater was sitting off to the side yet again, in the selfsame spot. His head was bowed as Linden Hess reviewed the first lesson and gave more handouts to the middle-aged woman on the far end of the front row, over where Christian had sat last time. She began to pass them down while the leader shared, much as he had last week, that the Lord is near to the brokenhearted. "I know this from experience," he said, then asked for volunteers who might have specific things to share regarding that.

After the testimonies, they began the night's lesson, which dealt with understanding "the seasons of grief." Linden also shared that grieving was like a tunnel, one longer than anyone who hadn't lived through loss could imagine. "It's a journey of the heart and the emotions," he added.

Christian listened, but his mind wandered back to Lucy, wishing she understood how much he cared for her, that he was sorry for the way he'd handled things. *Was it only three years ago?*

Linden changed the topic a bit now, discussing ways to change up the holidays, potentially emotional landmines. Grief could also peak around the anniversary of the death or the birthday of the deceased. "Women are more naturally able to express their emotions. We men, however, want to control things . . . especially our feelings. We need to know it's okay to break down. Letting your guard down is a beneficial part of the healing process . . . a gift from God."

Christian tuned him out. *This would've been a good session for Lucy*, he thought, wondering what he might have done differently to encourage her to join him.

Later, during the discussion time, Dale again shared openly about his father. "The loss seems more final as each day passes," he told Christian. "Sometimes I wonder how life can go on . . . but I know Dad wouldn't want me to live in the past. He'd want me to keep my eyes focused on the prize God has for me." Then, brightening some, he added, "The blessed hope of seeing him again one day really makes heaven seem closer."

Christian agreed. "I look forward to that reunion with my father, too, Lord willing."

After the meeting, Christian was in no rush to leave, since Dale seemed interested in talking about Amish life.

"I've been thinking about raising goats for milk and cheese, and chickens for eggs," Dale said. "Would you have some pointers for me, perhaps?"

Christian nodded.

"I'm also curious about hydraulic and pneumatic power," Dale added.

"Ah, that's Amish electricity," Christian said, going on to tell him about his own brother's tools, such as saws and planers, which were powered by a diesel-run line shaft system in the floor of his furniture shop. "Caleb owns the next farm up from me."

"Man, would I love to see that!" Dale's enthusiasm was palpable.

Christian tried to describe the setup at Caleb's place in more detail, explaining how the various machines in the shop drew power by connecting to a series of belts that rose from the line shaft. And, before he realized what he was doing, Christian had invited Dale to drop by after work tomorrow.

"Thanks." The young man's face lit up. "I never expected this."

Christian gave him directions to the farm, and Dale said he'd call before he came, most likely in the afternoon.

"No need. No telephones in my house or barn," Christian reminded him, trying to keep from grinning. "We're off grid, ya know."

Dale was laughing now. "Naturally!"

On the way home, Christian began to have second thoughts. Why on earth had he thought it was okay to invite a stranger to visit the farm, or to his brother's shop? He didn't actually know the man, even though Dale had seemed convincingly sincere.

"'Tis a *gut* thing Dale doesn't know I have three single daughters still at home," Christian whispered as he made the turn onto Witmer Road, hoping that might somehow excuse his decision.

CHAPTER 8

EARLY THE NEXT MORNING, instead of reading the Bible, Lucy removed her wall calendar from the nail and sat at her small writing desk to look over the upcoming week. She enjoyed reviewing where her charitable work and regular commitments would take her.

Lucy opened her journal, too, and took pleasure in writing about today's scheduled work downtown with the food truck. *I hope Kiana and Van show up again!*

Then, leaning her head into her hands, she sighed, wishing she could do more to help not only Kiana and her son, but all the weary homeless in Lancaster County. But she'd come to her wits' end about how to extend herself further. And, too, it wasn't as if she had oodles of money to fund her benevolent hopes. As it was, she brought in very little each month for her parents, only a portion of what she earned from Ray and Martie.

She put her journal and pen in the desk drawer, still determined to do her part to rescue as many people as was humanly possible. Then she returned the calendar to the wall, where she could see all of next week laid out before her, as well as the week following. If Lucy were someone whose prayers didn't bump the ceiling, she might have asked the Lord God for strength.

She stared at the pretty landscape on the calendar—Amish farmland in Ethridge, Tennessee, according to the small print. She rose to make her bed, recalling last month's cornhusking over at Bishop Smucker's, where the deacon's wife had told Mamm that over four hundred settlements in thirty-some states were now home to Amish. Mamm had seemed surprised at the time, but considering the desperate need—and diligent search—for adequate farmland in the more established communities, such as Lancaster County, Lucy thought it only made sense.

She got cleaned up and dressed for the day, then slipped quietly down the two flights of stairs to start breakfast with Mamm. Lettie and Faye had gone out to the hen house together, according to Mamm, who'd reassigned the early morning egg gathering to the twins to accommodate Lucy's schedule. Late afternoons, however, were still her responsibility.

"You've got yourself another big day," Mamm said, looking perky in her violet dress and matching apron, a color she didn't often wear.

Lucy nodded. "You must be goin' to market, all dressed up like that."

"Thought I'd sell some of my homemade soaps at your aunt Edna's market table. She's welcomed my company." Mamm washed her hands and went to peek outside. "Looks like a mild day—only a few clouds in sight."

"Does anyone ask why ya make soaps, when it prob'ly costs nearly the same as buying ready-made at Walmart?"

"Oh, they ask, all right. But I tell them makin' soap is part of my heritage. Besides that, I just like doin' it."

"And I like knowin' what's *in* it." Lucy laughed, glad for the small talk, something she appreciated all the more after the unfortunate flare-up with Lettie. Little conflicts were becoming more and more common.

Lucy stirred the batter real good before pouring an ample amount onto the cast-iron waffle maker. Lettie and Mamm stood side by side at the stove frying eggs in one skillet and potatoes in another while Faye set the table.

Dat walked in the back door, going to the deep wash sink to clean up in the mud room. He was earlier than usual, maybe hoping for a few nibbles before they all sat down for breakfast. Then, wandering into the kitchen, he peered down at the frying pans, smacking his lips. He said something to Mamm, then to Lettie, but Lucy couldn't hear what.

Finally, taking his place at the head of the table, he picked up the old German *Biewel,* which Faye had put near his placemat. He held it up as he began to read, as if hiding from them. Once again last evening, Lucy had experienced the ongoing awkwardness between them. He had startled her by suggesting that she get ready to go with him to his peculiar church group. She'd rarely heard of any other devout Amishmen doing such a thing. *So unnecessary, too!* Honestly, Dawdi Flaud died three years ago. Why seek out help now?

When Lucy had piled up all the hot waffles, she carried the platter to the table and took her usual place on the wooden bench next to the windows. Dat looked at Mamm before bowing his head for prayer once the rest of the food was ready to serve. Lucy bowed her head, too, feeling self-conscious—she knew all too well that she hadn't lived up to his expectations back when.

Pondering this anew took away her appetite, and she picked at her food, leaving most of the waffles and fried potatoes untouched.

"Is something the matter?" Mamm asked.

"Oh, the food's delicious, really."

"Well, then . . ." Lettie started, then stopped herself.

Undoubtedly, she remembered the last time she'd talked up to Lucy.

"Just ain't very hungry." Lucy pushed her plate back slightly.

Dat's head came up, and he finally looked her way, seemingly concerned—or was that annoyed?

"Are ya ill, honey?" Mamm asked Lucy.

She shook her head.

"James's apple orchard is just a-waitin' for you girls," Mamm said. "Lucy, you'd have time to go and pick a bushel or more with Lettie and Faye before goin' to Martie's later, I'm thinkin'. That is, if you're up to pickin'."

Nodding, Lucy said she would. "If I take my push scooter, that'll save time getting to Martie's."

Dat dished up a second helping of waffles, this time spreading strawberry jam over the top.

"*Gut* thinkin'," Mamm said, reaching for the jam herself and mimicking Dat.

Faye cast an encouraging smile at Lucy. "It'll be real nice to have you along, sister."

Lucy couldn't help noticing how pleasant, even helpful, the twins were as the three of them picked apples after they'd cleaned up Mamm's kitchen. It was encouraging so soon on the heels of what Lettie had gone and said Wednesday at breakfast.

Stopping to smell one of the delicious apples, Lucy pressed it right up against her nose and was tempted to take a big bite. The mildly tart flavor of a ripe, juicy McIntosh apple would do something for her, she was convinced, but she rejected the notion, determined to keep up her sisters' pace.

"Are ya feelin' some better?" Lettie paused to ask, looking over at Lucy.

"I'm getting my appetite back, surrounded by all these delicious apples." She wondered if Mamm had said something to Lettie, maybe.

"Hungry's a *gut* sign."

Lucy set down her bushel basket and went to give Lettie a hug. "You're a caring sister."

Pulling away, Lettie laughed.

"Well, so are you," Faye said.

Some time later it was Lettie, again, who seemed to want to talk. "You were out helpin' Dat hitch up last evening," she said, trying to sound casual-like.

"*Jah?*"

"Just curious if you know where he was off to."

"Did ya ask Mamm, maybe?"

"Oh, she seems to know, but . . ." Lettie stopped.

Lucy decided to tell what she knew, at least in part. "Dat signed up for a class at the nearby community church."

Faye's head popped up. "A class?"

"It's a support group," Lucy said, not revealing more. After all, she still had no idea why their father needed such a class in the first place.

"Really?" Faye looked astonished. "What for?"

Lucy felt cornered. Did anyone else in the family know about the meetings? Besides, wasn't it Dat's or Mamm's place to fill in the twins—and if so, they'd better get round to it quick! "Sometimes, I guess, certain folk need to draw support from others who've been through similar circumstances."

Faye shook her head like she didn't understand, and Lettie frowned. "*Certain* people," she murmured, staring at Lucy.

What's Lettie thinking? Lucy wondered.

Lucy reached higher into the tree and picked off the largest apple so far that morning. "That's a big one," she said, relieved her sisters had not pressed for more. "Is it overripe, though?"

Lettie frowned. "Looks kinda wormy to me."

They had a good laugh, and Lucy hoped that was the end of the questions about Dat's Thursday group. But knowing Lettie, there would be more to come.

⁓⌁⁓

After Lucy did her part serving hamburgers and baked beans to the homeless folk who'd come through the lunch line, she went out and visited with Kiana and Van. Kiana seemed more discouraged than usual. "You're struggling today," Lucy said softly.

"I'm sick of living like this." Kiana glanced at Van, who was busy with his second helping of baked beans. "The new shelter has a limit on how long you can stay, and frankly, I'm nervous there." She shook her head, tears welling up. "I have followed through with every lead for work—waitress, receptionist, whatever I can find—but I keep hitting a wall. Even if I do get a job, I don't know who to trust with Van."

"You need some help," Lucy whispered.

"And besides, service jobs don't bring in enough to pay for an apartment and childcare anywhere safe."

An idea came to Lucy. "What if I do some checkin' around for you out in the country, maybe? Would ya wanna move out of the city if something comes up?"

Kiana's face brightened, and she smiled at her son. "If I could find a way to get around, I'd love that."

Heartened by their conversation, Lucy agreed to get in touch if she located work and a place to stay for a while, till Kiana could get her feet on the ground.

On the ride home, the barns and silos on the east side of the road gleamed in the afternoon sunlight. Seeing the creek running through their pastureland, she remembered leaping in it as a girl, splashing about, and exploring grassy paths here and yon. *What a gut life that would be for little Van, too,* she thought. *Ideal . . . if I can find something.*

Her hunger pangs signaled suppertime. *Mamm will be pleased my appetite's returned.* Lucy was also eager to read what Martie had written for the week's column in *The Budget,* as well as to look through the newspaper for job opportunities and places to live.

She was smiling as the driver pulled into their treed lane. Immediately, Lucy spied a beat-up red pickup parked close to the back of the house. "What on earth?" She didn't know a single soul with a truck, let alone such a loud-looking vehicle. *Except little Jesse.* As she paid the driver, she had to laugh in spite of herself.

Hurrying around the opposite side of the house, Lucy avoided walking past the truck. It seemed out of place parked there. *Does it belong to the new feed salesman, just maybe?*

Slipping past flower beds golden with marigolds and mums, and over past the small white gazebo to the south, she heard her father's voice even before she saw anyone. Then there was another voice—an unfamiliar one—and Lucy could see Dat leading a tall blond man toward the stable. Dat was gesturing and talking right fast, more outgoing than she'd seen him in recent years.

Since he found out he couldn't trust me . . .

She went to the back door and stepped inside the house. There, Lettie and Faye and Mamma were huddled at one of the windows, peering out with gaping mouths, like birds waiting for worms. When they realized Lucy had appeared, they scattered, the twins rushing across the kitchen to finish setting the table, and Mamm to the gas range.

"What's goin' on?" asked Lucy, mystified by their odd behavior.

Mamm was first to speak. "Your father's got himself a new acquaintance—an *Englischer* fella who wants to learn to live like us."

"Well, not exactly like us," Lettie spoke up, eyes blinking.

Lucy was surprised and moved to the counter, where her mother's apple pie was ready for the oven. She pinched the crust to make the edges deeper, recalling the lighthearted time in the orchard that morning.

Mamm continued. "Your father met him at the community church over yonder."

The twins exchanged curious glances.

Mamm waved her hand. "Nothin' to fret over. Sounds like the young man's interested in God's grid."

"Solar energy?" Faye asked, forks in hand.

"I believe so." Mamm glanced at the twins, and Lucy wondered why she didn't say more. It made her all the more curious.

"I need to freshen up a bit," she said, leaving the kitchen and going all the way to the top floor, suddenly wanting to be alone. She was concerned why her father, of all people, was hosting such a guest.

She went immediately to the sunroom area upstairs and pinched off a few dead blossoms on her African violets, then sat in one of the cushioned white wicker chairs, trembling. *What's he thinking?*

She sighed heavily—but no, she wouldn't let herself fall into any of that. She simply could not. Getting up, Lucy crept to the window, then stepped back a bit so as not to be seen. It *was* possible to be spotted this high in the house, she recalled now, feeling ashamed anew.

Below, her father's face was animated as he and the clean-shaven fellow stood outside the stable now, near Hurricane Henry's stall, and not far from Sunshine, their older mare.

Lucy watched her father shake hands with the young man and, of all things, motion toward the house.

She cringed. "*Nee . . .*"

CHAPTER 9

MARTIE SMILED AT THE SIGHT of Ray reading her column in *The Budget* as he sat at the head of the table, waiting for an early supper. "I enjoyed readin' it. Too bad it's not out twice a week." He winked at her and set the paper aside.

"*Ach*, that'd be too often for this writer to keep up." She carried a platter of meatloaf to the table. "Did ya happen to see that red pickup go down the road earlier?" she asked.

Young Jesse's eyes went wide.

"I mean lickety-split," she added, reaching to tie the terry cloth bib around Josh's neck in the wooden high chair between her and Ray.

"I must've been out fillin' silo." Her husband folded his hands, ready to pray the silent grace and get on with the meal.

Martie bowed her head, her heart filled with gratitude for the plentiful meal and for her precious family. *These boys, lively as colts!*

Ray cleared his throat to signal the end of the prayer, and they lifted their heads on cue. Promptly, Martie reached for the platter of meatloaf and passed it to Ray, then dished up some for Jesse and Josh, and finally for herself. There were fluffy mashed

71

potatoes with creamy gravy, and buttered carrots with parsley sprinkled on top.

"What's this now about a pickup?" Ray asked when his plate was full.

"Aw, prob'ly nothin'," she said.

"Maybe it was the man your Dat invited to drop by the farm," Ray suggested casually. "Your brother James said he met a fella at a meetinghouse last week."

"James knows 'bout this?" Martie was surprised, but then again, everyone's business was known fairly quickly around here.

"Seems so." Ray smacked his lips and reached for more potatoes and gravy. "Says the young man's mighty curious 'bout simple ways."

"Goin' Plain, ya mean?"

"Well . . . not so far as that."

"What, then?" She'd never heard of an outsider interested in the Old Ways without also wanting church membership.

Ray glanced at her, gave her a smile, and returned his attention to his food. "Guess there are some English who wanna live more independently, is all. Not be so reliant on electricity and whatnot."

"S'posin' it's not too peculiar, what with some folk worryin' over the state of our world."

"We mustn't forget that this is God's green earth," Ray said, his meatloaf disappearing quickly from the plate. He looked at Jesse and Josh. "The Lord God has His mighty hands wrapped around the world He's created, protecting it—and us—till it's time to call us Home."

Ray certainly had a way of putting things back into perspective. Martie reached for the serving bowl of cooked carrots and put a small amount on young Josh's plate. "Lookee there," she cooed encouragingly. "You like these, *Bobbli.*"

"He'll use his fingers if you don't give him a fork, dear," Ray observed.

"*Jah*," she said, still marveling that her baby was old enough to hold a utensil.

Across the table, to Ray's left, there came a *thunk*. Young Jesse frowned like he might let loose with a wail—his toy pickup must have fallen off his lap. Quickly, he looked to his father for permission to get down and retrieve it. When Ray gave the nod, Jesse scrambled down off his stool. Jabbering in *Deitsch*, he happily retrieved the toy beneath the table and returned to his seat, all smiles once more.

I wonder when he'll stop insisting on bringing it to the table, Martie thought with a sigh. *Carries that truck nearly everywhere!*

Things had been much too quiet in the kitchen, yet Mamm and the twins were surely busy preparing supper downstairs as Lucy still stood at the largest window at the far end of her room. Earlier, she'd crept all the way down the two flights of stairs only to see that Dat was sitting on the back porch with the stranger. She'd also snatched up the *Intelligencer Journal*, hoping to look through the ads to find some work options for Kiana.

Silently, ever so cautiously now, she raised her bedroom window, impatient to overhear the conversation below. She couldn't remember feeling this nosy, not since she'd overheard the bishop's wife telling about their driving horses falling through the stable floor into the cellar below. Miraculously, the mares had survived.

Her body tense, Lucy leaned near the windowsill, careful not to bump the screen.

Dat's voice floated right up to her. "Oh, there's still a *Bann* on getting electric from the public grid. On radios and televisions, too."

"I noticed gas grills on a few Amish properties as I drove through the neighborhood to get here," the young man said, his voice smooth. "Is that common?"

"Perty much."

"I've also seen some Amish teens around town with cell phones. May I ask what your church's view is on that?"

"Plenty of unbaptized teens have 'em. And some contractors and businesspeople use 'em—folk whose livelihoods need a quick way for customers to reach them." Dat sighed. "It's a sore point with our ministerial brethren. I mean, how can we expect to keep anyone away from the Internet with a device ready in hand, twenty-four hours a day? Temptation's all wrapped up in a *schmaert* phone!"

Lucy certainly hoped her father wasn't getting too familiar with this man. She held her breath. How much longer would Dat linger? She must get out to the hen house soon . . . gather the late-afternoon eggs.

"Come again tomorrow, Dale, if you'd like," she heard Dat say. "I'll show ya how to raise chickens and goats, and take ya over to see my brother's shop, if you're still interested."

"Wouldn't want to be a bother."

"*Ach*, don't think thataway."

"Thanks again, Christian. I appreciate your time."

"Glad to help settle all this in your mind."

Lucy frowned. *Settle what?*

She stepped away from the window and went to sit at her corner writing desk, leaving the window open for now. She felt the air cooling the room and could hear the shuffle of feet as Dale Something took himself off to his truck and started it up with an unexpected roar.

⁘

After supper that evening, Christian sat longer than usual at the table, waiting for Lucy and the twins to redd things up. He occupied himself by reading Martie's column in *The Budget*, getting a kick out of how she was progressing these days as a scribe for the newspaper.

As Sarah returned for the last of the serving dishes, he leaned toward her. "Put your jacket on, love. Take a walk with me."

Sarah nodded and carried the dishes over to the counter, then made her way without delay to the enclosed porch adjoining the large kitchen. He slid back his chair and rose to meet her there. Reaching for his old work coat, he motioned to the back door, letting her step out first.

The sun's fading rays felt light on Christian's shoulders, and he chose to take the field lanes instead of the main road. The trees along the way were black with crows perched among the branches. He'd seen fewer hummingbirds around the flower beds in the last few days and felt the slight chill in the air, especially late at night when he awoke, restless, and went outdoors and sat on the back porch to pray.

"Autumn's officially here tomorrow," he commented.

Sarah gave him a sidelong glance. "Somethin' more than that on your mind?"

"There is, *jah*." Christian wasn't altogether sure how to bring this up. Knowing Sarah, though, it was best to just get it out and let the chips fall where they might, though he did have his qualms about it. Already he could sense her growing anxiety. "Nothin' to fret over," he prefaced what he wanted to say.

"Oh?" She let out a small laugh. "Well then, why are ya workin' your jaw like that?"

Not a gut start . . .

He sucked in a breath and began. "The fella who dropped by today—Dale Wyeth—well, I wondered what you'd think if I invited him to stay over for a couple days at some point."

"Whatever for?" Sarah's voice was suddenly shrill.

"Just to give him more time on the farm to observe and take him over to Caleb's shop, too, maybe. I'd like to teach him what he's itchin' to learn."

"Well, surely the man has a job."

"He owns a hardware store—doesn't have to be there all the time."

"Oh, Christian." She sounded downright mournful. "Have ya forgotten so soon 'bout—"

"How *could* I?"

Sarah folded her arms and looked down at the ground. "Seems to me it ain't a *gut* idea to let an *Englischer* near our family."

He'd guessed she might say as much. "Dale's different, though. He's not a bit pushy, and from what I gather, he's a devout Christian. And this is all my idea—I'm tellin' you first. Dale knows nothing about the possibility of staying here. He's just very curious 'bout our ways, is all." Christian slowed his pace. "And spending time with him is helping me like nothing else has."

"Helpin' what?"

"*Ach,* Sarah."

For a long time, she was silent. When she did speak, her voice cracked. "Just put yourself in Lucy's shoes—imagine how she might feel."

Christian considered that.

"I daresay you haven't given this enough thought, dear."

"Which is why I brought it up to you now," he replied as tactfully as possible. To her credit, Sarah had made a fair assessment of the situation.

"It was wise not to simply jump ahead and invite your friend," Sarah added.

So she wasn't budging. "Guess I'll just give him a few pointers, then," he replied.

If it had been dusk, he might have reached for her hand. But given the way she looked—her arms a protective shield about her—Christian realized that, dark or light, his wife was not keen on having her hand in his just now. He was sorry he'd ever brought up Dale Wyeth.

CHAPTER 10

LUCY OPENED THE BACK DOOR to her grandmother's small *Dawdi Haus* and stepped quietly inside. Mammi Flaud was sitting in her most comfortable chair, a gray recliner, a few feet from the oak hutch built by Lucy's grandfather decades ago. Mammi's eyes were closed and her gray-white head leaned back in sweet repose, but as Lucy moved inside, the floor creaked and Mammi awakened, her wrinkled face breaking into a sunshine of a smile.

"*Ach.* I was tryin' my best to be quiet."

"You're chust fine, child." Her grandmother leaned on the arms of the chair as she inched up to a stand, though still a bit stooped. "Your cousin Barbie Ann, over in New Holland, came by yesterday and dropped off a large bag of fabric leftovers," Mammi said as they went into the kitchen and sat down for some coffee.

"How nice for the quilter in you, *jah?*" Lucy was happy for this windfall her beloved grandmother had received. "Let's have a look-see."

Mammi began to lay out an array of fabrics: solids, florals, polka dots, plaids, and even a holiday pattern.

"Just imagine how much it would cost to purchase all this fabric," said Lucy. "About how many quilts can ya make with this?"

"At least two big ones, I'm guessin'." Mammi picked up a paisley print in maroon, indigo, and navy.

Lucy had to smile. "Like an early Christmas gift."

"Ain't that the truth!" Mammi's wrinkled face lit up. "Well, dear, how long can ya stay and help me organize?"

"Oh, an hour or so. I promised Martie I'd give her a hand with some baking."

"For after Preachin' service tomorrow?"

Lucy nodded. "Can't believe Martie offered to bring most of the snitz pies for the shared meal."

"Bless her heart." Mammi smiled, looking the picture of health in her pretty maroon-colored dress and black apron. "Martie's one ambitious woman."

Lucy recalled how, years back, Tobe Glick had helped his mother carry in dozens of snitz pies for a gathering of all the courting-age teens in the district. It was the night Lucy had agreed to go walking with him. They'd laughed and talked away the evening—a *gut* time for certain.

Life was so simple then. . . .

Shrugging off the memory, Lucy went to the walk-in pantry adjacent to the kitchen to get the leaves for her grandmother's table. After adding those, she began to spread out the material. Together, she and Mammi smoothed and folded and made tidy stacks according to style, color, and pattern. It was a delight doing this, and Lucy wished now she hadn't said she'd be at Martie's quite so early.

While they sorted, Mammi talked of the upcoming canning bee, then remarked that she was in the process of making a list of her dozens of grandchildren and greats, as well as their birthdays.

"Maybe you should sort *them* by personality or looks, instead of just age," Lucy suggested, laughing softly. "Or you could keep a worksheet like Dat has out in the barn—his breeding records for the livestock, ya know."

"Well, now!" Mammi's face turned red.

"*Ach*, I didn't mean it like it sounded." Lucy felt worse than embarrassed. "I just meant you could use an easy way to keep track of everyone."

"I'm not sure I've tallied up how many there are. 'Least, not lately."

"Well, I'm sure we could count them together—after all, they're my cousins, ya know."

Her grandmother nodded. "Meanwhile, I best be comin' up with a plan for all this fabric."

"Maybe you could make quilted potholders for each of the girls on your birthday list."

"I like that idea. Or for their hope chests, ain't?" Mammi clapped her frail hands. "What 'bout yours, Lucy—is there anything ya might need yet?"

"Not that I can think of," Lucy replied, relieved when Mammi let the topic drop.

Bidding Mammi good-bye, she headed to Martie's.

Lucy arrived at Ray and Martie's ten minutes later than planned that Saturday morning, since Mammi Flaud had talked her into staying a little longer. Typically, Lucy preferred to be prompt for work, if not early.

Quickly, she washed her hands in the gleaming white sink. Then she measured out the necessary ingredients to make a generous amount of pie dough, eventually rolling it out at one end of the long counter while Martie worked on the opposite side.

Meanwhile, young Jesse sat under the table playing, jabbering softly while Josh napped in a pack 'n' play in the corner, arms flung wide.

"I heard Dat had an English visitor yesterday," Martie said, resting her hands on the rolling pin.

Lucy was surprised Martie knew. Her own recollection of Dat's conversation with the young man rose up in her mind as vividly as some of Mammi Flaud's floral fabrics. "How'd ya hear?"

"Ray learned it from James."

"Well, it seemed rather strange" was all Lucy wanted to say.

"*Jah*, James said as much. And we'll just leave it right there," Martie said, waving a hand toward the stove. "By the way, I already soaked the dried apples overnight and cooked them on low heat to make our work go faster."

Lucy thanked her, glad that part of the chore was already done. And once the pie dough was ready to be pressed into the greased pie plates, she measured the sugar, salt, and cinnamon to mix with the apples in a large bowl, then added the lemon juice. "Remember when Mammi Flaud made all her meals on that old black cookstove?"

Martie grimaced. "I can't imagine cookin' and bakin' that-away."

"I'll never forget the day she gave in and got her gas-powered range and oven," Lucy added. "She declared they had a special place in her heart."

Nodding, Martie set the oven just as Jesse crawled out from under the table, still clinging to his truck. He asked for some pots and pans to play with.

"He likes to pretend he's drumming," Martie said, kissing his forehead.

"Like in a band?"

"Goodness knows how he came up with that."

This boy could be a handful, Lucy thought, but she didn't say a word. Instead, she asked her sister, "How many pots and pans?"

"Three's plenty." Martie motioned for Jesse to go and sit with his noisemakers in the far corner of the kitchen.

"Here, you'll need this, too." Lucy gave him a long, sturdy wooden spoon.

Jesse was still holding the truck as he tried unsuccessfully to pick up one of the pans. Lucy helped him out of the way and took time to arrange the pots and pans just so. Giving Lucy a determined look, he began to pound away.

After a moment, he stopped beating and asked for a second wooden spoon. "*Ich welle der Leffel. . . .*"

Lucy headed over to see if Martie had another wooden spoon, but her sister wagged her head. "Where does it end with this child?"

"He seems to know what he wants, *jah?*" *Something Mamm always said about me*, Lucy thought with a flash of recognition.

She and Martie laughed together, and Lucy was glad to spend the day with her closest sister.

On the way home that afternoon, Lucy could hear their Amish neighbors not far from her father's farm calling back and forth as they drove their heifers from one grazing area to another. Lucy enjoyed the pleasant sound, as well as that of the babbling brook that flowed along the roadside and down to Abe and Anna Mary Riehl's dairy farm. Lucy recalled wading barefoot in it when she and her sisters were younger. She sighed with the sweet memory, glad to be nearly home after helping Martie with the pies and a bit of other cooking for the better part of the day.

When Lucy rounded the bend and the familiar front yard came into view, she saw the red pickup parked in the driveway and stopped short. *Dat's friend is back.*

As before, she took the opposite route around the house, toward the back door, and was startled when she nearly bumped into the tall, blond *Englischer.* "Ach, goodness!" she burst out.

The man reached out to steady her, but she stepped backward, wanting nothing to do with him. "Are you all right, miss? I didn't see you coming."

"I'm fine," she said, embarrassed, and would have hurried on her way, but he was intent on speaking.

"You must be Christian's daughter."

She stiffened and turned slowly, reluctant to confirm his assumption.

"If you don't mind, I'd like to introduce myself." He pushed his hair away from his forehead with long, tanned fingers. "I'm Dale . . . Dale Wyeth." He smiled, eyeing her curiously. "You look a lot like your mother."

He's met Mamm?

"Did my father invite you back?"

Despite the obvious rudeness of her question, Dale smiled. "He offered to show me your uncle's woodworking shop—especially the diesel generator."

"Oh." She wondered if Uncle Caleb was expecting them.

"I was just headed back to my truck now for my cell phone—wanted to take pictures for my own reference, nothing more. Of course I'll be careful not to get your father or uncle in any of them."

"That's *gut*, but have ya considered that having a vehicle parked in our lane ain't the best thing?" she asked. "A poor witness to anyone ridin' by."

His face turned pink. "I never thought of that."

"*Nee.*" *An outsider wouldn't,* she wanted to say.

Why didn't he just skedaddle, or was Dale up to more than what he'd indicated?

"I meant no harm," he replied, his voice quieter now.

No harm? Past experience had taught her otherwise.

"I should get goin'." Without waiting for a good-bye, she abruptly turned and left him standing there.

Making the turn past her grandmother's kitchen window, she saw Mammi Flaud standing at her sink, a look of bewilderment on her face. Lucy backtracked to the *Dawdi Haus* and up the porch steps.

"I couldn't help seeing what happened," Mammi said, wiping her brow with the back of her hand.

"That fella nearly knocked me over." Lucy fanned her face with the hem of her apron.

Mammi gave her a discerning look. "You're all worked up."

"Am I?"

Mammi poured a glass of water and brought it over to her. "Sit yourself down and take a long drink before you say another word."

"But Mamm's expectin' me to gather eggs," Lucy countered.

"I daresay those eggs can wait." Her grandmother took a seat across the table. "I'm curious. Do ya think you might've been a bit inconsiderate with that nice young man?"

"He's *nice*, is he?" Lucy leaned forward. "Have you met him, then?"

"I took coffee to him and your father both, out in the barn."

Lucy shook her head and sighed. Was no one else bothered by this man's presence?

Mammi reached to touch the back of Lucy's hand. "You're angry, ain't so?"

"S'pose I shouldn't be, *jah*? After all, why do I care if Dat wants to be hospitable to a stranger?" Lucy lifted the glass to her lips and drank half the water right down.

Mammi's eyes grew soft. "But I witnessed your reaction, my dear, and it wasn't a'tall like ya." Mammi shook her head.

Lucy had no words in her. Mammi was right; she *had* been harsh to a man who'd done her no wrong.

Mammi folded her hands on the table. "As I understand it, the young fella just wants to learn how to take things back a notch. Wants to raise some produce . . . maybe get some goats."

She swallowed the lump in her throat. Mammi was undoubtedly right—there was nothing wrong with what Dat was doing, and Dale's intentions were surely innocent enough. Eventually, she'd have to find a way to apologize.

The special pink candy dish centered on the table caught her eye, and the sight reminded her of her childhood— in the past, the sweets in this same carnival glass bowl had often soothed her and her siblings. Mammi liked to bring it out whenever someone needed a good cry. *"Just let the tears fall,"* she would say, her face shining with sympathy. *"Some sugar always helps."*

Looking out the window, Lucy watched her father motion across the backyard to the stranger. She shivered, and in spite of her best intentions, she felt unsettled again—was Dat really so oblivious to the pain this dredged up for her? Why was *this* outsider acceptable to him?

～⁂～

In the hen house a while later, Lucy used a bit of sandpaper to gently scrape away pieces of straw stuck to the gathered eggs. She'd learned the helpful trick from her mother years ago, and the routine task seemed oddly comforting now.

Carefully, Lucy carried the egg basket out of the hen house and overheard her father and the *Englischer* talking just on the other side of the stable.

"Your daughter reminds me of someone I once knew," the young man was saying.

"That's hard to imagine," Dat said. "Lucy's one of a kind."

Dale chuckled. "I'm afraid I caught her off guard. I imagine she's very private—and unaccustomed to outsiders roaming about. I apologize for upsetting her."

"Aw . . . I should've known better," Dat replied. "It's my fault."

Not wanting to hear more, she made a beeline to the house. *Why's Dat discussing me with a stranger?*

She entered the kitchen and set the basket on the counter near her mother. "Plenty of eggs," she announced.

Mamm stared at her. "Well, for pity's sake, Lucy. Your face is all flushed."

"I just need to wash up," Lucy said, unwilling to bring any of this up with her mother. The emotions were too close to the surface.

"Well, there's a sink handy right here."

Lucy shook her head. "I'll head upstairs for a bit." She picked up her skirt and darted up the staircase, down the long hallway, and up the far flight of stairs to her room, closing the door firmly behind her.

Taking a few breaths, Lucy went to her desk, where she opened her journal, read the previous entry, then wrote, *Dat's* Englischer *showed up again today.*

She wrote for a few more minutes, giving herself time to calm. Then, feeling somewhat sheepish, she recalled what Mammi had said about that *"nice young man."*

Rising, she went to the window and looked down. The red pickup was gone.

CHAPTER 11

FOLLOWING PREACHING SERVICE the next day, Martie kept busy cutting pieces of her snitz pies and distributing them around the tables set up for the shared meal. She'd noticed Lucy out on the back porch, hanging back a bit with Lettie, a cluster of courting-age women nearby. Faye, however, was farther from the house, smiling and talking with Rose Anna Yoder. It seemed a bit odd, since Rose Anna was married and typically visited with the other married women.

"Need a helpin' hand?" Mammi Flaud asked, looking nice in her navy blue dress and black apron.

Martie thanked her. "I think we're ready for the table blessing once the elders and their wives are seated."

Her grandmother squeezed her arm, a twinkle in her eyes. "Come over sometime, and bring your boys, too, won't ya?"

"All right," she agreed, then whispered, "I have something to tell ya."

Mammi's eyes lit up. "Another little one on the way, maybe?"

Martie ran her thumb and pointer finger along her lips to seal them, then said they'd talk later. "This week, I promise."

Lucy felt cornered when Lettie pushed the note into her hands as they waited to go in to eat.

"You think I'm pullin' your leg, don't ya?" Lettie said, eyes bright. "Tobe Glick really *did* give me this for you."

Lucy stared at the folded piece of paper from a lined notebook, its edges rumpled. She stuffed it into her dress pocket. "Don't get any ideas."

Lettie's eyes danced. "Furthest thing from my mind!"

Lucy gave her a mock stink eye, and Lettie giggled.

With a wave to Rose Anna, Faye returned to them on the porch.

"I'm not the one with ideas, I daresay!" Lettie grinned and exchanged glances with her twin.

Faye caught on. "Watch yourself, Lettie —it's the Lord's Day."

Lettie's eyes twinkled. "Tobe's up to something; you mark my words."

"*Ach*, you two." Lucy left them standing there, not far from a whole batch of their girl cousins, as well as Rebekah Glick, all of them twittering and whispering.

Lucy patted the note through her dress as she strolled through the backyard.

What could Tobe want? she wondered, his note burning a hole in her pocket.

Christian folded his arms at the table, lingering where he'd sat for the common meal. He suddenly felt put upon, what with Deacon Edward Miller having singled him out. The deacon had taken a seat across from Christian, a deep frown on his ruddy face.

"What is it, Ed?" asked Christian, wondering why he was so sober.

Deacon Ed leaned forward, his voice low. "Something's come to the bishop's and my attention," he began, then glanced about them and motioned Christian toward the door with a bob of his head. "Let's go outdoors."

Christian wolfed down another bite of the delicious pie, wiped his mouth on the back of his hand, and rose to follow. *Now what?*

Outside, they meandered back toward the stable, where several road horses were quenching their thirst at a large galvanized tub full of water.

"I'll just say it right out—there are at least three families talkin' of pulling up stakes and movin' out west," Deacon said, grimacing. "Is this something you and Sarah might be thinkin' of doing, too?"

"Hadn't heard anything till now," Christian said, instantly curious. "Are these established farmers?"

"*Jah,* every one of 'em . . . which is what's most surprising."

Christian didn't know what to make of this. "Are they lookin' for land for their courting-age youth, maybe?"

"Seems so."

"Might be time to pay some visits . . . knock on doors," Christian suggested.

"Well, I've been askin' around here today, and so far only a few have gotten wind of it."

"Interesting." Christian said he'd keep his eyes and ears open. "So is this hush-hush?"

"*Nee*—it's all right to tell Sarah." Ed headed back to the farm-house, leaving Christian to scratch his head.

✦

After the third and final seating for the meal, the one for teenagers and older youth, Lucy stayed around to help Martie and the other designated women clean up the dishes, drying them and packing them away carefully into boxes, getting them ready for the men to carry out to the bench wagon at dawn tomorrow.

Martie went out of her way to include Lucy in conversations

with the married women there in the kitchen, and Lucy loved her all the more for it. Since their childhood, this sister had had a way of making Lucy feel comfortable enough to share her dearest thoughts . . . and some of her deepest heartaches. Martie listened not only with her ears but also with her heart, and most of the time, Lucy could tell Martie anything without her jumping to conclusions.

When the kitchen was put back in order, Martie offered for Ray to give Lucy a lift home, but Lucy politely declined. "I'd like to walk, if ya don't mind."

"Oh, we mind terribly," Martie joked. "*Nee* . . . do what you need to."

One buggy after another passed by as Lucy walked the long stretch back to her father's house. Folk kept waving and calling thoughtfully, offering to take her in theirs. Her brother Ammon and his wife, Sylvia, and their six children, the four young boys squeezed into the back of the carriage, fondly called her name in chorus. Fourteen-year-old Cora and twelve-year-old Emma Sue waved excitedly, their *Kapp* strings floating in the breeze, and Cora even pleaded for her to come over for a visit later.

"I will another time," Lucy told her, loving the fact that she was close to all her nieces, but especially Ammon's girls.

"*Geb mir dei Watt!*" Cora said, making her saddest face.

"Sure, I'll give you my word," Lucy said, realizing the walk wasn't at all what she'd intended. *They mean well,* she thought.

The truth was, despite her curiosity about Tobe's note, still hidden away, she was altogether distracted by what she'd seen earlier—Deacon Miller seeking out her father, and the two of them going together to the stable, Dat looking awfully solemn. She hadn't been able to get the image out of her mind—it stirred up memories she much preferred to erase. Memories of offering to put aside her church membership for as long as the brethren deemed necessary—a temporary shun—for having dated an outsider after her church baptism. But that wasn't the worst of it . . . she'd never told the deacon the full truth.

Just then a gust of wind worried the trees overhead, churning them into a whirl much like her own troubled thoughts. She remembered how nervous she had been the day she'd gone to speak with the deacon about her transgression. Yet it hadn't been nerves alone that had kept her from revealing all.

Near home, the expanse of grazing land came into view, and Uncle Caleb's barn dog howled at her. Lucy felt drawn into the landscape—the orderly stacks of firewood, the homemade scarecrow in the pumpkin patch. And observing Sunshine and Hurricane Henry, or Caney as most of the family called him, galloping gracefully in the large paddock, Lucy smiled. *Our beautiful pets*, she thought, glad their racing days were long past. She thought then of Kiana and Van, wondering if they were enjoying the outdoors, too. Thus far, her attempts to find anything affordable for them had failed, though she would continue to search the newspaper every day.

In the near distance, Lucy recognized Tobe Glick's father as he vigorously sang one of the *Ausbund* hymns while their family carriage rumbled down the road. She couldn't help but smile. It was as if the Almighty One had brought them along just now to cheer her up, like a small blessing. Mamm would be quick to point out that, no matter how hard it was to reconcile the past, there was always the Lord's Day to encourage and bring comfort. *"Like a tether between you and your heavenly Father, dear Lucy."*

Does Mamm even suspect how far away He often seems to me?

Lucy sighed and slipped her hand into her dress pocket as she continued walking, ready to see what Tobe's note might reveal.

Hi, Lucy,

Even if you're not interested in coming to Singing tonight, will ya at least consider meeting me on the road near your

*house afterward, and I'll pick you up in my buggy? No need
to let me know in advance—I'll come by either way. I'd really
like to talk with you privately.*

Your friend,
Tobe Glick

Maybe he wants my opinion . . . although it's been a long time.
She remembered back when Tobe had turned sixteen, dating age,
and he'd sought out her advice regarding certain girls. More than
once, he'd broken things off on Lucy's counsel alone.

And look where it's gotten him, she thought sadly. *My loyal
friend . . . still single.*

"This must be urgent. It's not every day I get a letter from
Tobe," she whispered.

Back at home, she made her way to the top of the house, where
she flung herself on her bed and wondered if Lettie imagined she
was playing matchmaker. *Wishful thinker . . .*

Lucy let herself rest awhile, recalling when she'd first started
going to Singings and other youth-related activities. Somehow
or other, she'd always ended up on the same volleyball or softball
team as Tobe, who had a way of making every gathering more fun.

Getting up to remove her hairpins, Lucy brushed her hair one
hundred times, just as Mamm had taught her to do. Quickly, she
put it back up neatly to go visit Mammi Flaud next door.

～✦～

Lucy's grandmother wanted to sit out on the wooden swing on
her small white porch to enjoy the weather. At either end of the
porch, a rusty yellow watering can was filled with an abundance
of orange marigolds. A robin's-egg-blue decorative birdhouse sat
in one corner, making for a cozy, inviting spot.

"Well, much to my surprise, I managed to recall even the most recent birth dates, including all my great-grandchildren," Mammi said. "So I'm on my way. I just hope I don't forget anyone."

"I knew you'd put that chart together, Mammi. By the way, Sylvia has an old cross-stitch from *her* grandmother with the names of each grandchild and their day of birth. It's hanging on the wall in Ammon's and her front room. It's really something to see."

"What a *gut* idea," Mammi said. "Next time I'm there, I'll look at it. More than likely I've seen it and just haven't paid close attention."

"Well, you won't miss it, now that you know." Lucy was glad she'd come to visit, though she knew there'd been several other visitors at her grandmother's door this week. It was the way of the People to look after widows, something for which Lucy had always been grateful, especially since Dawdi died. *If only it were that way for all the folk in hospice, too.*

"I only hope I'll be around when *you* finally bring a little one into the world," her grandmother said, the swing moving gently.

Lucy felt her cheeks warm. There had been more than a few times Mammi had dropped hints about marriage. "Well, I daresay you might have a long wait, Mammi."

"For pity's sake, what're ya saying, Lucy dear?"

"Just that . . . it's unlikely I'll be marryin'."

"Don't you *want* to?"

She has no idea, realized Lucy, feeling relieved her grandmother had been spared.

"Oh, I've given it some thought."

Mammi looked askance. "Well, now . . ."

Taking a breath, Lucy continued. "Back before Dawdi Flaud passed away and you moved here to be near Dat and Mamm, I suffered some real difficulties. I'd made some terrible choices . . . which I soon regretted." *Ones I might never be able to make up for . . .*

A silence passed between them; Mammi's expression was clearly *ferhoodled*.

"Oh, my precious girl, try an' remember that our Lord Jesus was a man of sorrows," Mammi said, her smile sweet as she patted her hand. "He's closer than a brother."

"I know, Mammi," Lucy whispered, tears welling up. "I know." *If only I could believe it . . .*

CHAPTER 12

BACK HOME, LUCY FOUND her mother sitting outside fanning herself on the porch. "Feels *gut* to just rest," Mamm said as she rocked.

"You don't have to make excuses, Mamm." Lucy sat in the old hickory chair next to her. "Not as hard as you work."

"You're starting to sound like your Mammi Flaud."

"I was just over there. Nice to have her near."

Mamm nodded. "She's so much more settled nowadays . . . used to the idea of living next door to us."

"And excited 'bout all that perty fabric she was given," Lucy said. "I have a feelin' we'll be over there quilting once it turns real cold."

"*Des gut*, then. A new project is always a joy."

Lucy considered the possibility of seeing Tobe, just the two of them, later tonight. And she mentioned it to Mamm. "He's probably sweet on someone and wants my opinion."

Mamm nodded, a smile breaking forth. "Maybe he's sweet on *you*."

"*Ach*, we've always been friends—that's all."

Her mother shrugged. "But still, your Dat's awful fond of Tobe."

"Well, it ain't what he might think."

Swallows buzzed about the trees, and everything seemed to move in perfect rhythm with this new season. Oh, Lucy loved the fall best of all, and she looked forward to helping the twins pick pumpkins and haul them in Dat's wheelbarrow out to the road, where they always put up a stand to sell the excess.

"Older folk often talk 'bout the autumn of their lives," Lucy found herself saying.

"'Tis true, and things can be even more beautiful toward the end of that season of life. The tree might be goin' dormant, but it certainly goes out in style!"

That's Mamm for you, Lucy thought. *Ever optimistic.*

The elderly gentleman Lucy had talked to at market came to mind. "I met an older *Englischer* man the other day." She told of having seen him at the footbridge up yonder, as well as at the farmers market. "He mentioned his wife is ill."

"Oh?"

Lucy nodded. "I could tell he was real worried."

Mamm looked her way. "Well, perhaps you were meant to meet him, honey-girl."

"It's not like I can help her, though."

"No, you can't fix everyone," Mamm replied. "But there is something you can do."

Pray, she means.

Mamm always seemed to have the right words to say. And not only that, she sincerely meant them. *"Sarah's one to be trusted,"* Mammi Flaud often said, pride in her voice.

"Have ya thought that certain things happen for a reason?" Lucy's mother asked. "And ofttimes for a very important one?"

Lucy swallowed hard. Not so long ago, she had.

From his spot in the barn, Christian took delight in observing his wife and Lucy relaxing on this beautiful Lord's Day afternoon. It was good to see they'd weathered the past storm, though Sarah had admitted to him recently that even their relationship had suffered from Lucy's unexpected engagement to an outsider . . . and the trials that came as an outgrowth of that.

He clenched his jaw, remembering the order of events almost like they'd happened just yesterday.

"Thank the Good Lord she's still amongst the People," he murmured, recalling the night Lucy told her mother she didn't think she would live to see the light of the next day.

Christian stepped closer to the open barn door, counting his blessings and soaking up the tranquil scene across the yard as his wife and daughter talked quietly, Sarah moving her hands now and then, and Lucy turning and nodding, smiling . . . even laughing.

In a few more hours, the sun would sink below the horizon, and dusk would fall. He recalled other Sundays, when Lucy had made a point of shadowing him, assisting with barn chores so he could spend more time with the family. How he missed those afternoons with her.

O Lord, he prayed, choking back tears. *If only she'd forgive me . . .*

⌘

Feeling a mixture of curiosity and confidence, Lucy walked up the road toward Uncle Caleb and Aunt Hannah Flaud's big farm and stood off to the side of the road, near the horse fence. She'd thought Tobe might already be there waiting, but the Singing part of the Sunday social gathering might have gone longer than usual.

Looking around, she recalled this was one of a handful of prearranged locations where she'd waited for another young man—her first beau. Her *Englischer* boyfriend, Travis Goodwin.

97

Seems like a lifetime ago, she thought, surprised she'd wandered up this way.

She wondered if Tobe would think to look there for her, though he had met her on foot close to this very spot once before, long before she'd ever thought of accepting Travis's charming words and invitations.

But Tobe had always had a way of finding her. Yet it seemed out of character for him to have slipped a note to Lettie, of all people. Like a few other fellows in the district, Tobe adhered a bit more to the old way of dating—keeping a lid on whom he was seeing. Maybe that was the reason Lucy had never heard of a steady girlfriend, not in the past few years. *And Rebekah certainly seems to want to keep the twins apprised of that.*

The world was ever so still at this hour. She thought she heard a carriage in the distance . . . or was it?

Her heart sped up a little, and the image of a silver convertible flying down the road with Travis at the wheel flashed in her mind.

Goodness, what was causing these memories to spring up now, after she'd sealed them away? Perhaps it was the time of evening . . . and this peaceful bend in the road where the tree-tops intertwined overhead. Uncle Caleb's beautiful horses had sometimes wandered over from the meadow to the fence, nuzzling her arm while she awaited the sound of Travis's Mustang on a Friday or Saturday night.

I stood here once in pouring rain, she recalled. The storm had come up quickly, and she was soaked to the bone by the time she'd finally seen the headlights.

Taking gulps of breath now, Lucy began to walk quickly, refusing to remember more. She even considered just going home until, as if by Providence, she saw the lights of a courting carriage coming this way.

"Out with Jerry Glick's boy, ya say?" Christian asked as he and Sarah rode over to visit their eldest son, Ammon, and his family on Horseshoe Road that evening. Sarah promptly shushed him, seeming to want him to keep this under his hat. "Well, now . . ."

Sarah patted his arm. "She does not want it known . . . says she has no idea what he wants to see her about."

"I 'spect Tobe's got a *gut* reason, *jah?*" Christian glanced at her as they sat in the family buggy.

"I agree, but it's not a date."

Christian laughed. "*Puh!* That's what we used to say, too, back when we were starting to see each other, remember?"

"Things of the heart don't change much, I guess."

Glad for the covering of night, he slipped his left arm around his wife, holding on to the driving lines with his right. "Well, lookee here: I've still got what it takes."

"You were quite an expert at one-handed drivin' back when we were courtin'," Sarah agreed.

"Ah, so ya haven't forgotten, love?"

Sarah slid closer. "*Niemols*—never."

"*Mei Lieb.*" Christian pointed out the moon, high over the eastern hills. "If Lucy's wise, she'll hear Tobe out, whatever it is."

Sarah smiled. "Are we back to that again?"

"*Ach*, love, come here." Christian drew her even closer.

CHAPTER 13

LUCY FELT AWKWARD sitting in Tobe's open courting buggy and left plenty of space between them. Tobe had gotten down from the black carriage to greet her and even helped her in, gentleman that he was. Yet as soon as they were on their way up Witmer Road, she could tell by the rigid way he held the driving lines that something was gnawing at him.

They talked about the usual things—who was courting whom and what snacks were served at tonight's Singing. He noted, "Your twin sisters went riding with the Mast brothers for the third time. Might be a double match."

"First I've heard it," she admitted.

"Well, if you came to Singings . . ."

"*Gut* one, Tobe."

"I'm serious." He gave her a quick smile.

She wanted to set her old friend at ease, but Tobe wasn't himself tonight, and she decided not to bide her time. "*Ach*, what *is* it? What's on your mind?"

Tobe laughed softly and shook his head.

"I *know* you, and you're *ferhoodled*." She waited, hoping he might loosen up.

Then he nodded. "All right." He turned and smiled at her, then suddenly looked timid. "It really wonders me, Lucy, if you might've already heard from the grapevine the news I'm gonna tell ya."

"Glory be! Tobe, the gossipmonger?"

He laughed again and caught her eye. "It's called news when ya get it straight from the horse's mouth. Ain't gossip at all."

She frowned, feeling her insides tighten. "Okay. What's the news?"

He changed his grip on the reins. "*Gut*, then . . . I hoped you'd hear it from me."

She stared at him. Was he going to reveal something really big, like an engagement? Was that why he wanted to talk privately? They were close friends, although they hadn't been confidants since her relationship with Travis.

"Just how much longer will ya keep me in the dark?"

He cleared his throat. "Well, my parents are seriously thinkin' of moving to Colorado next year, come early spring."

His parents? She frowned, letting this sink in.

"Remember when they were gone for ten days early last summer?" He explained that they'd gone to investigate the possibility of becoming established there. "There's *ungeheier* amounts of ranchland available," Tobe said. "Acres and acres of wide open space, Dat says."

Lucy wondered why he was telling *her* this. "Are they eager to live somewhere new?"

He stopped talking and looked straight ahead. The sudden silence was unsettling.

At length he said, "Thing is . . . I'm considerin' going with them."

She was speechless.

He held her gaze. "What do ya think, Lucy?"

Lucy wasn't sure how to respond. "I've heard nice things . . . 'bout Colorado. Mamm writes a circle letter with some cousins from out west."

"But what I'm askin' is," he continued, "do *you* think I should go?"

In her heart of hearts, she knew she had no right to keep her friend here. "Do you want to?"

He looked at her.

She shrugged. "I mean . . . if ya want to, why not?"

He was quiet again, seemingly sad, as if she'd given him the wrong response.

Again Lucy spoke, trying to sound more hopeful for Tobe's sake, yet feeling as if the ground were sinking around her. "The mountains are tall there, *jah?* And you've always talked 'bout conquering them, remember?"

He chuckled. "Like a mountain goat?"

She laughed and slapped the seat playfully. "You know what I mean! The Rocky Mountains might just be callin' you, Tobe."

Their laughter blended with the evening air, and they rode for a ways without saying more.

When he spoke again, his voice was somewhat hushed. "Actually, my father's giving me the opportunity to buy his farm here. If I decide to stay, that is." The struggle was evident in his tone.

"What I really want to say, Lucy, is I'd like to court you."

The word hit her like a bale of hay. Had she heard correctly? *Courtship—with Tobe?*

He kept right on going. "Because if there's any chance of that, I'd be willin' to consider staying on here."

Things were suddenly fuzzy, and she couldn't think of a sensible response.

"Uh, Lucy? Now's a *gut* time to say something."

She moved slightly in the seat, grasping for the right words. "I didn't expect this."

"Well, is it really a surprise—how I feel 'bout ya?"

Her voice escaped her. At last she replied, "I guess it is."

"Is it a *gut* surprise . . . or a bad surprise?"

She would not embarrass him—he was too nice for that. *Too wonderful, really.* But she didn't know what more to say. If Lettie and Faye—and Dat and Mamm—were here, they would be nodding their heads, encouraging her.

But the truth of the matter was simple: She couldn't just blurt out her past failings. Tobe wouldn't understand, and she could never fully explain.

"Lucy?" he asked softly. "Are you okay?"

"*Ach*, Tobe . . . I really don't know how to answer. It's just that . . ." Her words dried up like the tobacco hanging in their neighbors' shed.

"*Jah?*" Tobe prompted her.

She tried to say more, but it came out as little more than a sigh.

They rode past Ray and Martie's farmhouse on the hill, and the sound of the horse's hooves *clip-clop-clipp*ing on the pavement seemed to accentuate the stillness between them.

Eventually, Tobe spoke again. "I've put you on the spot, Lucy. Didn't mean to do that, believe me."

"*Nee*, it's really very nice of you to ask, but the truth is . . ." She stopped. *I'm not good enough for you,* she thought, pressing her lips together. "Listen, Tobe . . . I've given up on ever getting married."

"Why on earth?"

"I honestly don't think . . ." She hesitated and started again. "I'm just not the right girl for you."

"Well, I disagree."

She paused. "Honestly, I'm not."

"Won't ya let me be the judge of that?" Tobe sounded more confident now, not pleading but determined.

"Trust me, Tobe."

"I certainly do . . . and I admire ya, too."

Lucy felt terrible, but she absolutely could not let him change her mind. Tobe was such a good man—he deserved a better bride.

"Won't ya consider praying 'bout this?" His tone was soft, endearing.

She wavered long enough for Tobe to extract some kind of hope from her silence. "Let's not talk 'bout this anymore. *Please*."

He slowed the horse, sighing loudly. "Lucy, you're the dearest girl I know." Facing her, he went on. "You must've known how I felt."

She could no longer hold back the tears.

He leaned toward her as if he had the urge to touch her, but backed away just as quickly. "Lucy, how can I help ya? What are ya thinking right now?"

"No one can help me," she whispered.

Moving back in the seat, Tobe was quiet.

She brushed away her tears and took a deep breath, then said flatly, "Might be best if ya just took me home. I'm real sorry to spoil the evening."

Without another word, Tobe directed the horse to turn around at a wide spot in the road. The ride back to her father's house was a silent one.

Tobe halted his mare a short distance from the mailbox, then looked toward Lucy. "Will ya at least think about this?"

Swallowing hard, she nodded.

He gave her a winning smile.

"*Gut Nacht*," she said, nearly fleeing the buggy.

CHAPTER 14

MAMM LOOKED UP from the kitchen table, where she was writing a letter, all smiles until she saw Lucy. Immediately, she set her pen aside and asked, "Everything all right?"

Lucy mutely toyed with the idea of sitting for a while, but she felt too vulnerable and merely shook her head as Mamm held out her hand to gently pull her close and kiss her cheek.

"I don't know what got into me," Lucy whispered, struggling against more tears. "I'm afraid I hurt Tobe's feelings."

"You quarreled?"

"It wasn't like that."

Mamm considered this. "Want to talk about it?"

Lucy covered her face with one hand. "I'm just too tired right now—I know you understand." She paused. "I'll see you in the mornin', bright and early. . . . I'll be goin' over to help Martie with her washing, as usual."

Mamm's expression remained concerned. "You sure you're okay?"

Lucy ignored the question. "I hope you didn't wait up for me, Mamm."

"Well, I was just finishing up a circle letter to a cousin out in Montana—she has twin daughters, too. According to what she writes, the church districts out there are thrivin'." Mamm looked thoughtfully at her stationery. "Seems there's even more interest here lately amongst our own People in explorin' other settlements—'specially newly established communities out west."

Lucy wondered if Mamm was aware of the Glicks' plans to leave the area but didn't feel it was her place to share Tobe's news.

"*Ach*, enough 'bout that." Mamm smiled faintly. "I trust your worries, whatever they are, won't keep you from resting well, dear."

"*Denki*, Mamm. You rest well, too."

Trudging up the stairs, Lucy heard the twins chattering in their room, as they often did this time of night. *If only I could talk to Martie*, she thought, hurrying toward the door to the third floor. She'd enjoyed having her bedroom across from the twins prior to the months of her dating relationship with Travis. When her parents had found out about him, Mamm had been unyielding in her insistence Lucy be separated from her sisters. "*Better for Lettie and Faye not to know you're seein' an outsider.*"

Subconsciously counting the steps just now, Tobe's words played over in Lucy's mind. "*You must've known how I felt.*"

With her hand on the railing, Lucy lowered herself onto the stairs, trying to grasp what had just happened. "He wants to court me, and I basically refused," she whispered, leaning forward.

Three years ago, she'd thrown away her life, and she was still paying for it.

To think she'd almost told him how blemished she was. *Almost.* She shuddered. Tonight's ride with Tobe had certainly thrown open the window to her long-buried memories, things she hadn't thought about in so long.

She recalled her secret dates with Travis . . . slipping out of the house on weekends, changing into fancy clothes at a convenience store. Oh, she'd loved the wind in her long hair as they drove in his beautiful car, their expensive dinners, his irresistible attention, his kisses, his marriage proposal. *And our wedding plans . . . kept secret from the People, including my own family.*

Travis's family and friends knew, however, and were all for their wedding, assuming Lucy intended to walk away from her Amish upbringing and embrace theirs. Lucy had kept her engagement private, declining a ring. As a substitute, Travis had purchased a necklace with a large solitary diamond in the middle of a gold heart, which she wore only when out on dates with him, and sometimes alone in her room.

But she'd made a deplorable mistake one night. They both had. And once was all it took. . . .

Lucy limped up the stairs to her room and sat on the bed. She leaned against the headboard, reliving the first time she'd met Travis Goodwin, at Central Market at the square in downtown Lancaster. He'd looked like a lost puppy dog, and surprising herself, she'd gone right up to him to offer assistance. As it turned out, he was interested in locating a particular spicy homemade salsa his grandfather had purchased a while back at that market, Travis had explained shyly, glancing at her, then back at the note in his hand, where he'd written the name of the salsa.

The thing that had struck her was his obvious reticence. It was only after they became better acquainted—he showed up at market every weekend to see her—that Travis admitted he had been inhibited that first time because she was so beautiful. *"And so very Amish."* He'd been astonished when she approached him.

He was so different from Tobe or any other Amish fellow I knew, thought Lucy, getting up to light the lamp on her bedside table. She walked to the nearest window and reached for the dark green shade, lowering it to the windowsill, then did the same with the next two windows.

Turning, Lucy moved to the dresser and opened the middle

drawer, lifting up several clean nightgowns. Clear back in the right-hand corner, she retrieved the small fabric pouch she'd made for the engagement necklace. Opening the pretty thing, she pulled out Travis's expensive gift.

It had been years since she'd worn it. Staring at its splendor, she impulsively opened the fragile clasp. *Dare I put it on?*

The clasp got caught in her stray hairs, and she momentarily struggled to free it. When she finally looked into the mirror, she was struck by the strange combination of her Plain dress with the dazzling necklace. The showy jewelry no longer held the meaning it once had. In fact, she felt queasy at the sight of it around her neck. *How did I ever think this—or Travis—was right for me?*

Removing the necklace, she returned it to its pouch and decided to write in her journal. *I'm done with the past, and anything connected with Travis.*

She stopped writing, recalling tonight's ride with Tobe, still marveling at how genuine he was . . . and his misplaced confidence in her. To think he wanted *her* to decide his future— whether or not to take on his father's rolling farm. If she refused him, would he realize there might be better dating options out west? Evidently no one else here had caught his eye.

She groaned as she remembered the look on Tobe's face. *"Will ya at least think about this?"* he'd requested, expecting an answer. And if she refused, he would likely move away.

How do I feel about losing him?

Under other circumstances, Lucy might have happily accepted his offer to court. If only her past hadn't hindered her present . . . and her future.

Christian removed his suspenders as he sat on the bed, getting ready to retire for the night. He was keen on hearing whatever Lucy may have told Sarah when she arrived home tonight. "Did ya learn anything, love?"

Sarah was standing in front of the dresser mirror, busy unpinning her bodice. "Something happened, but not necessarily *gut*."

Christian drew in a quick breath. "And she didn't say what?"

Turning, Sarah shook her head. "Lucy was too distressed to talk 'bout it."

Truth be told, Christian had hoped for something special tonight. He hung his suspenders on the designated wall peg. "On a different topic, Deacon Ed approached me to say there are a few families in our district leanin' toward moving out of state, hopin' to acquire more land for the next generation," he said.

Sarah finished brushing her hair and came to bed. "Deacon Ed said this? I was just tellin' Lucy about my Montana relatives, in fact." He heard her sigh. "Do ya think this kind of interest will increase as time goes by?"

"Wouldn't be surprised, really." Christian hurried to pull on his pajamas, feeling drained just now. Why was Lucy so distressed after riding with a fine young man like Tobe Glick?

Sarah blew out the light and moved over next to him, and he slipped his arm around her while adding an extra silent prayer for their dear, lost Lucy. Things had been unresolved for much too long.

CHAPTER 15

FOR HOURS, LUCY RELIVED the time spent with Tobe and his unexpected question. She marveled that he had romantic feelings for her. True, they had always been wonderful friends, but how had she missed this?

Later, she fell asleep, only to awaken in fright from a bad dream, her face wet with tears. The room was still dark, and when she looked at her wind-up clock, she saw that it was only three o'clock in the morning.

Mamm had been concerned that Lucy might not be able to rest, and in the wake of the dream, Lucy didn't see how she could fall back to sleep. As she attempted to quiet herself, a most wonderful idea presented itself. She would sell her necklace . . . to help someone in desperate need.

Early *Weschdaag* morning was the ideal time for Martie to sort the dirty clothes by color; she wanted to get as much done as possible before Jesse and little Josh awakened.

Tomorrow, she could easily complete her next column, excited, as always, to see it published. Hearing of her sisters' tussle to see who might read it first was encouraging . . . even humorous. Somehow, she imagined Lettie was usually the first to get her hands on it.

Eyeing now the armload of blankets and coverlets she'd pulled out of the blanket chest upon rising, she carried them down to the cellar to launder them for the coming colder weather. She might also gauge Lucy's mood today and decide whether or not to tell what she'd only recently learned from her doctor—something Ray had laughed off as next to impossible.

"We'll just have to see." Deep in the cellar, Martie set the items down on the counter Ray had made. Then, picking up the empty laundry baskets, she carried them all the way up to the kitchen before returning upstairs to hers and Ray's room.

But what if my husband is wrong? she wondered, unnerved. *And the doctor is right?*

<hr />

Lucy nearly leaped from bed at the sound of her alarm clock. She felt excited about her plan for the necklace and eager to set things into motion as soon as possible.

Downstairs, she came upon the twins' bedroom and heard them stirring, although Lettie was still buried in quilts when Lucy peeked in. "It's Monday, an' we all know what that means," she said, smiling at Faye, who was sitting on the edge of the bed, rubbing her eyes with her fists like a child.

Lettie threw the covers back, sat up, and pushed her feet into her slippers. "I slept like a rock, the way I did when your bedroom was across from ours. Sometimes, when I was restless, I'd go in there and stand by your window and look over to Uncle Caleb's place. I've always thought the pasture is prettier from that view, even at night."

"And I was out cold?" Lucy laughed.

"Well, *jah*, since it seems you never knew." Lettie glanced at her with a frown. "I s'pose you like your privacy upstairs."

"It's all right."

"We do miss havin' ya nearby," Faye said.

"I never understood why ya moved up there," Lettie said, clearly probing now.

"Wanted my space," Lucy replied cautiously.

"And you always liked to move around," Faye said.

"Even out to Ohio for a time," Lettie added. "Remember that?"

Prickles went up Lucy's arm. *Does she presume to know something?*

Faye went over and pulled Lettie to her feet. "'Tis nothin' to fret 'bout. Don't ya remember she went to help Mamm's elderly cousin Sally? And Lucy's our oldest sister, so she deserves to have the upstairs bedroom."

Faye . . . always the peacemaker.

But Lettie held Lucy's gaze, intent on knowing more—Lucy could just sense it.

"Well, I'll see you two in the kitchen." And that quick, Lucy made her exit.

Lucy caught whiffs of cider and strudel as she rode past various farmhouses on her way toward Martie's. Pushing with one foot, she zipped along on her scooter, which to most English folk looked like a bicycle with large rubber tires and without pedals or a seat. Lucy noticed that Witmer Road was less busy than most days, and she guessed the womenfolk were taking advantage of the sunshine to get their washing hung out on the line.

At Martie's, wide-eyed Jesse met Lucy at the back door, opening it with a grin. "Hullo, Aendi Lucy," he said brightly.

She patted his head. "Looks like you're Mamma's little helper, *jah*?"

Giggling, Jesse walked with her into the kitchen. "Mamma's

down cellar." He pointed toward the door and went to sit on the floor, returning to his block building.

Downstairs, Martie looked up and smiled when she saw Lucy coming. "*Guder Mariye, Schweschder!*" The dank cellar was lit only by a single lantern as they worked together to put the whites into the washer for the first load. "I set aside a bunch of blankets, by the way," Martie mentioned.

"With cooler weather comin', prob'ly not a bad idea." Lucy went over to lift some off the pile and noticed a small quilted coverlet done in pastel yellows, greens, and blues. Intrigued, she held it up. "So perty! I've never seen this before."

Suddenly, Martie had the most peculiar expression, as if she were waking up from a nightmare.

"Is it Josh's—for his crib?" Lucy asked, confused by Martie's strange reaction to something so lovely.

"Lucy, oh, honey . . . I didn't realize that was in the pile," Martie said, her voice wavering as her gaze met Lucy's.

In that moment, Lucy understood. *This was supposed to be for me. . . .*

Martie crept closer. "Do ya remember writing that one letter to me from Ohio?"

Lucy knew what she meant—she'd shared yet another secret in that letter, one not another soul had known about, not even her parents.

Tears came to her eyes as she held up the coverlet. "You made this?"

"I kept it for ya, waiting for your return. It's yours if ya want it."

"Oh, Martie . . . it's ever so beautiful. *Denki.*"

Martie went to her and gave her a sweet hug. "We both know that the Lord sees the future, so just maybe it'll come in handy one day. . . ." Martie seemed to choose her words carefully. "You really can't know for sure."

"Just havin' it is enough," Lucy said, deeply touched.

CHAPTER 16

CHRISTIAN LINGERED OVER HIS COFFEE when Sarah asked Faye to go to the third floor and gather up Lucy's laundry. Lucy herself was well on her way to Martie's by now; she'd been in a big hurry to get out the door.

"Ain't like Lucy to forget," Faye remarked as she finished up the breakfast dishes.

"I daresay she has too much on her mind." Sarah rose from the table to freshen Christian's coffee cup.

"Sure, I'll help out, Mamm. First, I'll let Lettie know I'm comin' with more dirty clothes." Faye opened the cellar door and called down to her sister.

When Faye was gone, Christian said, "It's been years since I've been up there in the eaves." He chuckled. "How's Lucy keepin' things?"

"Well, her African violets thrive up there, and it's a nice spacious place to sit and read or sew."

Christian nodded. "Do ya think she might ever want to move back to her old room?"

"I think she's real settled." Sarah returned and placed his

coffee in front of him, then sat back down. "Why do ya ask, dear?"

"Oh, I would just hate for her to feel alienated all this time from the rest of us," he said softly.

"I doubt you have to worry 'bout that anymore."

Christian sighed. "She's come a long way. . . ." His voice trailed off.

Sarah was nodding her head. "Travis disappeared the moment we nixed the wedding." Looking toward the window, she whispered, "Well, the moment you had that talk with him."

His wife wasn't accusing him, Christian knew. They'd come to that agreement jointly, believing that asking Travis to join their church before any marriage was best for their daughter and the coming baby. *Lest Lucy be shunned . . .*

"Lucy did say at the time that she'd never love again," Sarah sadly reminded him.

"Surely she's changed her mind," Christian said.

"A mother can always pray, *jah?*"

He reached over and patted her hand. "Prayin's always best, my love."

***

The morning had wings as Lucy and Martie worked together, and soon they were hanging out the second washing on the clothesline. A breeze had picked up, and there was less humidity, too—ideal for drying.

One buggy after another rode past the house, and the closest neighbors waved, some calling "*Wie bischt?*" And Jesse, who played near his mother, waved back.

"I just can't imagine livin' in the city, can you?" Lucy asked Martie, pulling a clothespin from the corner of her mouth.

"Not in a hundred years of Sundays."

Lucy nodded. A small silence spooled out, and she thought

of the crib quilt and what it meant to her now, after these years of keeping her heartache to herself, burying it in relentless activity.

Shaking out a large towel, Martie smiled over at her. "What are ya thinking 'bout, Lucy?"

"Oh . . . city life, I guess."

Martie looked at her. "Why's that?"

"Just realizing again how close I came to givin' up the Old Ways for a *city* boy." Lucy rubbed her neck. "I would've missed the country . . . and my family, too."

Still holding the damp towel, Martie nodded. "The way it turned out, you avoided *die Meinding*—the shunning."

Jah, Lucy thought. *I avoided it, but some things are equally painful.*

"Mind you, what's done is done," said Martie, who seemed to sense Lucy's reticence. "*Ach,* sister, you're lost in thought."

"I saw Tobe last night," Lucy confided.

"What do you mean . . . *saw?*"

She told Martie about accepting a ride with Tobe Glick, how he'd wanted to talk. "He shared some things with me. And I opened up some, too. . . ."

Martie stopped what she was doing, her expression shocked. "You *told* him?"

Lucy shook her head. "*Ach, nee!* Never!"

Martie seemed relieved. "He wouldn't understand."

"You're right," Lucy admitted. "Who would?"

"So . . . may I ask what Tobe had on his mind?"

Lucy stopped short of telling Martie the whole of it, but she related some of Tobe's struggle with his parents' decision to move west—whether he should go or not, too. "And while he was tossing the notion round, something broke free in me . . . and I've been reliving everything that happened between Travis and me."

Martie listened and continued to hang up the mound of clothes, arranging them in order from little Josh's britches, then Jesse's, to Ray's. She and other womenfolk in the area made a clothesline look like "an art form," or so Lucy had once seen it described in the *Intelligencer Journal.* A reporter had written about the "home arts," including a mention of the perfectly hung washing on thousands of lines each week in Amish country.

"Well, don't forget I'm right here for you, Lucy."

"I appreciate that every day I live." Reconsidering her earlier reluctance, she forged ahead. "Tobe wants to court me."

"He does?" It was apparent from Martie's grin that she was all for it. "And what did ya say?"

Lucy told her everything she'd told Tobe. "You and I both know he's the perfect man for a girl who *hasn't* messed up her life."

Martie's eyes turned cheerless. "Oh, sister . . ."

Lucy forced a smile. "We'd better talk of somethin' else, *jah?*"

Sadly, her sister agreed, and they dropped the subject.

The minute Martie's basket was empty, she came over to help Lucy. "I have something to share with you, too, but I hope it won't hurt you further, sister," Martie said. "Never would I want to compound your sadness, past or present."

"*Ach,* no need to fret over me, Martie," Lucy said. "What's on your mind?"

"I've been ponderin' how to tell ya. . . ." Martie stopped, looked away, and wiped her eyes. "You seemed really glad to receive the crib quilt earlier, so I hope it's not the wrong time to tell you this."

"Go on."

Martie reached for her hand. "My doctor said recently that he thinks I might be carryin' twins," she said softly. "He thinks he heard a second heartbeat, so he's scheduled an ultrasound for this week."

Lucy smiled, wanting to be happy for her precious sister. With all of her heart, she yearned to be, but she could not find the right words. *Martie has two little boys already. Why should the Lord God see fit to give her two more . . . and both at once?*

"Sister?" Martie pleaded.

"You deserve this *gut* news."

Martie was sighing. "Oh, Lucy, I prob'ly shouldn't have brought this up, at least not today. Even so, if the ultrasound shows twins, you'd wonder why I hadn't told ya, close as we are."

Lucy nodded. "You did the right thing. Honest, ya did." Tears rolled down her cheeks and she brushed them away.

"Aw, Lucy." Martie opened her arms. "*Kumme* here!"

Lucy stumbled forward and sobbed on her shoulder.

Martie soothed her, stroking her back. "It's best to cry it out."

And at long last she did, finally allowing herself the comfort of crying in Martie's loving arms.

After she'd calmed some, Lucy finished hanging the clothes while Martie ran to the porch to check on the sleeping Josh. And soon, here she came with a tumbler of cold water for Lucy and a small cup for Jesse, who was chattering to himself in *Deitsch* all the while.

"*Denki.* What would I do without you?"

"Well, you've been a listening ear for me, too, remember?"

Lucy smiled. "Your uncertainty about marryin' Ray?"

"Seems like another world ago now."

Lucy offered a sip of the water to Martie, who drank from the opposite side of the tumbler.

"I have an idea." Martie patted Lucy's cheek. "What would you say 'bout goin' with Dat to those grief meetings Mamm told me about?" Martie asked gently. "Have ya given it any thought?"

"Not since he invited me last week."

Martie tilted her head. "I'm thinkin' it might just help ya."

Lucy took another drink, pondering Martie's suggestion. This grief she'd locked away was beginning to feel like a sickness, even a terminal disease.

"I'll think on it," she said, realizing she'd never let herself fully grieve the loss of her baby.

CHAPTER 17

LUCY PARKED HER SCOOTER in the barn as soon as she arrived home that afternoon, then hurried toward the hen house to collect the eggs. She was surprised to see her mother come strolling out of the house. "*Wie geht's*, Mamm?"

"Need some help, dear?"

"*Nee*, I'm fine."

Her mother nodded. "Just thought maybe—"

"You're still thinking 'bout last night, I s'pose."

"Well, you did seem upset . . . even a bit sad when you came in from your ride with Tobe."

Lucy felt a twinge of regret for having told Martie all about it yet hesitating now with Mamm. There was a time when she used to include her mother in so much more.

Just then, Lettie called from the house. "How many green peppers should I stuff for supper tonight, Mamm?"

Their mother sighed good-naturedly. "If it's not one thing, it's another."

"Go an' help Lettie. It's all right," Lucy assured her. "I'll be in with the eggs soon enough."

Her mother moved toward the hen house but turned back. "I'm here, Lucy, if you wanna talk."

"I know, and 'tis a comfort. *Denki*, Mamm."

~~~

When Lucy left the house on Wednesday after breakfast, Mamm handed her both her lunch and a thermos of orange juice for a pick-me-up that afternoon at the hospice center.

Wendell Keene slept through much of Lucy's reading the first hour, and when he did awaken, he was groggy and out of sorts, even failing to recognize her.

"His memory is fading as his body begins to shut down," one of the nurses told Lucy out in the hall. "But please keep reading to him. Hearing is one of the last senses to go."

That means I can still talk to him, Lucy thought, wishing the Lord God might put something significant into her mind to share with poor Wendell. But she had little hope of that.

At noon, Lucy ate her sandwich and apple in the large atrium downstairs, where the popular aviary was located. Glancing around, she realized yet again that she was the only Amishperson in the spacious area, although she'd met several Mennonite girls who dressed like they were more fancy than Plain.

On her way back upstairs, Lucy noticed an older gentleman in a red sweater coming out of the elevator pushing a wheelchair containing a very slender woman. The new patient was dressed in a white bathrobe with matching white socks and satin slippers. Upon second glance, Lucy realized that it was the friendly man from the bridge whom she'd met at the Bird-in-Hand Farmers Market.

Seeing the couple together made Lucy want to rush over to greet them, but she willed herself to walk slowly.

"Hullo again," she said to the man as they headed this way with Sandi Turner, one of Lucy's favorite nurses. "We met before, at—"

"Yes, hello." The man smiled readily. "I take it you must work here."

"I volunteer." She smiled down at the woman. "My name is Lucy Flaud."

"And we're Clinton and Dorothea Holtz." He gently touched his wife's shoulder. "We were known as Clint and Dottie when we were young," he added.

"I'm glad to meet ya both." Lucy accepted his handshake and nodded at Dorothea, whose pretty brown eyes twinkled up at her.

"My wife can hear quite well, but she sometimes struggles to speak," Clint told Lucy quietly, off to the side. "Dottie has a wonderful sense of humor, however, as you'll soon discover if you get better acquainted."

"I'll look forward to that."

Nurse Sandi motioned for Lucy to come along to Dorothea's assigned room, which had the sweet smell of a florist shop, thanks to a sizeable bouquet.

"Oh, darling, look at this!" Clinton said, picking up the accompanying card. "The church sent over flowers."

"Makes for a real cheery room," Sandi said as she set the brake on the wheelchair.

"B-beautiful," Dorothea whispered, putting both thumbs up.

Lucy scanned the pretty room, similar to the others but with a few personal touches like photographs, a leather Bible, and a colorful throw blanket. Despite the abundant sunlight and openness of the space, a momentary darkness fell over her.

Dorothea will most likely die here, she thought sadly. The large spray of autumn colors caught her attention yet again.

Sandi, who was always exceptionally caring, assisted Dorothea into bed at the woman's request, and Clinton and Lucy stepped into the hallway.

Lucy would have returned to Wendell's room, but Clinton asked, "Do you enjoy working here, Lucy?"

"'Tis really a special place, *jah*." She began to talk about the things she liked best—the soft background music, the little birds in the aviary, and the neat and tidy rooms, too. "It seems to be a *gut* choice for comfort care. Most of all, the compassionate staff makes it that way."

"My Dottie deserves the best of care." Clinton nodded slowly, a tear on his cheek. "She has looked after me all these years, and our four children when they were young—two boys and two girls, all grown and busy with their own families now." He stopped for a moment to gather his composure. "Next to the Lord Jesus, Dottie's my life . . . my reason to keep going."

Lucy had never heard anyone talk so, and she was intrigued. "I hope some of your family can come to visit here." She recalled how difficult it had been for Wendell to feel so alone, his family elsewhere, although the man had never actually admitted it.

"We're a close-knit bunch, I assure you," Clinton said, eyes shining. "As you and your family must be."

"We Amish do tend to stick together."

Nodding, he cracked a smile. "Dottie and I have read several books about the Plain culture, especially by Donald Kraybill. Have you read any of his work?"

"*Jah—The Riddle of Amish Culture*." Lucy knew the respected author was the longtime voice for the Lancaster County Amish community.

Clinton talked of the tough decision to bring his wife to hospice care, glancing at the closed door with concern in his eyes. "It's not easy saying good-bye," he told Lucy. "If I could do it all over again and live the last sixty years with my sweetheart, I would in an instant."

"You remind me of my father's parents," she told him. "They were real sweet on each other, too, up till the final hour."

"I'm sorry for your loss." He paused, offering a gentle smile. "Was this recent?"

"Dawdi died several years ago. And my grandmother still mourns him."

Clinton mentioned his church had an outreach for grieving folk. "I'm being helped by it, thankfully. Although things will get more difficult . . . especially in the coming weeks."

It sounded as though Dorothea didn't have long. "They'll keep her comfortable, I'm sure ya know," Lucy assured him.

He nodded. "Watching her suffer has been so hard. More than I can bear at times."

Lucy remembered her Mammi Flaud saying something similar about Dawdi before he passed away. She was touched that Clinton had opened up so freely to her—and so quickly, too. And she wondered, *Is it my Plainness that sets him at ease?*

When Sandi opened the door and invited them back inside, Lucy offered to read to Dorothea, who pointed toward the well-worn Bible on the table.

"My wife has cherished this Bible because I received it from my Sunday school teacher as a lad," Clinton said, picking it up. "At the time, I could recite whole chapters. But Dottie wasn't always impressed with my enthusiasm for the Lord."

Carefully, Clinton opened to Romans 8, where he indicated he'd stopped reading to his wife that morning. "She especially finds encouragement from the letter to the Romans," he said, "since it's all about the unearned gift of God's grace."

While Lucy read to Dorothea, Clinton went out to the car to bring in the last of his wife's personal items. "'For I reckon that the sufferings of this present time are not worthy to be compared with the glory which shall be revealed in us.'" Lucy paused to contemplate the verse and looked over at Dorothea, who had folded her hands, as if in prayer. Moved by this, Lucy continued reading with even more expression.

When it was time to leave, Lucy spotted Belinda Frey, one of the Mennonite volunteers, down the hall, also getting ready to head home. She asked Belinda if she might stop in and speak with Wendell Keene before leaving. "He's floundering," she said softly. "Seems to have lost hope."

Belinda nodded, her eyes sober but kind. "I'm afraid we've seen this too often, haven't we? But it's also true that it takes the loss of hope for some people to finally cry out to God."

Lucy knew such desperation for God's attention all too well. She swallowed hard. "Well, Wendell told me himself he'd had some experience with the Lord. But he's definitely troubled, and I'm not sure what to say."

Belinda's eyes showed her understanding, and Lucy was relieved. "I'll go in and see him right now."

Lucy watched her scurry off to Wendell's room, hating to think of the dear man in such a panic.

On the way home, Lucy felt distraught as the words *the sufferings of this present time* continued to echo in her mind. She thought of not only Wendell, but of Clinton and Dorothea and their impending final farewell. She'd witnessed the deep sorrow, even pain, in Clinton's eyes as he spoke so tenderly of his wife.

Lucy pondered the prospect of her future twilight years, decades from now, wondering what it would be like to have a man like Clinton to stay by her side, come what may.

CHAPTER 18

WHEN LUCY HAD RETURNED from the hospice, she recalled Mamm's seeking her out in the hen house the other day and decided to ask her for a bit of help upstairs. "I'd like to move my bed and dresser around, if it won't put ya out."

Faye was just around the corner sewing, the treadle of the sewing machine going mighty fast. Lettie, meanwhile, was chopping cabbage for a slaw and looked her way. Lucy waited, expecting her to comment on this, since everyone in the family knew that Lucy liked to change her room every six months or so. Surprisingly, Lettie returned her focus to her work, keeping mum.

"Sure," Mamm agreed with a smile. "I s'pose it's that time, ain't so? And I have some time before I'm needed back here in the kitchen."

When they got to the third floor, Lucy opened all the windows to air out the space.

"Seems to me if I leave something in the same spot for too long, I quit seein' it anymore," Lucy said to her mother.

"That's true of more things in life than just furniture,"

Mamm replied with a glance around. "You do have a cozy nest up here."

"Lettie asked me recently why I moved my bedroom upstairs in the first place," Lucy told her. "Has she ever mentioned this to you?"

Mamm shook her head. "It's beyond me why she'd bring that up now."

They pushed the bed into the middle of the room, all four legs on coasters. Next, they moved the dresser out and away from the wall, sliding it carefully across the floor. Dat had put sliders beneath all of her heavy furniture, making it easier for Lucy and her sisters or whoever helped with the seasonal task.

When the two pieces had been switched, Mamm brushed her hands on her apron. "That took no time at all."

Lucy caught her mother's eye. "This might sound silly, but talkin' with Tobe on Sunday night set me to pondering many things."

"How could I think it silly, my dear, knowin' what you've gone through?"

Lucy flushed. "Honestly, I don't think I can ever move forward with a new fella. Maybe never." The last words caught in her throat, and she drew in a deep breath. "The truth is, Tobe wants to court me."

"Oh my." Mamm seemed taken aback. "He *said* as much?"

"*Jah*, asked me right out." She felt so vulnerable telling Mamm this. "Obviously he doesn't know anything 'bout my past."

"I daresay no one amongst the People knows."

In the distance, Lucy could hear Lettie and Faye laughing about something below, an odd contrast to the tension swirling in this room.

"How could I possibly agree, Mamm?"

"Are ya sure you can't?" Her mother's eyes bored into her.

"It's not possible, *nee*." Lucy didn't have it in her to explain everything that was erupting inside. "There's more, too," she added quickly. "I want to sell my necklace. The one from Travis."

Mamm managed a smile. "*Ach*, I didn't even realize ya still had it."

"I'd like to give the money to a young homeless mother and her little boy."

"Perhaps you should consider puttin' it in the alms box at church on communion Sunday. *Jah?*"

Lucy remembered the way Kiana had looked at her upon receiving the scarves and mittens. "Kiana has nothin' 'cept her little boy, Mamm."

She told her about trying to locate somewhere safe for Kiana and her son to live, and a job, too. So far, nothing feasible had come up.

"Has the Lord *Gott* put this on your mind?" Mamm's expression was soft now.

"Ain't sure, really." Lucy rose and went to the dresser, found the necklace in the little fabric pouch, and showed it to her mother. "This cost a perty penny."

Mamm shrugged at that. "You're kind and generous to think of doin' this, Lucy. But just how would you give her this money you're talkin' about? In cash? And then what, Lucy? She could be robbed."

"Well, I'd deposit it for her in a bank to keep it safe. They have so many needs: decent clothes, an apartment, household items, a car . . . things like that." Lucy folded her hands, pleading. "Oh, Mamm, if only you could meet Kiana and Van—all those poor, precious people I see every Friday. They deserve a gift of hope." Lucy surprised herself as the words spilled out. "If Kiana could just get back on her feet, maybe return to her family . . . if her father could lay eyes on his little grandson—well, things could soon change for the better."

"Remember that Kiana has to want this for herself and for her son. It can't be just your doin'."

"I believe she does. A girl in her situation—with a young child—wouldn't she want to live a normal life?"

"You might want to talk this over with your father." Mamm scooted forward to perch on the edge of the settee.

Lucy prickled at the notion and got up to put away the necklace. Frustrated, she accompanied her mother down the two long flights of stairs. "There is something I do want to talk to Dat 'bout later tonight," she said.

Mamm looked her way but did not inquire.

"*Denki* for helpin' me with the furniture, Mamm. And for hearin' me out."

Her mother gave her a quick squeeze. "I care 'bout ya, Lucy. Your Dat, too. Please don't forget."

⁓⁂⁓

Christian walked back from Caleb's place, choosing to take the narrow path that ran along the edge of the vast meadow south of his barn. The sky was clear blue, without a single cloud, and a flock of birds cut across a patch of sky right over his head. "Gonna be a nice, clear evening," he murmured as he observed.

Back in the barn, he was happy to see Lucy wander out to help feed the livestock. She rarely came on her own anymore. "Nice weather, ain't?" he said as she moved from each of the mule's feeding troughs to the driving horses.

Lucy glanced over and smiled but said nothing.

Normally her reticence pricked at his heart, but he let it go. *It can't be easy to still live at home, what with all she's gone through.*

Christian forged ahead regardless, mentioning the forecast for the week. "Of course, we trust the Lord's hand of provision, as always. For the weather . . . for everything."

"*Jah.*" Lucy leaned her face against Caney's long nose.

Christian collected the feed buckets and stacked them high.

"I was wonderin' if I might go with ya tomorrow night," Lucy said, blinking in his direction, as though hesitant. "If you don't mind."

At first he was speechless, reeling at her request. "Why, of course you can, Lucy." His heart rejoiced. "You're always welcome."

Long after his daughter had wandered back to the house, Christian found himself praying over this news, wondering what had transpired to change her mind.

CHAPTER 19

RIDING ALONE WITH DAT to the community church the next evening wasn't nearly as uncomfortable as Lucy thought it might be, partly because her father had called for a driver to take them. It was easier because Dat sat up front in the passenger's seat and Lucy sat behind him with another Amishwoman, her babe in arms. Lucy didn't know the woman, who was visiting her sister-in-law on Hunsecker Road, but she was friendly and her baby boy was adorable—a thick head of brown hair and bright blue eyes. Seeing the infant, Lucy's insides turned to Jell-O, and she had to look away.

She'd noticed her father's notebook and folder on his lap and was glad she'd brought along a pen and a small tablet in her purse. Dat had said he was confident she, too, would receive the materials from the previous two class sessions if she wished. Lucy just hoped she wouldn't be viewed as barging in on the rest of the group.

The trip was quick compared to the same distance in a horse and buggy, and before getting out of the van, Lucy said good-bye to the sweet-faced mother and went to walk with her father toward the meetinghouse. Dat was quiet, even contemplative, his face solemn.

"Are ya sure this won't be a problem?" she asked. "My coming for the *third* class?"

Dat shook his head. "I doubt the minister will mind at all. He's very welcoming, as is everyone."

"How many more weeks will the course last?"

He told her there were eleven more sessions in the outline.

As they approached the church building, she suddenly blurted, "I've decided to sell Travis's engagement necklace. Mamm wants you to advise me 'bout my plan to give the money to a young homeless mother."

Her father jerked his head to look at her, mouth agape. "You still have it?"

"*Jah*," Lucy replied, wishing now that she had chosen a better time to bring up such a many-layered subject.

"We best be talking 'bout this another time. Don't want to be late for your first class."

She nodded in agreement—at least she'd managed to voice the words. Now Dat could think about it and maybe come up with a good solution for how to sell the necklace. *Anything to get Kiana on a more stable footing.*

Lucy followed him into the entrance and immediately spotted his friend, Dale Wyeth, standing near the door, smiling and greeting two others ahead of them. She gasped—one was Clinton Holtz. *My word, this must be the support group he mentioned!* she thought. *We keep running into each other.*

Dale's face lit up when he saw Lucy and her father, but she let her father do the talking, still feeling a bit tense at the *Englischer*'s attention, especially after their run-in. *Outsiders are way too friendly. . . .*

Just as her father had said, the group's leader, Linden Hess, made Lucy feel welcome by introducing himself and talking with her and Dat, and offering the handouts for the previous meetings.

"Let's sit there," her father said, motioning to some vacant chairs.

Dale took a place on the opposite side of Dat. Baffled by their obvious friendliness, she scanned through the pages of the sessions she'd missed.

When it was time to start, Linden bowed his head to open in prayer. "Our heavenly Father, all of us here tonight are broken and hurting. We ask for Thy presence in this meeting—in the words we speak and in the way we open our hearts to one another. Guide our ways, and lift our spirits, in the name of our Savior and Lord. Amen."

Lucy purposely kept her face forward, hoping her father and his friend wouldn't notice how distracted she felt. Her mind kept returning to Wendell Keene, hoping Belinda had been able to give him the help he needed. Working at the hospice had made death and loss an ever-present part of Lucy's days.

"What types of feelings have surprised you this week in your grief recovery?" Linden asked the group after his talk was finished.

"Loneliness," offered a woman on the far right.

Another woman said, "Bitterness."

Clinton Holtz raised his hand. "Self-pity." He paused and the leader waited. Lucy could see the older man's shoulders rise and fall repeatedly, and knowing the source of his sadness, she felt more than a twinge of empathy. "My wife is so cheerful and sweet, yet she's really suffering." Clinton wiped his tears with a handkerchief. "I feel quite helpless . . . wish I might find a way to alleviate her pain . . . take it on myself."

Later, when Lucy was partnered with two other women— Sue Kaiser and Janey Marshall—they discussed the holes left when someone beloved passed away. Lucy listened as they talked about dreading the future, something she realized she had also experienced.

Sue, the younger of the two, asked Lucy, "How has the Lord encouraged you this week?"

Lucy forced a smile, trying to think of something pertinent to say, but nothing came to mind.

Sue encouraged Lucy to join the conversation whenever she felt ready. "After all, this is your first time here. If you're anything like I was, you're second-guessing coming at all." Opening her Bible, she read aloud Second Corinthians four, verses seventeen and eighteen. "'For our light affliction, which is but for a moment, worketh for us a far more exceeding and eternal weight of glory; While we look not at the things which are seen, but at the things which are not seen: for the things which are seen are temporal; but the things which are not seen are eternal.'"

Lucy jotted down the reference in her little tablet, drawing encouragement from it. *When our work is done and our suffering is finished, we can rest.*

Janey moved on to the next discussion question. "Are we able to relinquish our fears to God?" she asked.

Easier said than done, Lucy thought, then chided herself.

The week's assignment was to make a list of all the blessings the Lord had brought into their lives—anything for which they could be thankful.

When they disbanded, Sue lightly touched Lucy's arm, smiling through her tears. "I'll keep you in my prayers this week, Lucy. Remember, we're all in the same boat."

Am I even coming back? Lucy thought as she thanked Sue.

"It's a surprise to see you here, young lady." Clinton was standing right behind her.

Lucy explained that her father had been coming to the classes, and she'd asked to join him.

Nodding thoughtfully, Clinton motioned toward Dat. "That must be your father."

"*Jah*, since we're the only Plain folk here," she said, laughing a little. "Come, I'll introduce you."

"Oh, we've met already, but I'd like to introduce you to the young man he's talking to, my good friend Dale Wyeth . . . the salt of the earth."

She felt embarrassed. "Actually, I guess you could say we've already met. . . ."

Clinton didn't seem to hear her and led the way to Dale, who stood next to her father. She was relieved when Clinton took up the conversation, telling both Lucy and Dat that Dale's father had been Clinton's devoted friend.

Dale added emphatically, "Mr. Holtz here took my dad under his wing, helping my father to get his hardware store up and running many years ago."

Lucy realized Clinton had likely loaned Dale's father some money, charitable as Clinton seemed. And she took it all in, observing the seemingly effortless interaction between the three men—three generations connecting as friends.

Dale looked her way and caught her eye.

Feeling uncomfortable, Lucy glanced away.

The last thing she needed was another fancy fellow flirting with her, no matter what praises Clinton Holtz had spoken about Dale Wyeth and his father.

CHAPTER 20

AFTER LUCY AND DAT ARRIVED HOME, they spent some time with Mamm in the kitchen, where cookies and hot cider were waiting. As soon as she could reasonably excuse herself, though, Lucy dashed off to her room. She was too on edge to discuss the possible sale of the necklace tonight, assuming Dat might've brought it up. Instead, she took a moment to read the latest job classifieds, searching for something that might be a springboard to a better life for Kiana and her son.

Finding nothing, Lucy decided not to put off writing to Tobe Glick any longer. Before she changed her mind, she sat down at her desk and took out some nice stationery: *Dear Tobe, I hope you'll overlook my delay,* she wrote. *This week has nearly gotten away from me, but I've been thinking about what you asked me . . . and I have prayed about it, as you requested.*

In her best handwriting, she gave her reply. And when she'd signed off, Lucy slipped the letter into an envelope and sealed it shut. Tomorrow morning, her response would be in the mail.

Tobe should have this by Saturday afternoon.

The next afternoon, Martie hitched up the family buggy for the visit to Mammi Flaud's, thinking she might arrive around the time Lucy got home from her work downtown with the homeless. Often the last person to finish up, Lucy had told Martie how important it was to make sure each pot and pan was scrubbed and everything put back in order. Martie smiled at the thought. *Lucy could probably oversee the whole thing!*

When Martie pulled into Dat's driveway, she directed the horse over behind Mammi's cozy house. Getting out of the carriage, she tied the mare to the hitching post and helped little Josh out next as Jesse clambered down on his own. "We'll mind our manners, *Yunge*, ya hear?" she said as they walked up the stone path.

Her grandmother's face brightened the minute she saw them. "Oh, *kumme* right in! I chust read your column, Martie. You do a fine job of representin' our community round the country." She leaned down to peck Jesse's head, and Martie picked up Josh so he could also receive a kiss on his chubby cheek. "My, yous are all dressed up nice."

Recalling Jesse's howls at having a bath before leaving home, Martie smiled. "They got scrubbed real *gut*, let me tell ya."

Mammi Flaud beamed as she led the boys to the table and brought out some applesauce cookies she'd made just that morning.

Martie waited for Jesse to get seated, hoping to goodness he would be polite; then she sat with Josh on her lap. "We had us a busy mornin' of baking while Jesse made mud pies just out the back door," she said, grinning at her firstborn. "Ain't so, Jesse?"

Jesse nodded, then held up his toy truck to show Mammi.

"Well, I declare!" Mammi said. "Say now, if ya stay long enough, you might just see a big truck pull right into the driveway."

Martie sighed at this.

Mammi continued with a glance at Martie. "Your father invited that young man from the classes he goes to on Thursdays to come by . . . Dale Wyeth. The fella with the pickup."

Jesse raised his eyebrows. "*Bloh?*"

"Not blue, *nee*. You'll see what color 'tis, *Bobbli*."

Frowning, Martie attempted to signal her grandmother not to go on anymore about Dale Wyeth and his truck. Alas, Mammi didn't seem to understand, because she kept talking about that "*Englischer* with the loud truck—in color and otherwise."

Fortunately, Jesse himself somewhat changed the subject by telling Mammi in a faltering yet lengthy description about getting all the mud off his toy truck, and himself, in the bathtub earlier.

By now, Mammi was laughing, her head tilted back. And since her grandmother was having such a good time, Martie didn't have the heart to put a stop to the frivolous talk.

Later, when the boys were finished with their snacks, Mammi went to her utility closet and brought out two big wooden puzzles for Jesse to play with on the floor. Josh, sitting not far from his brother, had been fighting off sleep, and soon conked out with his blanket next to his rosy cheek, his legs sprawled out.

"I'm real glad yous came," Mammi said, still sitting across the table from Martie, her wrinkled hands folded on the plastic placemat. "I get lonely for ya, dear. Miss seein' you."

"Well, I'd like to visit more often, 'specially now that Jesse and Josh are older."

"I look forward to that." Mamm nodded her head, really studying her. "You look so fit, Martha. Such a healthy glow to your face."

Martie wondered if she'd guessed her baby news. "Well, it seems I'm carryin' twins."

"Two wee babes! Well, now, I had a hunch you were in the family way. How's Ray takin' all this?"

"Oh, he was in denial for a week, let me tell ya. But now that I've had the ultrasound to confirm twins, he's struttin' round like

Dat's rooster." Martie bobbed her head in the direction of the hen house. "Which is funny, 'cause initially he really doubted this could be . . . when the doctor first suspected it."

Mammi grinned. "Well, now, the Lord *Gott* knew ya needed that big house on the hill, ain't so?"

"I'll say."

"Keep me in mind to help once the babies come, won't ya?"

"Oh, I will . . . 'specially the first few months."

Mammi bobbed her head. "Just think, it won't be many more years and I'll be helpin' your sisters with their little ones, too."

Martie wondered if, or when, her grandmother might ever be told of Lucy's past secret. As far as Martie knew, it was a closed issue . . . Mamm and Dat's earnest wish. *Lucy's too.*

When they'd exhausted the topic of twins, Mammi excused herself to go to her sewing room around the corner. She returned with piles of fabrics. "Aren't these perty?" She shook out a few pieces, holding them up. "These here are for potholders—Lucy's idea. All the rest, I'm thinkin', can be used for quilts to sell. I've already done up three potholders." She displayed those next.

Martie marveled at her grandmother's tiny quilting stitches, running her fingers over them.

"Honestly, I need to keep my hands—and heart—busy." Mammi's eyes squinted shut for a moment.

"Maybe I can help ya stitch up one of the quilts later this fall," Martie offered.

Immediately, Mammi brightened. "I could invite some of the womenfolk for a quilting bee, in fact. We'd have a big meal at noon, and then homemade popcorn balls and a variety of treats for later. What do ya say?"

Martie felt like smiling now, too.

Just then, they heard a vehicle coming into the driveway next door. Jesse jumped up and ran to the back door to peer out, his nose pressed against the pane.

"Didn't I tell ya that fancy truck would show up here, Jesse?" Mammi chortled.

In spite of herself, Martie was intrigued. So her father's friend was back for yet *another* visit? *He's becoming quite chummy. Awful peculiar for Dat to befriend an outsider like this.*

"How often does Dale visit?" Martie asked.

"It's the third time that I know of. Your mother tells me that if your father had his way, he'd ask the young man to stay for a weekend."

"*Emschtlich*—seriously?"

"Oh *jah*. Your father's ever so keen on helpin' the fella learn to be less dependent on the world. The young man says it's a way to reconnect with his roots." Mammi went to the sink and washed her hands.

"Why does he want to do that? Just feeling nostalgic, like some *Englischers?*" Martie walked to the back door, where she stood with Jesse, even more dumbfounded to see Dale walking out toward the chicken coop with not only Dat, but with Lucy, too.

What the world?

CHAPTER 21

RELUCTANTLY, LUCY MOTIONED for Dale Wyeth to follow her to their large chicken coop when her father was called away to the barn in the midst of the so-called tour. *Be nice*, she told herself. Trying not to reveal how ill at ease she felt, Lucy pointed out the fenced-in chicken run to Dale.

She supposed her father believed there was no harm in showing this man around the hen house. Even so, she wished she had gone directly indoors upon arriving home, instead of going with Dat when he'd called to her. If so, she would be busy now with Mamm and her sisters, helping to make supper, biding time until Dat and his *Englischer* friend finished their latest visit before she headed out to gather the afternoon eggs.

And Dale would be wandering about by himself, she thought.

"I'd like to build something similar to what you have here." Dale crouched down to peer through the chicken wire, his blond hair resembling new bedding straw in the afternoon light. "On a much smaller scale, though."

"I haven't seen 'em much smaller," she told him.

Dale stood up and flashed his winning smile. He'd worn pressed navy khakis instead of jeans, and a pale yellow long-sleeved Oxford shirt, probably having come straight from work. "Would you mind terribly if I asked you a question?"

She'd hoped this tour wouldn't involve much conversation. "S'pose not."

"In your opinion, what's the best thing about living the simple life?"

An odd question. "Actually, never thought 'bout it."

He instantly looked apologetic. "It's all you know, of course."

"Most folk round here would prob'ly say they enjoy a slower pace," she said.

"In some ways, it seems harder." The kindness in his light brown eyes caught her off guard.

"Well, more sweat and discipline, I 'spect. But not necessarily slow. My life's anything but." She moved toward the hen house, offhandedly mentioning that volunteer work often kept her busy.

"Charity work?" Dale asked, sounding impressed. "So then, you must be quite comfortable with non-Amish folk."

"*Englischers* is what we call them . . . well, you."

He laughed. "I stand corrected."

"These days, we Amish rely on tourism and other means to supplement farming income. Things like craft and quilt shops, or selling candles, and jams and jellies. Men sometimes have to find work other than farming, too. A number do woodworking or construction, masonry or welding. Why, some even build solar panels."

"I've noticed that but hadn't really thought about it before. And this has happened in the past few years?"

"More than just a few," she explained, "clear back since we started to run out of farmland here in Lancaster County."

"Fascinating."

She shrugged. "What we really need is more land. We aren't so isolated anymore."

He nodded. "Or insulated."

She ducked to enter the chicken coop, where the nesting boxes were located, and Dale followed, observing carefully. She pointed out the wire-covered ventilation door and the long roosting bar, too.

"Did your father build this coop?" asked Dale, inspecting the floor, where straw had spilled over.

"Back before I was born."

He ran his hand over a small section. "Do you have any idea what type of flooring goes into newer coops? Is it like this?"

Dale's serious interest in raising chickens took her aback. "You could ask my father or one of the English farmers on Oak View or Harvest Road. Those are all Yankee farms over there."

Dale stood up and reached to open the wide, horizontal ventilation door. "I'm looking into getting plans online."

She found his dependence on complicated technology in order to discover how to live more simply rather amusing, considering. *Is he aware of the irony?*

Moving slowly and quietly past the still-nesting hens, Dale mentioned having done some research on various breeds of chickens and their behaviors.

She thought of telling him that reading up on this was one thing, but actually doing it was another. Dale Wyeth had lots to learn, she decided. Then again, he was doing exactly what he should and learning from those who were already doing it.

When they were outside again, he stepped off the dimensions of the chicken run. His sporty gray tennis shoes seemed ridiculously out of place.

"How do you live so simply in a complex world?" Dale asked brightly.

Another strange question, she thought. "It isn't just a matter of simple versus complex," she said. In all truth, some of the ways they did things were *more* complicated, and sometimes technology could actually simplify certain tasks. "The People have chosen a path that honors our forefathers and is a silent witness to the world," she told him. "That's our intention . . . rather than simplicity. For instance, it would be simpler and faster to buy our produce at a grocery store than to grow our own."

"True." He scratched his head. "I get your point."

She wanted to remind Dale that whatever he was doing here was between him and her father. But his steady, friendly gaze appealed to her, and she believed he was sincere. "Surely you've noticed some of our unique ways of doing things, like our propane-powered fans in the barn and stable, for one. There are also some Amish farmers who have solar panels for their houses." She paused, thinking of all the things she took for granted every day. "Of course, all Amish grow produce as much as possible and stock up at least a year's worth of canned goods. It's important to plan ahead."

"I certainly agree with that," Dale said. "Your dad was kind enough to show me around the rest of the farm so I could see how you manage without electricity. He even took me over to see your uncle Caleb's workshop. What a fascinating setup!"

"So, you've seen something of how we live."

"Your dad also mentioned something called a Candelier . . . thought it might come in handy." Dale smiled at her again.

"Well, we haven't had ours for long." She motioned him toward the house, where she suggested he sit on the back porch while she got the lightweight three-candle lantern. "Here 'tis." She carried the candle lantern out to him. "This produces a mighty strong light . . . you can even heat water on its top."

Dale peered inside the glass and tapped on it lightly. "Someone was very ingenious to create this," he said softly, shaking his head in amazement. "I'd like to see it lit up at night."

"Think of a hundred lightning bugs. That's how bright it'll be in the dark."

He returned the large lantern to her. Then she excused herself and returned it to the house.

Inside the kitchen, Lettie was stirring something in a big pot on the stove. "Looks like you've made a new friend, sister," she said in a singsongy voice.

Lucy ignored her. "Where are Mamm and Faye?"

"Down cellar getting some jars of chowchow and pickles." Lettie smiled at her again. "But Dale's waitin' out on the porch for ya. . . ."

"Keep in mind he's Dat's friend."

"What's the problem, Lucy? Our father's doin' the same thing you do all week long, helpin' others."

"Well, this is different—you don't know *Englischers* the way I do," Lucy snapped.

"Why, 'cause ya volunteer?"

Refusing to get into a pointless disagreement, Lucy headed back outside, hoping Dale wouldn't expect her to make further small talk. She was glad the screen door wasn't the only door stopping her and Lettie's conversation from leaking out to the porch.

Dale was leaning on the banister when she stepped outside again. "I'm curious," he said, arms folded. "You mentioned volunteering."

"*Jah*, for church-approved organizations."

"And you've been doing this for a while?"

"Three years next month."

"Do others in your family or circle of friends also volunteer?"

She realized she could either tell him to mind his own business, or try to stop feeling so annoyed with him. The question seemed innocent enough.

Maybe he really is curious, like he said.

"Plenty of us volunteer at the Mennonite Central Committee up in Ephrata—makin' quilts and checking donated kits for shipping overseas." She went on to describe some other activities she

151

was involved in, but felt increasingly uncomfortable. She wasn't used to talking so much about herself.

"Wow," Dale replied. "You must be awfully busy."

Not busy enough . . .

She mentioned wanting to take her grandmother to the hospice where she helped out a couple times a week. "Mammi Flaud would be so *gut* with the patients, I'm sure of it."

"Spending time with people who are dying?"

"Comforting them, ya know." She sighed.

Dale's expression grew thoughtful. "I'm sure they appreciate you offering them some hope."

He'd touched on a nerve, though she had no idea how they'd landed on this topic. "Honestly, I have a Mennonite friend who's *gut* at calming the patients with Scripture or prayer."

Lucy braced herself for the next question, for surely it was on the tip of his tongue. Dale's attentive eyes searched hers, and she wished now that she hadn't shared so much.

My prayers don't seem to matter anymore, she thought. *Otherwise, God would answer.* But she certainly wasn't going to tell *him* that.

"Well, I need to get back to the store. It's been great getting acquainted with you, Lucy. Thanks for your time." Moving toward the steps, Dale smiled and said good-bye.

He made his way toward the truck and was just about to get in when little Jesse came darting out of Mammi's back door, running as fast as he could toward Dale and the truck.

"Slow down, there!" Lucy called to the boy. "For goodness' sake!"

But Jesse had eyes only for the red pickup.

Dale reached down and scooped Jesse up to show him the bed of the truck, then brought him over to the driver's-side window, letting him peer inside.

Lucy stepped forward, surprised.

"Does he belong to your family?" Dale turned to her.

"That's Jesse, my sister Martie's boy."

And here came Martie this minute, white *Kapp* strings waving as she flew over the sidewalk from the *Dawdi Haus*, hands outstretched toward Jesse.

"Jesse!" Martie called, her cheeks pink.

Dale looked downright *ferhoodled*, caught between the exuberance of the boy and the concern of his mother. "I apologize if I stepped out of bounds."

"*Nee*, ain't your fault." Martie lifted Jesse down from Dale's arms. "What were ya doin', running off like that, son?" She held him near, scolding him in *Deitsch* all the way back to Mammi's place.

Dale shrugged ruefully in Lucy's direction. "I'm real sorry," he said again.

Lucy hardly knew what to do or say, so she turned and headed into the house. *Next time, wear your work boots and jeans,* she thought with a titter. *Then again, maybe there won't be a next time.*

CHAPTER 22

LATER THAT EVENING, Lucy went out to help feed and water the livestock with the twins. She recalled the pleased look on Dale's face as little Jesse charged over to the red truck, and the way Dale had ruffled Jesse's bangs, not hesitating to reach down and pick him up.

"Ach, sister, you're daydreaming," Lettie said, glancing across the stable. "Ya thinking 'bout something?" she asked, then smirked. "Or some*one*?" She paused dramatically. "Someone Tobe would *never* approve of?"

Lucy ignored her, murmuring to the livestock as she made her way to each trough, carrying the bucket of feed.

"Ain't becoming to ya, Lettie," Faye said.

"Do you ever get the feelin' we're on the outside, tryin' to look in?" Lettie persisted, much to Lucy's annoyance. "It seems like forever since the three of us curled up in our room and talked after Dat and Mamm retired for the night, ya know?"

Lettie refilled her bucket, returning quickly. "So, Lucy, are ya just going to pretend I'm not here?"

"We're here to work, not talk," Lucy said at last.

"She's right, Lettie. Finish up so you can join me back at the house," Faye said, taking her leave.

Lucy hoped Lettie might take the hint and go, too, but Lettie remained, eyes fixed on Lucy.

"Okay, now that it's just the two of us," her sister said, "you haven't mentioned anything 'bout your time with Tobe on Sunday. Surely yous had a nice evening together."

"It was nice enough." Lucy moved on to the next trough.

"Seems like you might have two young men interested in you just now. But one's off limits . . . as you should well know." Lettie gave her a sly look. "Haven't ya had a little experience with that?"

Lucy worried this conversation was heading in a troublesome direction. "If you mean Dale Wyeth, I don't know why you're bringin' him up."

Lettie nodded. "Just want to be sure ya don't cast Tobe aside for someone outside the People. Rebekah told Faye and me that her brother really hoped to see you after the Singing. So . . . did Tobe have something special to ask?" Lettie was inching this way as she filled the troughs opposite Lucy.

"Aren't you the *naasich* one?" Lucy asked, feeling increasingly put out with her.

"Nosy? It's only natural to be curious about your big sister, don'tcha think?" Lettie sighed. "I wonder if Rebekah will go along when the Glicks move out west. Word has it more families are talkin' of leaving to join a small *Gmay* out there," she said suddenly.

Lucy was surprised. "How do you know 'bout that?"

Her sister frowned. "How do ya think?"

Rebekah, Lucy realized. *Of course!*

Lucy wondered how much Tobe's sister was privy to her parents' plans. But it was impossible to get another word in, since Lettie kept rattling on until she finally slipped back to the house, leaving Lucy to put away her bucket and the watering hose, feeling terribly on edge.

–––––––

Christian waited for Lettie to return to the house before moseying out to the barn to check on Lucy. He found her with Sunshine, grooming the mare. Often after evening family worship, Lucy came out and brushed down the horses. *Maybe it's her way of working off frustration, like it is for me.*

Scuffing his feet, Christian moved into the area of the stable, his pulse heightened and jaw clenched. How ridiculous it was to feel anxious around the daughter he'd once been so at ease with!

She looked his way but kept working the rubber curry brush from the horse's neck to its rear, loosening the dirt.

He leaned both arms on the door to Sunshine's stall. "Is this a *gut* time to talk about the necklace?" He had no idea what she was thinking other than what little she'd spouted to him earlier. *. . . And as we walked into the community church, no less!*

At first, Lucy didn't respond, but her motions became more determined . . . rigorous. Finally, she spoke. "I hope you don't intend to talk me out of what I want to do."

Startled by her outspoken manner, Christian considered turning tail and talking with her another time. "*Ach*, Lucy . . . the necklace is yours to keep, sell, or give away as you see fit."

Lucy switched to the currycomb, working through Sunshine's mane till it was smooth and gleaming. "Mamm thought I should get your wisdom first, before deciding to give away whatever I might get for it." Lucy paused and shook her head. "It doesn't make sense for me to keep a necklace I no longer want . . . and shouldn't have accepted in the first place. Not when the money could possibly change someone's life—someone who needs more than her family will give."

Christian watched Lucy tend to the horse. "If you're settled about this, I won't stand in your way."

"Tomorrow, after I finish at Martie's, I'll hire a driver to take me to the jewelry store to get an appraisal, maybe sell it outright."

"Will you be okay . . . goin' alone?" His heart went out to her.

She took her time before she spoke again. "I'm always alone in here." She tapped her temple. "No one else understands."

Her admission took Christian by surprise. "Oh, Lucy, other women have suffered, too—"

"I'm not *them*, Dat! I couldn't just bounce back after Travis rejected the baby growin' in me . . . and then you called off the wedding."

"Lucy," Christian said firmly. "*Genunk*—enough!"

Flinching, Lucy pressed her lips together, as if to keep any further words inside.

"It's time for us to slam the door on the past," Christian declared. "Dredging this up now can't solve anything."

Eyes glistening, Lucy looked at him again, her chin raised. She slipped around to the other side of Sunshine and set to work once more. "You wanted Travis to become Amish for me . . . for my baby's sake."

"It was the only right way for you to marry him."

"That was never the plan, though." Lucy shook her head. "I wanted to go fancy for him, Dat. To join *his* world. Not the other way around."

Christian felt the air go out of him, yet he understood. He, too, had flirted with the idea of leaving the Old Order Amish church as a youth. "You must've loved him very much. . . ."

"It's so hard to rehash all this, Dat."

He saw the red rising from Lucy's neck into her face. "I'm honestly sorry I pushed the father of your child away. But I'm not sorry you remained with the People."

She shook her head. "It felt so cruel . . . cut off from everyone I loved, and who loved me."

Christian drew a long breath, trying to calm his nerves. This was the most Lucy had spoken of that devastating time, the most she'd talked to him about anything in years. "Ain't easy to think 'bout those days and months. Not for me, nor your mother. And certainly not for you, Lucy."

When he was rather sure she would not say more, Lucy glanced at him, then away.

He turned to go. "I'd better call it a night."

"*Jah*, Mamm will wonder what's keepin' ya."

He nodded. Lucy was absolutely right.

Lucy watched as her father trudged off. He, too, was still stuck in the mire of yesterday.

Dawdi Flaud had passed away just days after Lucy was put on a bus for Cherry Valley, Ohio, to stay with her mother's distant cousin Sally. Her misery was heightened by having missed out on the funeral.

She cringed as she recalled Dat's mention that *"other women have suffered, too."* Could he possibly have realized how offensive it sounded?

Oh, and she *had* suffered, trying her best to be brave when confronted with the loss of the baby no one seemed to want but her. And when she eventually did come home, she was expected to resume her usual cheery attitude. *"For the sake of your twin sisters . . . and everyone else who is better off not knowing,"* her father had told her after the long bus ride home.

She had been ever so compliant upon her return, willing to abide by his and Mamm's mandate never to reveal her secret to anyone but the brethren. So very eager had she been to remain in East Lampeter . . . where she had finally understood she belonged.

Where my heart was supposed to heal, given enough time.

Lucy patted Sunshine's silky neck and lifted each leg to pick out the stones in her hooves, letting her tears fall onto the bedding straw below.

When she was finished, she left the stall to put away the grooming implements. "I know one thing, and I know it with all my heart," Lucy whispered as she walked out of the stable and past the hen house. "If I had a daughter who needed my love at a desperate time, I would never push her out the door! *Ni net!*"

CHAPTER 23

BEFORE BREAKFAST THE NEXT MORNING, Christian welcomed his three eldest—Ammon, James, and Solomon—inside for coffee, out of the heavy rainstorm. Sarah was still upstairs dressing, and Christian had come down to read his Bible and drink his first cup of coffee when the back door opened and in they walked, soaked from head to toe.

"It's makin' down mighty hard," Ammon said, removing his straw hat over the sink while James and Solomon were still shaking out their jackets in the mud room.

But the weather seemed to be the last thing on his sons' minds. "There's talk that some families are thinkin' of moving to the San Luis Valley in Colorado," Ammon said when they all sat down at the table.

"You can't really blame folk," James said, twiddling his thick thumbs. "After all, it's a *schmaert* idea for families needing land for their courting-age children to broaden their horizons."

"There's plenty-a land there," Sol agreed as he got up and poured coffee for his brothers.

The younger serves the older. Christian smiled.

"Is this somethin' you and Mamm would ever consider doin'?" asked Sol, bringing the full mugs to Ammon and James.

"Moving has never crossed my mind," Christian replied.

"I thought maybe since Lucy and the twins are still single, and it doesn't look like they've got serious beaus yet, well . . ."

"Oh, there're enough young Amishmen here locally." Christian raised the mug to his lips. "Besides, your mother is content here . . . and we have your Mammi Flaud to look after."

This seemed to satisfy Sol and Ammon, but James asked, "What if *I* was to pull up stakes with my family and go? What would ya think of that?"

Ammon and Sol began to murmur between themselves.

"Listen, son, nobody's gonna stop you from doin' God's will, if that's where He's leading ya," Christian said. "But I daresay you should beseech the heavenly Father for His blessing before going ahead with such a sweeping decision."

James nodded and glanced at his brothers. "I wouldn't think of doin' otherwise. You taught us well, Dat."

"All right, then, let's talk this through," Christian said, rising to get some sticky buns leftover from yesterday. Then, bringing them over on a plate, he set it down, still standing at the head of the table. "Is this something you've also tossed round with Reuben and Ezra?" Christian was mighty curious what his other sons might be thinking about all this, especially when they hadn't shown up here, too. How had what seemed to be a rather private matter spread so quickly . . . and to his own sons? *That Amish grapevine!* he thought, knowing Deacon Ed had surely anticipated this.

Ammon was nodding his head, his bush of a beard touching his chest. "Ezra thinks the families making noises 'bout leaving are *Dummkepp*, to put it plainly. He wonders if they're disgruntled over something." He shrugged his broad shoulders.

"'Tis a reason why some new start-up settlements wither and

die in only a few years," Christian said. "And if at least a dozen or so families aren't recruited to a new settlement within a decent timeframe, then very likely others will steer clear of joinin' them, for fear of failing. There's just too much at stake."

"Ain't any common discontent amongst the People round here that I know of," James observed.

Ammon and Solomon nodded their heads.

"Reuben wishes Godspeed to Jerry Glick and the others goin'. But he's also mentally filing the possibility for down the road at some point. So's Ray," added Sol.

"Is that right?" Christian said, surprised.

"Well, I doubt Martie knows anything 'bout it," James piped up.

"She'd be upset, to say the least." Christian couldn't imagine one of his daughters going out to the wild West. He dismissed it as something that sensible Ray Zook would never consider.

"It's comin' close to the time to divide up our district—nearly too many folk to fit into one house for Preaching anymore. But if a few families do end up leavin', we could push that off," James said.

Christian reached for a sticky bun. "Hadn't even thought of that."

"My guess is the bishop has," Sol suggested with a chuckle.

"Well, he may lose some of the older, more established families, though. Jerry, for example—his family's been round here for generations," Ammon pointed out.

This jolted Christian, recalling Sarah's whispers that Tobe had asked Lucy to court. *Surely Tobe didn't ask her to go to Colorado with him and his family!*

He tuned out his sons' talk, lost in thought until Sarah appeared in the doorway and set to work making breakfast.

⌘

Lucy was itching to get to Martie's early that Saturday morning. She donned her old black raincoat with the hood to keep her black outer bonnet dry, politely refusing her father's offer to take her in the family buggy. As she guessed would happen, her shoes and socks got sopping wet on the way over on her scooter. Thankfully, she'd brought along dry socks, thinking ahead especially to the trip to the jewelry store that afternoon.

Since she knew precisely what Martie wanted done, Lucy began polishing four sets of black church shoes for the family, who would be going to visit Ray's parents tomorrow for his father's birthday. All of Ray's ten siblings and their families would be present, Martie told her while Lucy worked, Jesse chiming in about going to visit Dawdi and Mammi Zook.

"Be sure to go out and see the piggies when you're there," Lucy told Jesse.

"*Huss Sau!*" Jesse gave the pig call that Ray, no doubt, had taught him, and she laughed, glad to see her young nephew in such good spirits.

Along with redding up the house, Lucy also entertained the boys in the kitchen, the rain pattering against the windowpanes while Martie baked a three-layer German chocolate cake for her father-in-law. The kitchen felt cozy, what with the stormy weather and the sweet aroma of the baking dessert.

Later, when Martie had a chance to get off her feet for a few minutes, she asked Lucy, "What do ya think if I include in my column something 'bout the chatter of families moving west?"

"Maybe it'd be wise to wait and see if anyone actually goes," Lucy suggested.

Martie frowned quizzically. "Do ya think some might back out?"

"Well, it's possible things will change." Lucy thought of Tobe, who should receive her letter today, if the postman wasn't delayed by the driving rain.

Nodding, Martie agreed. "I just thought it'd make for some interesting reading."

Lucy smiled. "You're always lookin' for the next big thing to report round here, ain't so, sister? Like journalists out there in the world."

Martie gave her a sideways glance. "How would ya know that?"

Lucy caught herself. "Oh, I can *imagine* it, can't I?" But the truth was, during the year she and Travis had spent time together, she'd seen television shows at his townhouse—including some news. But there was no sense in bringing that up.

She glanced over at her pocketbook hanging on a wooden peg, the necklace tucked inside. *Time to say good-bye . . .*

When he found a free half hour that rainy morning, Christian took the horse and carriage up to Jerry Glick's farm, interested to find out if his lifelong friend had truly decided to pull up stakes and move to Colorado.

He found Jerry in the milk house scrubbing down the equipment, including the bulk tank, singing loudly. Christian pitched in to help, remarking about the muddy road on the way over there.

"If you're really thinkin' of going west, I s'pose you'll have just the opposite—less rain, more wind."

"Even times of drought, from what I'm gathering," Jerry said, his old straw hat perched on his head. "Although drought was one reason why an early attempt at settling in Cheyenne County disbanded way back in 1914. The community of Wild Horse folded after only five years. Things are working out better for the folk in the San Luis Valley, however."

"Sounds mighty challenging."

"Guess we'll find out. And there's always irrigation, if necessary."

"Oh, I'm sure it will be. Can't grow much in a desert, ya know." Christian glanced at Jerry. "S'pose the inducement is the land, *jah?*"

Jerry nodded, and when they'd finished cleaning, he motioned for Christian to have a look at his new foals.

Christian was impressed. "I might be interested in buying these from ya, whenever you're ready."

Laughing, Jerry assured him. "I'll give ya first pick, how's that? Unless Tobe stays and takes over the farm. . . . He's still deciding that."

"Oh?" Christian looked around the stable, still finding it hard to believe his old friend wanted to uproot his family. But this tidbit Jerry had dropped about Tobe was news. "Mighty glad you'll still be round through the fall and winter," he said, wondering if Jerry might say more about his plan.

"Ain't a reasonable time to move the family, that's certain."

"*Nee*, you're right on that," Christian said. "Let me know how I can help out."

"I'll keep that in mind."

Christian said he should get back to work and headed to his carriage in the rain. He noticed Tobe pulling into the lane in his father's enclosed buggy.

Tobe waved to Christian, who stopped to talk a bit. "It's makin' down right *gut* now," Tobe said, dipping his head politely, always respectful to his elders.

Tobe mentioned that their English neighbor to the south was looking for some help putting on a new roof this coming Wednesday.

"With my brothers, two uncles, and a few other Amish neighbors, I think we've nearly got a full crew. We'll knock it out in a day or so."

"I'm not a young buck anymore, but I can throw down a few shingles if need be. Maybe get Lucy to provide some refreshments."

Tobe brightened. "Think she could spare the time?"

Christian laughed. "Hard to say anymore, considering how much time she spends on all her charities."

A strong wind rattled the leaves, and Tobe seemed momentarily lost for words. "Well," he said slowly, "you can't really fault Lucy for wanting to help folk. She has a *gut* heart."

In that instant, Christian was reminded of why he'd often felt as connected to Jerry's gem of a son as he did to his own boys. "I couldn't agree more," he said, then bid Tobe good-bye, his heart heavy at Lucy's rejecting his offer to court.

To think they might've married already if Travis hadn't come along. . . .

Lucy was thankful for such a pleasant and grandfatherly jeweler to assist her midmorning, when she quietly revealed that her fiancé had purchased the necklace less than four years ago. "I've scarcely worn it, and I'd like to sell it today."

Nodding cordially, the white-haired gentleman reached for his jeweler's loupe and held it up to one eye. Leaning forward, he took his time examining the solitaire diamond for its size, color, and quality.

Lucy had decided on the ride over in the Mennonite driver's van to accept whatever amount might be offered. It wasn't her nature to haggle over price.

The jeweler looked at her with kind, even sympathetic eyes as he lowered the loupe and placed the necklace carefully on a navy blue velvet cloth. "This is a remarkable gem—a brilliant stone with no flaws," he said. "The gold is also of exceptional quality. Are you sure you want to give up this fine piece of jewelry?"

"*Jah*," she assured him. "I'm ready."

"It is, after all, a very large stone for . . . such a Plain girl."

Lucy had thought much the same when Travis had presented her with the piece, but she was grateful now, because it would probably mean more money for Kiana.

"I would be remiss if I didn't say that you could get more for its value if you received a credit toward another purchase here in the store."

She shook her head. "*Denki*—er, thank you for the offer, but I don't need any other jewelry." She really just wanted to be done with this.

"One other suggestion, miss, if I may: You could easily get more for this necklace than I'm authorized to give if you—or someone you know—could advertise it on eBay or Craigslist."

"Well, I don't have access to any of that."

When Lucy signed her name to the agreement and, later, when the kind jeweler gave her a check, she had a sense of severing the last ties to Travis, and it felt ever so good. She could hardly wait to deposit the funds into her checking account. To satisfy her mother's wishes, she planned to put a portion into the alms box somehow or other, even if she didn't attend the Sunday the devout observed communion and the afternoon foot-washing service. Lucy shuddered to think that yet another six months had come and gone, and her heart was not right with the church. *Or the Lord God.*

CHAPTER 24

THE DRIVE-THROUGH WINDOW at the bank where Lucy and her family did their banking was still open when her driver pulled into the line of cars close to noon. She noticed an Amish carriage two cars ahead, but that was nothing unusual—her father often made transactions when he was out with the horse and buggy. Even so, Lucy noticed a man off to one side of the lot in his car, taking a video or photo of the horse and carriage with his cell phone. "Well, look at that," she said to the Amish girl next to her in the van. "I wonder if he asked permission."

"Everybody's doin' that," the brunette teenager said, pulling out her own phone and poking this and that, swishing her pointer finger across the face of the phone. Then, just that quickly, she was filming the man holding up his phone. "See how easy 'tis? And nobody asks anyone if it's all right."

Lucy wondered how long she'd had the phone but guessed it was something that would have to be put away and forgotten about once the girl joined church. Just looking at her, Lucy guessed she was no more than sixteen, which meant she must be in *Rumschpringe*.

"My parents don't know I have this," the girl whispered, brown eyes serious.

Lucy didn't know whether to say anything or not, but she wanted to. Oh, did she ever!

"You really don't know what you're missin' if you can't text friends at a moment's notice," the girl added.

"Well, I can't miss what I've never had, ain't?" Lucy said. The phone promptly disappeared into the girl's red shoulder bag, and she turned to look the other way.

Between the stop at the bank and dropping the Amish teen-ager off at the end of her lane, the wind picked up even more. Rain hammered the windshield so hard the wipers couldn't keep up.

The driver slowed and pulled onto the shoulder for a while to wait out the worst. Lucy watched the rainwater swirl in dark pools along the road and shivered. She looked off to the right and saw a scooter leaning against a horse fence, a bright red reflective vest hanging off its handle. Next thing, here came a young blond boy running to get it, with only his little straw hat to shield his head from the fierce weather.

Lucy's thoughts turned to Tobe, recalling his first-ever invitation, years ago. She was in fifth grade and he in fourth when he'd asked to race scooters one warm springtime afternoon on their way back from school. Tobe had boldly left the group of other boys his age to stick his neck out to talk to her while she rode her scooter beside Martie and the twins, who were on foot.

An invitation I accepted . . . and I managed to win the race! she thought, realizing anew how often Tobe had sought her out during those years. *But just as a friend . . . or so I thought.*

After a time, the rain let up to some extent, and her driver pulled out onto the road again. They crept along, hugging the right side of the road like the other cars in their lane, with the exception of one that sped up and swerved around them, sending enormous waves onto the van's windshield.

Cautiously, the driver slowed. "What's that driver thinking?" he muttered.

Lucy had seen her share of unnecessary accidents caused by cars. Fortunately, she had never been alone in the family carriage when a squall like this one blew in. She wondered if she might be able to adequately handle the horse on her own if that should ever happen.

I told Travis my concerns over that, she let herself reminisce. She had even shown him how to hitch up, and right outside Mamm's kitchen window, with Mamm watching. *My poor mother surely wondered if she was going to lose her eldest daughter to an outsider without a speck of interest in the ways of the Lord—or the Plain ways.*

Yet after her father had confronted Travis, Lucy never heard from him again.

Abruptly, Lucy's driver slammed on the brakes. Her head lurched forward as she grabbed hold of the seat. Before her eyes, another car flew around the horse and buggy that was less than a single car length in front of them. The horse reared up, and Lucy watched in horror as the buggy flipped over onto its right side, crashing against the rain-saturated road, and the helpless horse was pulled to the ground. In one terrible instant, it was over.

"*Gott* help them!" Lucy cried, thinking of the driver and any passengers. *Are they hurt? How could they not be?*

Instinctively, she knew the struggling horse must be kept calm so the buggy wouldn't be jolted again, further jeopardizing anyone inside. "Have mercy, Lord!" she cried, and without considering the consequences to herself, she scrambled out of the van into the needlelike rain, running straight to the thrashing animal pinned down against the road in its harness.

Drivers from cars in the opposite lane got out and ran to the overturned buggy as Lucy knelt on the wet road, beside the frightened mare, careful of the potentially dangerous hooves. She stroked the thick, wet mane, attempting to soothe the horse, its large russet eyes registering terror.

Lucy leaned her wet cheek against the horse's long, wet nose. "*Psch!* Be still—*ach*, please try to be still," she said in her most reassuring voice. "It won't be long now . . . we'll get you out of the harness. *Psch!*"

Now she could see the Amish driver emerging from the fallen buggy, the right side of his face red and swollen. Behind him, two small children climbed out, seemingly unhurt. The three of them huddled together, appearing somewhat dazed.

Lucy rose to her feet as several people came over and unhitched the terrified mare, freeing her.

Then, of all things, Lucy saw Dale Wyeth straining to right the buggy with two other men. *What's he doing here?* But in the next second it came to her: Dale must have been visiting her father yet again.

Still standing beside the shaken horse, soothing and stroking, Lucy was surprised to see Dale talking to the Amish driver, as if they knew each other. Suddenly, Dale leaned down and picked up the tiny Amish girl, and then the not much older brother, taking them both into his arms and carrying them to his pickup.

"Lucy Flaud!" She heard her name as the children's father hurried toward her and the horse. She recognized him as their neighbor Abe Riehl, who appeared to be walking normally, not seriously injured. "Lucy, please go with that young man . . . take Judah and Suzie home. I'll bring the horse later."

"*Jah* . . . I'll go with them," she said, crossing the road. More cars were backed up now along the narrow road.

The rain had slowed considerably as she opened the door to the red pickup, still stunned at what she had witnessed. Dale waved her in, and she got onto the front bench seat and gently put soggy little Suzie on her lap. Three-year-old Judah sat cradling his elbow and shivering uncontrollably between Lucy and Dale, whimpering.

"Shouldn't they be checked out at the hospital?" Dale said, eyes filled with concern as he turned the key in the ignition. Lucy was thankful for her raincoat, since the rest of them were completely soaked to the skin.

"Just take them home like Abe said—I'll show you the way." She cradled Suzie in her arms, trying to warm her.

The truck moved cautiously forward around the long lineup of gawkers. Lucy was relieved to see the mare much calmer and the carriage on its wheels again. The windshield looked like great cobwebs where the glass had shattered, and two of the wheels were badly bent.

"Are ya hurt, honey-girl?" she asked Suzie in *Deitsch*.

The little girl pointed to her dimpled hand, the back of which was all red and brush burned.

"My elbow hurts," Judah said, showing her, his face still wet from the rain . . . and tears.

"Any other boo-boos?" asked Lucy, trying for the children's sake to be calm.

Judah rubbed his eyes and pressed his lips together so he wouldn't cry.

"You've got yourself a little bruise, is all," she said, eyeing his forehead. She wondered now how badly Abe might have been hurt, even though he'd said he was fine. She had known of drivers, and passengers, too, depending on where they were sitting in the carriage, to have suffered head injuries and even death from such an accident. The children must have fallen on their father when the buggy tipped over. How else were they okay?

"Did you get the license plate of the car at fault?" Lucy asked Dale.

He shook his head. "It happened so fast. Was tough to see."

Now that she'd taken a deep breath or two and felt less

frightened, the whole thing angered her. She wished to good-ness cars would slow down around horses, especially on such a stormy day.

"The Lord's angels were present," Dale said with conviction.

"*Jah*, there's no other explanation for Abe's and the children's safety." She continued to stroke Suzie's arm. "Turn left at the next dirt lane," Lucy directed.

Little Judah looked at Lucy. "Ada-Girl was all shook up, ain't so?" he said in his small voice. "But I saw ya calmin' her real *gut.* . . ."

Lucy assured him that graceful Ada would be all right. *Or so I hope* . . . Quickly, she changed the subject. "Your Mamma will be so glad to see you two safe and sound," she told them, "she'll prob'ly let ya have an extra cookie."

This brought a half smile to Judah's face, and Suzie let out a small giggle.

"Perfect timing, Lucy—most people wouldn't know how to calm a horse," Dale said, glancing her way.

"Maybe not most fancy folk," she said, suddenly remembering her driver. He had surely seen her rush off with the children and Dale. *I'll pay him later.* . . .

At the Riehls' dairy farm, Dale stopped the pickup and reached for Judah, carrying him out of the truck through the subsiding rain to the back porch. Lucy took Suzie, moving as quickly as she could without further jostling the poor girl.

Anna Mary Riehl came right out the back door, frowning and wiping her hands on her long black apron. "Well, what's this?" Her gaze darted from Lucy to Dale, then back again.

Lucy introduced Dale as her father's friend. "Abe asked Dale to bring the little ones home. Ya see, there's been an accident." Swiftly, and in an unruffled tone, she explained in English, to spare the children, what had happened in the torrential rain. "Abe said he'll be comin' shortly with Ada-Girl."

"Well, thank the Lord yous were there to help out." Anna Mary held Suzie close and waved them inside.

Dale shrugged as if unsure he should go along, but Lucy motioned him to follow.

Indoors, Anna Mary set Suzie on the counter and pushed a nearby footstool up to the sink for Judah. "Let's get ya washed off *gut*, make sure you're both all right."

Gently, Anna Mary washed her son's elbow and inspected the bruise on his forehead, finally rolling up his pant legs to check his knees, discovering the right one was bruised. She asked him to move various parts of his body before she seemed satisfied that nothing was broken.

"*Kumme* now, Suzie. Your turn." She went through the same process, kissing Suzie's rosy little cheeks in between checking. She wrapped Suzie in a towel she brought from the nearby bathroom and asked Judah to go into his room and change his clothes.

When the children were reckoned all right, Anna Mary offered a dry shirt and a pair of broadfall trousers to Dale, who said he would be fine. "Are ya sure?" she asked, looking incredulous at him. "It'll be awfully wet sittin' in your truck to drive home, or wherever you're headed."

Lucy smiled at Anna Mary's dogged persistence, and in the end, Dale agreed and headed upstairs to change just as Judah returned to the kitchen.

"Is there anything else we can do for you or the children?" Dale asked when he returned, looking astonishingly Plain in Abe's green shirt, black broadfall trousers, and black suspenders.

"I'm ever so grateful." Anna Mary smiled, though she seemed puzzled by the fact that Lucy was obviously familiar with the *Englischer*.

Another one, she must be thinking, Lucy lamented. *Ach!*

"You must drop by again sometime, Mr. Wyeth . . . maybe for dessert, as a thank-you from Abe and me. You too, Lucy."

Little Judah was starting to cry and said he'd lost his hat.

"We'll find it," Anna Mary assured him. "Someone will rescue it, I'm sure."

Wiping his tears, Judah marched over and shook Dale's hand. "*Denki, Mann.*"

"You can call me Dale," he replied, and Anna Mary quickly translated for the boy, which brought a big smile to Judah's little face.

"*Denki,* Dale," said Judah, bobbing his still-wet head.

"You have two very brave children," Dale said, thanking Anna Mary for the dry clothes, his own in the plastic bag she'd given him.

"You're so kind," Lucy said.

"*I'm* kind?" Anna Mary exclaimed. "How can I ever thank the both of you?"

Lucy protested, and the next words out of her mouth surprised even her. "It'd be hard not to believe that the Lord planned for us to be right where He meant us to be."

"We can always trust the Good Lord, no matter the outcome, *jah?*" Anna Mary smiled.

"*Jah,*" Lucy replied, surprising herself once more. *The Good Lord.*

CHAPTER 25

MARTIE STILL FELT SHAKEN, having watched the accident unfold—the wild driver spooking the Riehls' road horse. She had been standing in the window before the accident happened, swaying gently with Josh in her arms, trying to soothe him to sleep after he and Jesse had fought over a toy.

When Abe Riehl's horse reared high on its hind legs, Martie's heart had dropped. Yet, seeing Dale Wyeth's colorful pickup yet again, and then him drive away with Lucy, as well as Abe's two children, gave Martie pause. *This young man keeps showing up,* she thought, recalling the times she'd seen him around the area in the space of a week or so. "Is Lucy helpin' him learn to live more simply now, too?" she murmured.

Looking down at her angel-faced toddler, she was tempted to kiss his cheek, but she didn't dare wake him. Not before he'd had his full nap.

She found it surprising that no one had called the police— surely some drivers had carried phones. Maybe because no one was hurt and there wasn't any need. *Abe Riehl would much prefer it that way,* she knew. The staunchest church members liked to handle things their way.

Turning from the window, Martie was thankful the rain had ceased for now. She carried Josh to the sofa at the other end of the long front room where she and Ray had hosted church some months back. Ray and other men had removed the wall partitions to the room behind it to open things up to accommodate the more than a hundred and fifty people. She remembered getting the house and grounds, even the barn, prepared prior to that particular Lord's Day. What a humbling feeling she and Ray had experienced, having the bishop, their district's two preachers, and the deacon all present and looking dignified in their black *Mutze*—split-tail coats—and Sunday broadfall trousers.

She'd noticed on the calendar that morning there wouldn't be too many more days and their fall communion service would take place—the Sunday after St. Michael's Day, following their day of fasting and prayer. *Will the People be unified . . . in one accord?* She prayed that Lucy might participate this time. *It's been too long. . . .*

<hr>

When they were alone in Dale's pickup, Lucy marveled again that everyone had been spared. *And to think that Dale was there at just the right time.* Just this morning, she might have considered Dale Wyeth a bit of a nosy nuisance.

Somehow, Dale and the other men had managed to get Abe's buggy back on its twisted wheels. *It took teamwork.* Indeed, there were many thoughts flying around in Lucy's head.

One thought in particular surprised her: Dale, self-professed seeker of a simpler life, appeared quite comfortable in Abe Riehl's clothing. Lucy suppressed a smile.

"Cute kids," Dale said as they backed out of the Riehls' long driveway.

"Aren't they?"

"That accident could've been much worse."

Lucy agreed. She could only imagine how frightened she would have been if she'd been inside that tipped-over buggy, but Judah and Suzie had seemed remarkably calm. She wondered if they might cry now that they were with their mother, being given such tender sympathy.

Turning right out of the Riehls' lane, she spotted Abe headed this way on Witmer Road, walking alongside the limping mare.

Dale slowed to a stop and rolled down his window, waving his hand to get the man's attention. "Will the horse be okay?" he asked.

"I believe so." Abe nodded, eyeing Dale's shirt. "*Denki* again. Mighty kind of yous to help." He bobbed his head toward his farm. "Nearly home, so I'll give the vet a call from the shanty right away."

"By the way," Dale said, "your wife *insisted* I change into dry clothing—yours, I'm afraid."

Abe grinned and waved it away like it was nothing.

"What about you?" Dale asked. "Are you all right?"

Abe cracked a smile. "I've experienced worse. But the carriage didn't fare as well—I left it by the side of the road till it can get hauled to the buggy maker's for repair."

They bid farewell and started on their way again. Lucy assured Dale that the vets were real quick about going to check on a horse involved in an accident. She was noticing Dale's compassionate way with everyone, from her young nephew to the Riehl family today.

"I need to run a quick errand," Dale said. "I promised a farmer out off Route 896 I'd drop off a ladder he ordered, and I'm already late as is."

It was too early for egg gathering, and Lucy was otherwise caught up on her expected home chores. She thought for a second.

"That's fine. It's a real perty area." She looked at his shirt. "That is, if ya don't mind bein' seen in Amish attire."

Dale snapped his suspenders. "Don't you think it adds a little something?"

Lucy laughed, and he joined in, setting his hands firmly on the wheel.

———

"Look over there." As Dale drove away from his farmer friend's place, Lucy pointed out a silo-like cell phone tower. "I've heard 'bout these towers—some farmers are makin' more on lease rates than they can make farming," she said, gawking at it. "It's amazing how high they are, even taller than those two silos."

"I should take a picture." Dale got out of the truck and took several shots with his phone.

She observed him over near the white horse fence and thought how funny he looked snapping photos while dressed Plain. She got out of the truck. "Getting some interesting ones?"

"Horses and ponies grazing in the paddock, the two-story barn . . . you name it. It's a photographer's paradise."

"That's a bank barn—two stories, with one side built into the hill."

He glanced at her and smiled. "You forget that I've always lived around here. The hayloft is in the second level, right?"

Lucy nodded. "And some farming equipment, too. Our Sunday night Singings are usually held up there, as well."

He caught her eye. "So is it okay to ask what's sung?"

She laughed. "At least two hours' worth of gospel songs. And, depending on which family is hosting, sometimes there's volleyball or a game of Dutch Blitz first, maybe even a hot dog roast."

"And this is something all the young people attend?"

"*Jah*, from age sixteen till ya marry." She paused a moment. "I quit goin' a while back, though." She went on to say that the gatherings were lots of fun, a way to connect with friends or pair up. She sighed. "I guess you could say the Singings are how we find our life mates."

Dale seemed to consider this. "So why did you stop going?"

She'd walked right into that one.

"It's okay if you'd rather not say," he added quickly.

"You know what? I oughta take *your* picture, so you can show your employees your new uniform, not just the cell phone tower."

Grinning, Dale shook his head. "Uh, no thanks. I'd never live it down. As it is, some of the guys at the hardware store already wonder about me."

They headed back to the truck, the reprieve from rain short-lived as another dark layer of swiftly moving clouds blocked any hope of sunshine.

As they turned and headed north, Lucy hoped that was the end of Dale's questions.

CHAPTER 26

CHRISTIAN HAD BEEN CHEWING THE FAT with Graham Weaver, his longtime vet, when the man's cell phone jingled. Not wanting to eavesdrop, Christian turned away, wondering what was keeping Lucy. She hadn't returned for the noon meal, though Lucy had warned that her trip to the jeweler might take a while. *Especially in this weather.*

Looking over at the chicken coop, Christian recalled Dale's interest in a coop of his own. From what Dale had told him, it wouldn't be too long and he'd have his own hen house up and be ready to purchase some chickens from Christian.

For sure and for certain, he'd made a mistake inviting Dale over here. True, he was an upstanding young man, but Christian had failed to take Lucy's feelings into account.

I'm a Dummkopp! Sarah had made it mighty clear to him.

Even so, Lucy's on the mend, he thought, taking comfort in her decision to sell the necklace. Alas, the matter with Tobe was another thing altogether.

Christian sighed. *Best to stay out of it.* Removing his straw hat, he fiddled with it.

"I'll come right over," Graham was saying. "Keep Ada-Girl as quiet as you can. Good-bye." He clicked off his phone. "Abe Riehl's horse got spooked just up the road north of here . . . turned over Abe's carriage with him and the little ones inside."

"Was anyone hurt?" Christian asked, alarmed.

"The buggy got the worst of it, or so it sounds from Abe." Graham waved and hurried to his car.

"Let me know if there's anything I can do," Christian called after him, following him partway down the driveway.

⁓⌒〜⌒〜〜⌒〜⁓

After a quick bite to eat at a fast food place, since both she and Dale had missed lunch, Lucy realized they would be driving right past the hospice.

"Would you mind droppin' me off?" she asked. "Since we're so close, I'd like to check on one of the patients I read to."

"Of course," Dale said. "Tell me more about your charity work. I'm really interested."

"*Ach*, my face is red," she said, then began rather reluctantly. "I spend a fair amount of time at the hospice, but my number-one priority right now is trying to help a homeless young mother get settled with a job. Her name is Kiana, and she has a little boy named Van." She shared with Dale how she'd met the two while working on the food truck downtown. "I've been reading the help-wanted ads in the newspaper every day, but when I call to respond to an ad on Kiana's behalf, I'm basically told she must apply online, or that the job has already been filled." She sighed. "It seems there's no way for her to get ahead if that's the case."

Dale listened, nodding. "What if I filled out the online forms for her?"

"You'd do that?"

"Sure." He smiled. "Glad to help." Then he asked if Kiana was looking for a place to live.

"That too, *jah*. I've been wading through notices for apartments or room and board."

Dale looked her way, studying her. "What if we prayed about this, Lucy, asking God to lead Kiana's steps . . . and ours, as we attempt to help her?"

Lucy didn't have much hope in any answers, but she agreed.

When Dale pulled up to the curb in front of the hospice, he bowed his head and did just that, offering a heartfelt prayer for divine assistance for Kiana and her precious child.

"Amen," said Lucy softly, unaccustomed to hearing such personal-sounding prayers said aloud.

Dale glanced at the hospice entrance and remarked that a group of young adults from his church had recently sponsored a marathon to raise money for this particular center.

Lucy was surprised but pleased. "If I could only volunteer at one place, this would be it."

Dale glanced toward the road. "It must be a couple of miles from here to your house."

"Oh, I walk it all the time . . . or take my scooter, which I left this morning at my sister Martie's. It was too rainy—and too far—to take it to town," she said. "I'll stay just long enough to say hello to one of the patients I visit."

"Well, I don't mind waiting for you."

How could she refuse? "I shouldn't be more than a half hour."

He turned off the ignition. "No problem."

"Actually, why don't you come in, and I'll show you around."

He considered this, tugging comically on the suspenders. "Wouldn't they find my outfit a little strange?"

"They'll never know you're *not* Amish."

"Good point." Chuckling, Dale got out of the pickup. "This should be interesting." He opened her door, and she got out.

"Of course, you might just run into someone you know, and then you'll have some questions to answer."

He grinned. "I think you're enjoying this too much."

"Hey, you want the simple life, right?"

"Touché."

Lucy couldn't help but laugh as they headed toward the front entrance, where exiting visitors gave them the once-over.

They surely notice that Dale-the-Amishman is letting his hair grow out real fancy-like, Lucy thought. *And has misplaced his hat!*

Inside the reception area, two nurses waved to Lucy, who offered to give Dale a tour of the main level, including the large aviary. A few patients in wheelchairs sat enjoying the beauty surrounding them. Some were accompanied by a relative or friend while others dozed in their chairs, propped up by plump white pillows.

"Notice the fresh smell of flowers everywhere," Lucy told Dale.

Nodding, he gazed up at a pair of yellow finches perched high in the aviary.

"Fine little friends of the facility." She spoke softly, as she always did in this area. "They serenade me during my lunch break."

Lucy took Dale around to the coffee shop and snack bar, then pointed out the gift store.

"It's a peaceful place," he said. But it was the aviary he seemed most captivated by, and she returned there with him.

"The serenity of this environment is one reason why many folk choose to come here for their final days."

"I can see why."

Then, eager to see how Wendell was doing, she excused herself. "Don't forget your friend Clinton's wife is here, too. Room 205, if you want to slip up there to see her."

Dale said he might do just that, and Lucy was delighted.

<hr>

There had already been a few times when Martie wondered how she would possibly manage with four children under the age of four. And the greater with child she became, the less energy she had.

Will I be able to continue as a scribe for The Budget? she wondered. The column brought her joy and was a small departure from her daily chores and mothering duties.

As Martie prepared ham and potatoes for the evening meal, she wished for just a moment to sit down and put her legs up.

Meanwhile, little Josh crawled out from beneath the table, wide-eyed again and whimpering. Today's nap had been all too brief, though Jesse, at least, still slept. Josh reached up for her, and she took him into her arms, going to the back door window to point out the "birdies." She told him gently that soon many of them would fly away for the winter. "The Lord above looks after the birds . . . takes care of them," she murmured into the fleshy creases of his damp little neck. "And *Gott* cares for you and Jesse, too."

Returning to the sink, Martie washed his face and hands and set him in his high chair for a snack. Then, thinking again of the Riehl children following the overturned buggy, and Lucy there with an outsider, Martie trembled to think another troublesome friendship might be brewing. Oh, for dear Lucy's sake, she hoped not. How could she bear to see her sister hurt again—and how could Lucy not be?

"Plain and fancy usually don't mix in happily ever after," she whispered, praying that the Lord might watch over her sister and keep her from making further mistakes with an *Englischer.*

❧

Upstairs, a cluster of folk were sitting in a spacious living area; some looked solemn, and others were struggling not to cry. One had lost that battle and was wiping away tears, reaching for a box of the tissues provided on each lamp table.

As Lucy passed Dorothea's room, she saw two ladies in with her. There was no sign of Clinton.

Making her way down the hall, Lucy's heart beat faster at the prospect of seeing Wendell again. His door was ajar, and one of the housekeeping staff, a stout redheaded woman in a white skirt and blouse and a black tailored apron was coming out. The woman smiled, but she was not familiar to Lucy. "Is Wendell awake?" Lucy asked as she waited to enter the room.

The woman shook her head. "I'm very sorry, miss. Wendell passed away this morning."

Lucy looked forlornly into the room from the doorway, noting the newly made bed, the two leather chairs moved near the window, the privacy curtain pushed all the way back. "He's gone," she whispered. "And I didn't get a chance to say good-bye. . . ."

She inched into the room where she'd spent hours reading and lending her ear . . . and heart. She tiptoed to the tan chair—the one she'd sat in for months, right beside Wendell's bed, where he liked it—and stared down, tears threatening.

"Are you all right?" the older woman asked.

Lucy turned. "Did Wendell's family arrive in time?"

"I really don't know." The housekeeper shook her head and left the room. "I'm so sorry."

Lucy lowered herself into the familiar chair; it seemed to embrace her. This very day, she had gone to sell her engagement necklace, relinquishing its grip on her heart. Wanting, even craving, a new start.

And all the while, Wendell Keene was making his own new beginning in the next life.

Did Wendell make his peace with God?

Lucy held her breath, hoping, even praying, it was so.

CHAPTER 27

BELINDA FREY WAS JUST COMING OUT of Dorothea's room when Lucy spotted her. "Have a minute?" Lucy gestured at the far end of the sitting area adjacent to the patients' rooms. "It's about Wendell," she said quietly as they sat down together.

"You must've heard." Belinda's eyes were solemn.

Lucy nodded and bowed her head.

"His son flew in from Chicago . . . made it here by the skin of his teeth," Belinda said. Smiling now, she reached over and tapped Lucy on the wrist. "And you won't believe it. No sooner did Newton Keene walk in the door in his business suit than Wendell asked him if he knew the way to heaven."

"Wendell did?" Lucy exclaimed.

"He sure did. Remember that afternoon?" Belinda asked. "Wendell not only wanted to talk over many things with me, but in the end, he prayed for *me*, thanking God for the Scripture verses I shared. Isn't that something? Quite a turnaround."

Lucy was relieved but also torn—she still felt inadequate, unable to have helped Wendell when it was most essential. "*Denki*, Belinda." She struggled to express her gratitude. "Hearing this means so much."

"Well, and seeing Wendell witness to his son of God's compassion and grace was powerful. It wasn't long after, that Wendell breathed his last."

"You must've been with him, then?"

Belinda nodded. "He was so peaceful, Lucy."

"I'm thankful for you. And I'm sure Wendell expressed that, too."

"It's the reason I volunteer here." Belinda smiled sweetly. "Not just to bring comfort but to speak life-giving words."

Just then, coming up the stairs, Lucy saw Dale, who waved to her as he came toward them, carrying a folded newspaper. "We'll talk again, I hope," Lucy told Belinda, rising.

"I hope so, too."

Why couldn't I have done what Belinda did? Lucy still felt defeated as Dale approached.

"Are you okay?" he asked, a slight frown on his face.

She mentioned Wendell's death.

"I'm sorry to hear it." Then, waiting a moment, he showed her the newspaper he'd purchased in the coffee shop downstairs, and the five help-wanted classifieds he'd already circled with Kiana in mind. "We can use my phone to call . . . leave a message, perhaps."

"Sure, that'd be a big help."

Then, looking in the direction of Dorothea's room, Lucy said she'd like to stop in and visit her. "Since I'm here. Would you wanna come, too?"

"Are you sure you're up to it?" He touched her elbow. "I'll visit Dorothea another time."

"Honestly, this could be your last opportunity. We just never know. . . ." Lucy had to turn away, lest he see her tears.

The white blinds in Dorothea's room had been drawn halfway, and Lucy smiled at her as she entered the room with Dale. "Hullo," she said. "You've had your share of visitors today, *jah?*"

Sitting up in a chair and wearing a pretty pink and lavender duster, Dorothea smiled in return. Her eyes looked brighter than the day she was admitted. "How nice . . . of you to come, Lucy," she said falteringly. Then, looking toward Dale, she smiled more broadly, pointing as if she recognized him.

Dale stepped forward, offering to shake her hand. "Dale Wyeth, from church."

Lucy covered her mouth, realizing he'd forgotten how Plain he looked.

"Well, now, that's one way . . . to get noticed by a pretty Amish girl," Dorothea managed to say. She chortled along with Lucy, who felt herself blush.

Quickly, Lucy made a point of telling Dorothea about helping at the scene of a buggy accident in the drenching rain . . . and how kindhearted Anna Mary had loaned dry clothing to Dale.

"I see." Dorothea coyly leaned her chin on her folded hands. "You two could pass . . . for brother and sister."

Lucy hadn't thought of that.

"There's . . . a sweetness in . . . your faces." Dorothea coughed, patting her chest lightly and shaking her head.

"There certainly is in Lucy's," Dale agreed.

Lucy heard footsteps in the hall, and she turned to see Clinton in the doorway, shedding his red cardigan as he came in. "Goodness, the staff must keep the thermostat sky high in this building."

Dale stepped over to greet him, and right away Clinton complimented his "new look."

"Dale's gone Amish . . . on us, dear," Dorothea said, bobbing her head at Dale.

"Well, I'd never have guessed." Clinton played along. "You'd forsake the grid for the girl?" He winked at Lucy.

Dale was quick to set the record straight, recounting the events that had led to his unlikely ensemble.

Clinton went over to kiss Dorothea on the forehead. He

stepped back a moment, looked into her face, and kissed her cheek this time. "How are you feeling today, darling?"

"Entertained," she replied, smiling again at Dale.

"You certainly wear the Plain garb well, my friend," Clinton said with another chuckle, and Dorothea nodded, then pointed to her Bible. "Will you read to us, Dale?" Clinton suggested. "You'll see where I placed the bookmark."

Dale promptly pulled up a chair so Clinton could sit next to his wife. Clinton leaned hard on his cane as he lowered himself onto the chair as Dale announced John fourteen and began to read slowly, emphasizing each thought. "'Let not your heart be troubled: ye believe in God, believe also in me. In my Father's house are many mansions: if it were not so, I would have told you. I go to prepare a place for you. And if I go and prepare a place for you, I will come again, and receive you unto myself; that where I am, there ye may be also. And whither I go ye know, and the way ye know. Thomas saith unto him, Lord, we know not whither thou goest; and how can we know the way? Jesus saith unto him, I am the way, the truth, and the life: no man cometh unto the Father, but by me.'"

Thinking of Wendell, Lucy did her best not to cry again, glad for the comfort in the promise Dale had read.

Once they returned to Dale's pickup, Lucy was ready to start making phone calls on Kiana's behalf. She soon learned the first two waitressing jobs she inquired about had been filled that morning. "This is what I've run into before," she said to Dale, feeling frustrated. "I'm always too late."

"I understand that, but it's been my experience that God is never too late. Sometimes it seems like the eleventh hour has just chimed, and then the answer comes."

Lucy tried to keep a positive outlook. "I can just imagine what

Kiana would say if something fell into place for her. I know she's not givin' up."

"And neither are we," Dale added, pointing to the next circled ad.

She dialed the number, and it rang six times on the other end before going to voicemail. "I'm not sure what to leave as a message—I don't really have a phone number they can use to contact me," she admitted, hanging up.

"Use my number as a callback," he suggested, jotting it down on a small note pad he pulled out of the glove box. "And leave your name rather than Kiana's."

Lucy dialed the number again, and this time it was busy.

Dale placed the last two calls. The final one was answered by a hiring manager who suggested Kiana come in person to interview for a retail position at a craft store in Bird-in-Hand, tending to shelves and welcoming and assisting customers. Lucy found herself holding her breath as Dale took it upon himself to say that he would see to it that Kiana got to the interview this coming Monday afternoon.

Is he doing this for Kiana . . . or to impress me? Lucy wondered.

When Dale put away his phone, he asked how to locate Kiana to tell her about this possible breakthrough. "I can drive you to the shelter where she stays," he offered.

"If she's still there." Lucy considered several other locations where Kiana might have gone, one of which was the Salvation Army's program. "No matter what, if we can find her, I know she'll be thrilled about this news."

"We could go in search of her tomorrow afternoon," Dale said now. "Since there's so little time before the interview."

"Well, it's our visiting Sunday, so maybe after my family returns home."

They decided on a time before supper when Kiana would perhaps be at one of the soup kitchens. "One way or other, I think we can find her," Lucy said, excited about Dale's help.

On the ride home, Lucy pointed out Ray and Martie's house. "My sister's a writer for a newspaper based in Ohio," she explained. "She has a weekly column."

"So, like an Amish blogger?" Dale asked, a twinkle in his eye when he turned to glance her way.

"A what?"

He explained, but Lucy still didn't understand.

"I'd be hard-pressed to have ever seen a blog," she said.

"You'd be surprised what people write about. Some have whole blogs dedicated to old-fashioned topics like the art of preserving food or raising livestock."

Lucy laughed. "Seems like a peculiar place to learn 'bout all that. My Dawdi used to say you learn the most just by doin'. Why, think of what you're going to learn once you get your laying hens!"

Dale chuckled. "I need to finish building my chicken house first. Once it's complete, your father has said I can purchase some hens from him." He also mentioned the goats he was planning to purchase from a Mennonite family in Conestoga.

Lucy found this very interesting. "Do *you* own a plot of land?"

He laughed. "A plot? I guess that's the best description of a patch that's just big enough to plant the necessary vegetables. I had a good crop of lettuce, radishes, tomatoes, cucumbers, and squash this year, by the way."

"Round this time of year, I'm always amazed to think our lovely garden is the culmination of my spring plans. Well, my twin sisters' and mine."

"With the three of you planting, weeding, and harvesting, it must be more fun. Working together always is." He grinned.

"It's how we've done it since I could pick up a hoe," Lucy said. "A *gut* way to help out Mamm, too."

He talked about his drafty old farmhouse then, saying it was on the outskirts of Bird-in-Hand, only a few miles from his store. "It's about a third as large as your father's."

"You might need only a modest coal stove to make it toasty—if you're thinkin' of disconnecting from central heating. That or a woodstove could heat the main level real nice."

Dale nodded brightly. "Things are starting to fall into place, thanks to all the help I've gotten, especially from your dad."

When her father's farm came into view, Lucy thanked Dale for the ride home.

"It was my pleasure," he said, looking her way.

She smiled and pointed at his homemade shirt. "Do ya remember how to get to Riehls' to return Abe's clothes when you're ready?"

Dale said he did. Then his eyes grew serious. "Do you plan to attend the next grief group?"

"I'm not sure yet."

He made the turn into their lane. "If you do, would you like to discuss the class together sometime?"

"Well, I'm awful busy," she said, surprised Dale would ask her. Besides, she'd already looked ahead to the rest of the curriculum and wasn't sure she was brave enough to attend.

Thanking him again, Lucy got out of the truck before he could come around to open her door for her, as he had last time.

Then, swiftly, lest her family observe her with Dale and misunderstand, she hurried around the side of the house and up the steps to the porch. It was too chilly to sit outside and brood, but she would have much preferred time to just sit and contemplate the day's events, particularly Wendell's passing. *Thank goodness it was peaceful.*

"Someone needs to gather the eggs," she heard Mamm say as she poked her head out the back door, meeting Lucy as she came in.

Quickly, Lucy dropped her purse at the door, briefly telling about her trip to town, as well as the frightening accident. However, Lucy did not mention Dale Wyeth, nor the time they'd spent together. *No sense in calling any attention to that. . . .*

CHAPTER 28

ALL THROUGH SUPPER, and afterward during family worship, Lucy remained preoccupied with the events of the day. She was relieved no one asked about her lack of conversation at the meal, not to mention her arrival home in a red pickup truck with an *Englischer*!

She recalled Dale's question and wondered if she ought to return to the grief group. *I can do the assignment, at least,* she thought. *That way I can change my mind later if I decide to go.*

Lucy headed upstairs to begin the requested list and sat for a moment, thinking, *What am I thankful for?*

The old frustrations began to build as more and more of the things she was not thankful about crept in.

Just start writing, she told herself.

Ignoring the first thing that came to mind, she scribbled down the obvious: food, shelter, good health, and family, then decided to elaborate. She included Martie's encouragement and love, and Faye, but felt convicted that she hadn't thought of Lettie just as quickly, so she jotted down her name, too, along with Mamm . . . and Lucy's many nieces and nephews. *And beloved Dawdi Flaud and Mammi, too.* Her thoughts went then to Wendell, and she was thankful that he hadn't suffered in his passing, as well as that Belinda had been there to comfort him by sharing about God's grace. *Kiana and little Van are also people I'm grateful for.* Last of all, Lucy wrote the name of her friend Tobe Glick.

"Tobe," she said and felt a strange wave of sadness mixed with sincerest appreciation. *I should've listed him first.*

Sighing, she opened the desk drawer and slipped the list inside, then went to stand beside the middle window. Lucy looked out over the farmland as far as she could see to the south. There was still faint light in the fading sky, and she decided the best way to further contemplate the week's blessings was to take a walk.

Downstairs, she donned her warm black jacket and let Mamm know she was going out for a while.

"Might wanna take along a flashlight," Faye said, overhearing.

Lucy nodded. "*Gut* idea."

"You all right?" Mamm asked, clearly concerned.

"No need to worry."

Ever since she'd divulged that Tobe had asked to court her, Mamm had been hovering like a mother hen.

Dear Mamm, she thought. *I know she cares.*

Outside, Lucy was met by the familiar smell of woodsmoke as she meandered south on Witmer Road, toward the much-traveled Lincoln Highway in the distance. Tourists populated the main thoroughfares this time of year, eating out and spending the day at Dutch Wonderland with their children before returning to hotels or bed-and-breakfasts.

She briskly walked past Uncle Caleb's property, then down toward the sheep farm next door to him, on past to the local blacksmith's shop, too. She was glad Faye had suggested the flashlight, knowing now she'd be out long enough to use it. *For sure.*

In the distance, a train whistle blew, the sound melancholy this late-September evening. Soon, the leaves would color to gold, orange, and red, eventually falling and drying up, to be crunched underfoot. As a child, Lucy had always looked forward to that. She thought now of her school-age nieces Cora and Emma Sue and recalled her promise to visit, making a mental note to do so.

As twilight fell, she heard a catbird's song, its faltering series of short notes coming from the blacksmith's woodshed, it seemed. Lucy knew the bell-like sound by heart, and on this night, it soothed her just as Dale's reading about the heavenly Father's many mansions had reached into her heart. Very soon that catbird would be flying away, just as Wendell Keene had left . . . and Lucy's own Dawdi Flaud. The forest would shed its leaves and open up, permitting autumn sunlight to shine down into its depths.

A dog's yapping startled her. As the barking grew louder, she guessed it might be the Glicks' red spotted spaniel. *Running loose?*

Shining the flashlight down the road, Lucy searched for the dog. She passed a stand of mature trees, and her brother James's apple orchard, the sound of crickets, tree frogs, and locusts thick as she went. Farther along, there was another farmhouse, one built with a greenhouse off the south side of the main house. It belonged to Leon Miller—Lucy knew from Mamm that Dat had been sweet on his daughter Minerva many years ago. It had been strange for Mamm to mention that another girl had caught Dat's eye back when. *Does my father know whether Mamm was courted by anyone before him? Or was Dat her one and only love?*

These thoughts stirred up Lucy's memory of selling her engagement necklace. Now, if only her plans for Kiana and her little boy might pan out.

The woodsmoke seemed to thicken overhead, and the dog barked again, much nearer this time. "Who's there?" she called into the dusk.

"Spotty Glick . . . and his dutiful master" came the reply.

Lucy couldn't help but smile. "Out walkin' your dog, Tobe?" she said even before she could see her friend.

"I was comin' to see you. Was thinkin' of storming your house." Tobe chuckled, his silhouette outlined in the dim light. "Just jokin'."

She stopped to wait for him and Spotty to cross the road, thinking how nice it was that she'd bumped into him like this.

"Here," she said, giving him the flashlight. "Since it looks like we're walkin' together."

He accepted it. "Which direction do you want to head—the same or back toward your house?"

"The way I'm goin', if that's all right with you."

"So, I received your letter." He paused, the words hanging in the air between them.

He doesn't seem upset, she thought.

"I'd like to talk about it."

She murmured her agreement.

"You made an interesting point, Lucy. You don't feel you should tie me down . . . but that wasn't what I asked you. And what's all this talk about not bein' right for me? Help me understand what you mean."

"You'll just have to trust me."

"No explanation at all?"

She sighed. This wasn't what she needed tonight, but maybe it was good to talk it out in person. "I honestly think you should only stay to purchase your father's farm if that's what *you* want."

Tobe was silent. She could hear his footsteps on the pavement, and the dog's tags tinkling. "You never said I wasn't right for *you*," he replied at last. "Is that what you really meant?"

She inhaled sharply, wishing she could change the subject. "What if we courted and it didn't work out, and you were stuck here?"

"I'm willing to take that chance."

She sighed. "Well, it ain't fair to you, Tobe."

"That's what people do when they care 'bout someone," he said.

"They take a risk. It's the same with anything in life. Nothing's guaranteed except the love of our Father in heaven."

She felt like she could cry. *You wouldn't want me. Not if you really knew me.*

"I *can't* take the risk," she said, her voice pinched. She sniffled.

"Are you okay?" Tobe asked.

She nodded, then realized he probably couldn't see her.

"So there's nothin' I can say to convince you otherwise?"

"Nothin' at all."

He paused a moment, then said, "Well, wherever you're walkin', I'll go with you, till you're ready to head home."

"It's getting late." She could hardly talk, she felt so sad. Next to Martie, this was her best friend, and she was rejecting him. "I should head home."

"Then I'll walk ya back," Tobe said.

He shone the light as they crossed the road to the opposite side, and halfway between there and the lane into her father's house, Tobe picked up the spaniel and carried him. She was touched by his sympathetic nature. Tobe was as considerate of the family pet as of anyone who was weary, suffering, or downtrodden.

Tobe talked about helping his father—and hers—drive their cows that afternoon from one pasture into another. His Dat had carried an old walking stick, he said, as they made their way across to the other meadow. "It has a wide crook in one end and is as smooth as ivory. Dat's had that walking stick since I was a boy, and he's talkin' of letting me have it . . . if I decide to stay with the farm."

"Oh, you would cherish that," Lucy said.

"Well, the farm's got a long history with our family, too, but none of that's enough to keep me here."

She felt torn between getting back to the safety of home, and saying good-bye to this wonderful friend.

When they reached the end of Dat's lane, she gave Tobe a

quick hug, something she'd never done before. "Be happy," she whispered, worse than blue.

"Hey, still friends, *jah?*"

"Of course," she agreed, certain things would never be the same. *I've caused him such disappointment.*

"*Gut Nacht*, Lucy."

"*Denki* for walkin' with me."

He turned to go, then came back to hand her the flashlight.

"Can you find your way without it?" she asked.

"*This* road? I could walk it in my sleep."

She smiled through her tears. That was Tobe. And to think she'd just given up her chance for a lifetime of happiness as his bride.

CHAPTER 29

"I HELPED JERRY GLICK move some of his cows and their calves to his westerly pasture today, but some of the calves got separated," Christian told Sarah as they sat alone in the front room. Lettie and Faye had already gone upstairs, and he could hear them laughing and having themselves a good time. "Ach, you should've heard those calvies carryin' on—crying and mooin' like there was no tomorrow."

"The poor things." Sarah sat on the rocking chair near the sofa, knitting a brown sweater for their grandson Josh.

"Then, soon as we drove the last calf through the gateway, there was a grand reunion, and the cries subsided that quick."

Sarah reached over and squeezed his hand. Looking down at her knitting, she observed, "Young ones need their Mammas, ain't?"

"That's so," he agreed. "Jerry Glick told me something this morning that was real surprisin'."

Sarah glanced up, her knitting needles poised in midair.

"A while back, he offered Tobe a chance to take over the farm completely, eventually buy it outright. But Jerry's downright perplexed—said Tobe didn't jump. Tobe's waiting, needs to think 'bout it."

"I wonder why."

Christian ran his big hand through his hair. "I mean, honest to Pete, this just don't sound like Tobe to me. Does it to you?"

"What . . . that he might want to go with his family?" Sarah asked. "Why's that so surprising?"

"But you know how Tobe's always loved that farm. Besides, I thought he might have second thoughts 'bout leaving Lancaster County."

Sarah gave a pensive smile. "Perhaps he can't bear to stick around, considering . . ."

"Lucy sayin' no?"

She nodded.

Christian shook his head. "I wish you'd seen him brighten up like a solar lamp when I mentioned Lucy's name today."

"Tobe's always been crazy 'bout her," Sarah replied softly.

What's Lucy thinkin'? Christian wondered.

According to the grapevine, Tobe had dated a few girls, but nothing had come of it, leading many, including Lucy, to speculate that Tobe was too finicky. But Christian doubted it. He had his own opinions regarding Tobe, but he would never call him prideful.

Won't be long, and Tobe could be gone for good.

―――――――

Lucy slipped indoors without being noticed, partly because her father was sitting in the front room with his head back, mouth wide open, snoring. Mamm's hands drifted into her lap with her knitting, her head bobbing.

Upstairs, Lucy said good-night to Lettie and Faye, who said the same, mercifully not prying tonight.

Lucy hurried to the third-floor staircase, put out with herself for having forgotten to remove her jacket downstairs. Going to the row of wooden wall pegs, she hung it there, then sat with a thump at her desk. Dare she try to finish her list of blessings?

She glanced toward the window and saw only the stars and the rising moon. "I'm in no mood," she murmured, opening her desk drawer and staring at the short list. Of course she was grateful for these people in her life, but when it came to listing less tangible blessings, she didn't know where to start.

Instead, she fretted over her conversation with Tobe. She saw it now for what it was—two lifetime friends moving away from each other. *Since he's probably leaving.* Just the thought of never seeing him again made her feel depressed. But what could be done? It wasn't as if she could expect him to stay in touch when he was clearly looking to marry and settle down. She was ever so sure he would find someone out west. *Considerate and caring as he is . . . my best-ever friend.*

She liked the idea of putting that on her list and pulled the page out of her drawer. *Friendship, loyal and true,* she wrote.

"What else?" She twiddled with the pen. Were there any blessings that had come from her time of grief? After all, she was fairly sure that focusing on those unexpected blessings was the purpose of the assignment. *"Saying good-bye takes time,"* the leader had made a point of saying. *"It's a process that can't be measured."*

Thinking of that, Lucy realized she now had yet another loss to grieve, even though she'd never had Tobe as a beau. Still, the idea of being courted by him had taken up a large part of her reflection here lately. And now that, too, was gone.

───※───

Upon Lucy's suggestion, she and her family went to visit Ammon and Sylvia and their children on the no-Preaching Sunday afternoon. When they arrived, Cora and Emma Sue ran to Lucy first, then to Lettie and Faye, obviously eager to spend time with their aunts.

Ammon shook hands with Dat, and he and Sylvia quickly pulled up a few chairs, making a large enough circle for all of them in the spacious kitchen. Lucy noticed they'd redone their linoleum in a muted pattern similar to others' in the community. The long oak table, even the overall layout, looked almost identical to Mamm's.

Lucy and her family greeted each of Ammon's six children, all of them dressed up for Sunday, in case visitors dropped in. The fair-haired boys—Ammon, Jr., ten; Benuel, eight and a half; and twins Cyrus and Crist, six—quietly slipped out onto the back porch after a respectable amount of time visiting. It wasn't long before Lettie and Faye did the same.

Leaning toward Lucy, Cora whispered that she and Emma Sue wanted her to go upstairs with them. "We have a surprise to show ya." Cora beckoned.

Lucy caught Mamm's eye and gestured toward Cora and Emma Sue, indicating that she was leaving to visit with her nieces.

Up in their shared room, a brand-new quilt covered the double bed, a Nine Patch pattern done in reds, blues, and greens. "Do ya mean to say yous made this?"

"Emma Sue and I pieced it inch by inch, with a bit of help from Mamma," Cora said, soft blue eyes shining. "We've been wanting you to see it."

"Cora and I are thinkin' of starting a quilt shop when we grow up," Emma Sue said shyly, playing with a tendril of light brown hair that had escaped her bun. "What do ya think?"

Lucy clapped her hands. "Sounds just *wunnerbaar.*" Then, remembering Rose Anna Yoder's new shop, she asked if they'd been over there yet. "Mamm dropped by there recently, and I guess Rose Anna has some real interesting crazy quilts she's made from scraps of old neckties and hatbands she's gotten from Mennonite relatives, as well as other fabrics," Lucy said. "Come to think of it, you might get some ideas of your own to file away for later."

"*Jah*, Mamma said she'd take us over there soon," Cora said, resting against the footboard. "Would ya like to see the stitching pattern on the back, too?"

"Absolutely." Lucy could tell they were pleased with the result of many hours of work.

The girls simultaneously reached for the border of the quilt and gently pulled it back to show off the cotton backing, with its stitching of hearts.

"This can't be your first-ever quilt." Lucy was amazed.

"It is," Cora assured her, "but like I said, we had some help from Mamma."

"Not very much, though," Emma Sue admitted quietly.

"Well, I'll say you're on your way to becoming master quilters." Lucy smiled. "I'll know who to come to for my next new one."

"A Double Wedding Ring quilt, maybe?" Cora asked, eyes dancing.

Lucy gave a small shrug. "You never know."

"Surely there's a nice Amishman just waitin' for ya," Cora replied.

There was, Lucy thought, but she could not manage any further mention of bridal quilts and nice Amish fellows. "I'm impressed with your neat stitching," she complimented.

Cora took the hint and left the room, returning with the pattern. "I s'pose anyone could make these stitches with this for help . . . don't you think, Emma Sue?"

Emma Sue frowned. "I doubt I could've done it on my own. Would probably take at least two people workin' together."

"Has Mammi Flaud seen this?" Lucy asked.

"Not just yet," Cora said. "But she's heard 'bout it, that's for sure."

Lucy knew the girls' great-Grandmammi would be delighted at their workmanship. "Oh, you must show her, and soon. In fact, she's planning a little quilting bee, so be sure to come with your Mamma, if you'd like."

"When?" Emma Sue asked, brown eyes radiant.

"She hasn't said just yet, but with the colder weather and shorter days, I wouldn't be surprised if it's soon." Lucy thanked her darling nieces for giving her a private showing. "I think Lettie and Faye would enjoy seein' your quilt, too."

Emma Sue nodded and hurried out of the room and downstairs to get them.

"I'm sorry, Aendi Lucy," Cora said, reaching for her hand.

"Whatever for?"

"Well"—and here she ducked her head—"for speakin' out of turn . . . 'bout the Wedding Ring quilt."

Lucy waved it off. "Don't worry yourself over that, honey-girl."

Cora's pretty smile reemerged, and she wrapped her arms around Lucy. "I've always loved ya the best of all my aunties, ya know."

"Ain't you sweet." As Lucy slipped out of the room to join the rest of the family below, she wondered why that was.

<hr />

Christian had relished visiting with his eldest son and wife and seeing his grandsons having such a good time when they'd come inside to play jacks on the floor. He'd been delighted to go over and show them a trick or two.

All in all, it had been a relaxing and peaceful afternoon.

Unfortunately, that was not the situation during the buggy ride home. Lettie, in particular, was making too much of her and Faye's recent match-up with two of the Mast boys—Matthew and Mark—which was downright peculiar, even though Christian knew not all dating couples kept to the old hush-hush ways of courtship anymore.

First Lettie, then Faye told Lucy how many times they'd double-dated, and he knew it was bothering Sarah, as well, because she glanced at him twice, eyes flashing.

He took it upon himself to look over his shoulder, frowning at Lettie. But it was only a short time before Lettie piped up again, mentioning some plans the four of them had together in the coming week.

All the while, Lucy, poor girl, sat quietly, saying nothing at all. Christian didn't have to wonder how she felt. He could nearly feel the tension radiating through the back of his seat.

The courting years have nearly passed her by, he realized anew. *Does this worry her?*

Sarah had shown him something that had arrived in the mail from an Amish singles group in Big Valley, Pennsylvania. Sarah had been so worried the mailing might upset Lucy, she'd held on to it for the time being.

Truth be told, he had no idea what went through his eldest daughter's mind anymore. Even so, he knew one thing for sure: It was altogether beneficial for her to attend the Thursday night meetings. The group's warm reception of her might just give Lucy some confidence again.

⁕

Lucy heard Dale's pickup pull into the driveway, right on time. She had been sitting on the porch, watching the barn cats romp in the high grass behind the corncrib, waiting for him.

He waved to her, and she smiled.

Just then, the screen door flew open, and Mamm stood there. "Lucy . . . dear?"

She greeted her mother and said that Dale was giving her a lift to Lancaster.

Frowning, Mamm reminded her, "The People don't ride in a vehicle on the Lord's Day, Lucy. Just ain't right."

"I know, Mamm, but this is a one-time exception," she assured her. "I really need to find Kiana, the young homeless woman I told you 'bout. I have important news for her." She didn't spell out that Kiana had an opportunity for a job interview tomorrow afternoon.

"I wish you'd heed the *Ordnung* all the same. It's the Lord's Day, after all," her mother said, upset.

"I wish it was any other day, Mamm. I truly do." She didn't know how to further justify this. "Please, Mamm . . . I won't make it a habit."

Mamm looked miserable but made no move to stop Lucy as she hurried past, going inside to get her black jacket. A glance into the kitchen showed her father sitting at the table with his German *Biewel* open, head bowed. A thought crossed her mind, but she shook it off. *I wish they wouldn't worry I was going to fall for another* Englischer.

Turning, she opened the door and made her way down the porch steps to Dale, who walked to meet her in black dress pants, crisp white shirt, and black tie.

Feeling guilty, Lucy turned back toward the house to wave to Mamm, but she was nowhere in sight.

≈≈≈

Just as Lucy had feared, Kiana and Van were no longer staying at the most recent shelter Kiana had mentioned, and when Dale inquired of them at the front desk, the receptionist suggested other possibilities, including the Water Street Mission. The helpful woman reached for a notepad and jotted down the locations.

Dale thanked her and escorted Lucy out the front door amidst strange looks. Back in the pickup, they drove to the first two shelters but quickly discovered that Kiana and her son were not there, either.

Is this a wild-goose chase? Lucy wondered, attempting to draw courage from Dale's determination and hope.

At the Water Street Mission, the last of the suggested locations, Dale asked again about Kiana and her son. This time, the well-dressed woman in charge confirmed that Kiana and Van were indeed registered in the program, which offered temporary housing, food, and medical care.

Lucy fidgeted while they waited for Kiana to come downstairs, hoping her friend wouldn't be too shocked at having been tracked down this way. *Surely she'll be pleased.*

Dale smiled encouragingly. "I'm looking forward to meeting Kiana."

"Thanks for bringing me here," Lucy said. "She and others like her just need someone to take an interest and truly care, and you've done exactly that."

Dale nodded but waved off her compliment.

In a few moments, Kiana appeared in the doorway, her pretty eyes wide when she spotted Lucy, who introduced her to Dale and wasted no time in filling her in about the job interview at the craft store.

"Are you serious?" The young woman brushed away tears. "Do you really think they'd *want* me?"

"You can only try, *jah*?" said Lucy.

"Oh, believe me, I'm up for trying. I've filled out many applications, but it's hard to get a job unless you're already employed . . . and not having a permanent address has been a stumbling block, too." She folded her arms against her tiny waist. "But, hey, they can't *all* turn me down, right?"

Lucy felt heartened by Kiana's optimistic response, and Dale gave her the contact information for the country store.

Kiana shook her head repeatedly. "How can I ever thank you two?"

"Let's just hope something *gut* comes of this." Lucy smiled at Kiana, then at Dale, who nodded.

When Dale offered to pick her up for tomorrow's interview,

211

Kiana said the center would arrange for transportation, as well as some appropriate clothing. "They'll even look after Van while I'm gone—there's a daycare on site. I'm going to cross my fingers and hope for the best."

Kiana's anticipation tempted Lucy to reveal her plan for a down payment on a used car, but she bit her tongue. *First things first,* she thought, feeling as happy as Kiana looked.

Dale gave Kiana his cell phone number to report back on how the interview went. "I'll keep you in my prayers," he added.

Kiana blinked away tears. "I need all the help I can get."

⌒⌒⌒

On the ride back to East Lampeter, Lucy thanked Dale several times. "Do you think she'll land this job?"

"Well, considering her attitude and ambition, she has a decent chance. Even if she doesn't end up with this position, I believe the Lord has something in mind for her." Dale chuckled. "I can see you're already on to Kiana's next hurdle."

"And what a hurdle 'tis!" Lucy joined in the laughter, but inwardly, she was holding her proverbial breath that poor Kiana might get this break.

CHAPTER 30

DALE WYETH'S A GUT MAN, Lucy thought early Monday morning as she stared ahead to the spot up the road from Ray and Martie's where the buggy had overturned. She steered her scooter onto the steep lane leading to the striking white farmhouse high on the hill, thankful again that Abe and his children had gotten safely home.

Lucy hugged her nephews as she came into the kitchen, and Martie called a greeting to her from down cellar.

"Aren't you bright-eyed today?" Lucy said to Jesse, seeing that Josh was content in his pack 'n' play.

Martie was in a hurry to have Lucy help her get the second load in the washer and then hang out the first load, already washed. "I want to beat the rain that's comin'," she said, then asked if Lucy had brought her raincoat.

Lucy assured her that it, along with a few snacks, was in her scooter basket on the porch. "Dat never said anything 'bout rain. Where'd ya hear?"

"Well, Eppie Stoltzfus dropped by right after breakfast this mornin', warning of a big storm a-brewin'."

Lucy waved it off. "Ah well, you know Eppie."

"Still, the livestock seem mighty riled up."

Lucy distributed the clothes evenly into the wringer washer, then followed her sister upstairs, the wicker basket overflowing with damp clothes. Smiling at Jesse, she leaned over to watch him color at the kitchen table.

"Dat wants me to help him in the barn later on," Jesse said, eyes sparkling.

"Oh?"

"*Jah*, gonna learn to sweep."

"Startin' young," she said, patting his shoulder.

Ray wants to help Martie out, too, no doubt, Lucy guessed.

The rain had yet to materialize when Lucy left for the hospice. Dorothea was significantly weaker this visit, but Clinton said she wanted to be read to from the Bible, which Lucy did while Clinton left to run a few errands. It occurred to Lucy that Dorothea was not long for this world.

Later that afternoon, once Lucy was home again, her shoes damp from a light and steady rain, she took time to redd up her room and put away the clothes Lettie and Faye had taken down from the line and folded so neatly earlier. She'd made a point of going down to thank her sisters before heading back upstairs. Lettie had nodded abruptly, but Faye smiled, saying it was awful nice to see her home this soon.

She went out to collect the eggs, then returned to the barn to help feed and water the livestock. Faye came too, eventually, but Lettie remained inside with Mamm to peel potatoes for supper.

"Dat said his friend has started to build his chicken coop," Faye told her as they worked.

"Dale?"

Faye nodded. "I guess Dat went over to his place and took a look at the diagram."

"Sounds like he's making some good steps toward living the way he's been wanting to." Lucy wondered if Dale had decided yet how he planned to heat his home this coming winter.

"Dat says Dale ain't the only one talking like this. Quite a number of folk are worried 'bout unexpected interruptions in the national grid." Faye frowned and stopped to wipe her cheek with the back of her hand. "Know anything 'bout that?"

Lucy shrugged. "Maybe you could ask Dale next time we see him."

"Or maybe you could." Faye looked serious. "Heard he picked you up yesterday and took ya somewhere downtown. On a Sunday to boot."

Lucy quickly told her about Kiana, then added, "Dale's just a casual friend."

"Friendly's how it always starts, right?"

Lucy was a bit startled by Faye's pointed remark.

⁓

Dale's pickup pulled into the lane after supper, and suddenly buoyed, Lucy grabbed her jacket and headed out to meet him. As she rounded the corner of the house to the driveway, she stopped abruptly, feeling foolish—most likely Dale was coming to see her father.

She turned and headed back to the house and was just reaching for the back door when Dale called to her. "Lucy, I have some news from Kiana. She left a message on my phone."

"Did she get the job?" Lucy held her breath, hoping.

Dale shook his head, coming up the porch steps toward her. "Mind if we talk?"

She motioned for them to sit on the rockers. "How'd Kiana sound?"

"Frustrated."

Lucy shook her head. "I wonder what happened."

He explained. "Evidently she didn't get the job because she wasn't well versed on yarn and fabrics."

Lucy groaned. "Why didn't I think of that? I could've filled her in a bit."

Dale took out his phone. "It's not the end of the world. There are many more options in the classifieds, which is another reason why I dropped by. If you have some time, let's look and see what might be a good fit for Kiana."

Lucy agreed. "Do you know any of the retailers listed?" she asked, thinking he might, since he was in that line of business.

"None of them rings a bell. I can certainly do some more poking around."

"Kind of you." She paused and wondered if she ought to bring this up, then went ahead. "Faye mentioned that you've started buildin' your chicken coop."

"Yes, and it's not easy, let me tell you." Dale also volunteered that he'd returned Abe's clothing. "When I stopped by, Abe gave me some info on the going price for goats."

Recalling Dale's "new look," as Clinton had described it, Lucy smiled.

"I see why the Amish grapevine works so effectively," he said, grinning and rocking a little. "And I could *really* get used to these. How hard is it to build a rocking chair?"

Lucy laughed. "My Dat has the plans, so just ask."

"I'll do that." He smiled again. "Might be a good idea to build two, though."

"Or even more," she said, mentioning how often her family sat out there together. "I've been thinking 'bout doing something special for Kiana," she added.

"You already are by helping arrange interviews and encouraging her," he replied. "And praying, too, which is vital."

Lucy had thought he might say that. "Well, I mean something concrete . . . like helpin' her purchase a used car."

Dale stopped rocking, studying her. "You're really something, you know that, Lucy?"

She paused, embarrassed at his remark. "I really believe it's something I'm s'posed to do."

He shook his head, clearly taken aback. "Kiana will probably view it as a God-thing, if she thinks along those lines. You're a witness to the Lord's loving care."

She shrugged, blushing.

"You are, you know. According to the apostle James, pure and faultless religion is taking care of widows and orphans. That's straight out of Scripture, and I'd say Kiana and her son fall into that category."

Pure religion? Lucy had never heard it stated that way.

Suddenly, Dale turned. "You know what? We could go looking at some used car lots—I found my pickup at one." He grinned. "Not that I'd expect Kiana to drive a car that needs a paint job."

"I guess if it runs well and has some life in it, she wouldn't mind. Sure, let's do that."

He asked when would be a good time.

Lucy was stymied. "I'm busy all week, but after supper Wednesday could work, maybe . . . if it's not too late in the day."

"Better yet, we could pick up something to eat and get an even earlier start."

She thanked Dale enthusiastically, thinking of her high hopes for Kiana. It would be wonderful to find something.

"I'll come by for you around four o'clock. How's that?"

"You'll be just in time to help gather eggs," she joked.

"It's a deal."

Watching him leave, Lucy thought how very fortunate she was to have a friend who was as eager as she to help others.

Maybe Dale's the God-thing.

CHAPTER 31

TEN MINUTES HAD COME AND GONE, and little Josh, who was teething, began to cry again from the pack 'n' play. Lifting him out, Martie quietly carried him to the sink and washed his streaked face. It was all she could do not to splash some cool water on hers, too. *Lord, please, I need more patience!*

She dried Josh's plump cheeks and held him near, her chest wracked with sobs. *What's the matter with me?* She had to get control of her emotions before her boys noticed.

Martie set Josh down, giving him a few favorite toys before hurrying to the washroom to pat her face with a cold, wet wash-cloth. She looked into the mirror, staring at her reflection. "This is the face of a woman who's got twins in her belly and is stretched too thin to handle her household duties. Whatever will I do if I'm uprooted to parts unknown come spring?"

She recalled how shocked she'd been yesterday afternoon when Eppie had told her that Martie's own husband was among those contemplating a move west. Thus far, Ray had said nothing to her, but Martie guessed it could well be true. Sighing deeply, she realized it was the prospect of leaving her extended family that made her the most blue . . . and fretful.

She ran the water in the sink, concealing her muffled sobs, and let her tears drip down into the sink, mingling with the water from the faucet. Oh, she couldn't think of moving, let alone raising twins without the help of her family, especially Lucy.

Once Martie had cried sufficiently, she returned to the kitchen, where Jesse came and tugged on her dress and offered a hug. Then she began to cook dinner for the noon meal.

⁓

Lucy headed north in a van filled with other Plain women that morning to the Mennonite Central Committee Material Resources Center in Ephrata. The notion of looking for a used car with Dale tomorrow evening made her more hopeful than she had felt in a while. She was also looking forward to working with enthusiastic volunteers today, all of them eager to make a difference for others less fortunate.

Today would be fun, but she especially enjoyed the annual first Saturday of May workday, nicknamed Chatter, Chow, and Cheerful Service. The day began with worship and fellowship, and everyone brought homemade soup to share—vegetable beef or chicken corn—mixing each kind all together for the noon meal. On that particular day, volunteers worked assembly lines to put together donated items for various kits—infant care, hygiene, relief, school supplies, or sewing. They checked expiration dates and made sure all of the designated items were included before putting them into the handmade drawstring bags. The kits were then packed in boxes to be shipped.

This morning, however, Lucy was assigned to the room where long strips of donated blue jeans were being recycled into rag rugs to be sold at MCC thrift shops around the country. Lucy thought of Mammi Flaud, who liked to say: *"Living simply means buying less, wasting less . . . and wanting less."*

"Waste not, want not," Lucy said, smiling as she glanced over at the young Mennonite woman nearby.

"I heard that growin' up, too," the woman replied with a grin.

Quickly, they exchanged names, and Lucy was soon telling Isabella about the joy she experienced in turning donated items into something usable. "Don'tcha just love to give things a second life?"

Isabella nodded and said she also liked working on the Christmas boxes to be sent overseas to faraway places like Colombia and Tanzania. "My sisters and I do that together every year," she said.

"I should invite my twin sisters to come along sometime," Lucy said, wondering if perhaps Mamm could occasionally spare them, too.

During the midmorning break, Lucy heard Gracie Friesen, a Mennonite woman whom she'd worked with before, talking about a small guesthouse she had for rent. "I'd even consider exchanging rent for housekeeping and cooking and a bit of outdoor work," Gracie was telling another woman. "Do you know of anyone—maybe a single girl?"

"Where's your guesthouse located?" Lucy spoke up, going right over to her.

"Oh, not so far from the Amish schoolhouse on Gibbons Road, near Bird-in-Hand," Gracie seemed happy to tell her. "The place is right cozy—only one large bedroom. You'd like it, Lucy."

"Well, it ain't for me." Lucy took a moment to ponder the consequences, then forged ahead. "But would ya consider renting to a homeless person? She's a young mother my age with a small child."

"Homeless, ya say? An *Englischer*?"

221

"She is," Lucy admitted. "But I know her well enough to say she'd respect any rules you might require for a tenant."

"Well, having someone who doesn't smoke or drink is one thing my husband and I won't budge on. What else do you know about her?"

"She has a darling two-and-a-half-year-old who's as polite as can be." Lucy swallowed hard, just thinking about Kiana's plight. "Kiana's decision to keep her son is why she has no family support."

"Aw, the dear girl." Gracie patted Lucy's hand. "If she's anything like you, Lucy Flaud, she'll be a great fit."

Lucy blushed. "I could vouch for her, if she'll let me. Honestly, I have a strong feelin' she would work out fine."

"When can I meet her?"

Lucy was so excited, she could hardly keep from grinning. "I'll find out as soon as I can."

"Just drop by—no need to phone ahead, all right?" Gracie wrote out the address on a piece of paper she took from her purse. "This might just be the answer to our prayers."

"And mine!"

"The Lord certainly works in unexpected ways." Gracie's smile lit up the whole room.

Lucy agreed, shaking her head in amazement.

When break time was up, she found herself working faster than usual, so energized by this prospect, she even caught herself humming. No two days were the same, that was certain. And as far as Lucy was concerned, this was one of the best days in a long time. She could hardly wait to tell Dale the news.

Is God hearing my prayers, after all?

❧

Christian didn't know how to react when Lucy announced that Dale had offered to take her to look at used cars that Wednesday evening. He appreciated Lucy's willingness to spend her money on a homeless friend but was becoming worried that Dale was showing up fairly often lately. *And not to see me, either.*

Sarah hadn't said a word, but Christian assumed she would at some point, especially if it seemed Dale was pursuing Lucy romantically.

Thus far, though, Christian hadn't noticed any signs of familiarity between Lucy and Dale—nothing like what one would expect from a courting couple.

At least this time won't be on the Lord's Day. . . .

Christian considered talking man-to-man with Dale, yet knowing how respectable a fellow he was, he wondered if it was necessary. On the other hand, Dale was clearly yearning for an uncomplicated life, so maybe he was also looking for a Plain wife.

Glancing at Sarah, Christian held his peace, saying nothing as Lucy met Dale at the back door. *A fellow I'm responsible for bringing into our lives. Have I complicated things?*

He sighed and slipped out to the porch, waiting till the pickup backed out of the lane before wandering out to the stable.

❦

"Have you ever wanted to learn to drive?" Dale asked as they headed toward the used car lot after stopping for burgers and milkshakes.

"I considered it, *jah* . . . several years ago, in fact." She wanted to be careful how much more she shared about that period of her life. "I was younger, obviously, and inquisitive about the outside world."

"I never would have guessed."

"Truth be told, I wasn't always too terribly interested in the Old Ways." *And that's all I best be saying,* Lucy thought, hoping this conversation wasn't leading her down a slippery slope. The last person she wanted to know about her lack of discretion was an outsider.

"But you must've grown into the Amish tradition at some point," Dale said, making the turn into the lot.

"I learned some hard lessons, that's for sure."

"Well, here we are." Inching slowly along, Dale drove up and down the lines of cars and SUVs.

"Do ya see any *gut* choices?" she asked, glad she'd come with an *Englischer* instead of by van with a hired driver. This way, she might have more bargaining power!

"We should walk around and read the sticker prices," he said. "Okay with you?"

She nodded, hoping he might guide her through the maze of vehicles.

They wandered about the brightly lit lot, and Dale jotted down three options. It was around that time a salesman came out, shaking their hands and greeting them like they were the only customers he'd ever had the pleasure of meeting.

Later, on the way to a second car lot, Dale warned her to be prepared for the same sort of royal treatment again. "I'm not sure what adrenaline rushes these car salesmen experience, but they tend to come across as very similar, if you ask me."

They took longer to peruse the second lot, and by the time they were headed back to Witmer Road, Lucy couldn't keep all the vehicles straight in her mind. She said she hoped it wouldn't overwhelm Kiana, as well, but Dale waved his notepad and assured her that one or two would be just right. "If she lands a job soon."

"I really appreciate you doin' this," she said. "You have no idea what this'll mean to her."

Dale made little of it but was gracious all the same.

"I have some interesting news," she said, telling him now about the country guesthouse for rent. "I can't wait to let Kiana know, but what do you think?"

"Could be an answer to prayer," Dale remarked.

This didn't happen till Dale joined me in praying, too, she thought, admiring him for taking Kiana's concerns straight to the Lord last Saturday afternoon.

"If it's a go, then Kiana might need only a part-time job for incidentals," Dale replied. "Especially if she qualifies for food stamps."

"Right, and with the car we're gonna find her, she'll be in *gut* shape."

Assuming Gracie and her husband accept Kiana as a renter.

Lucy glanced at Dale. "Does the Lord always answer your prayers so quick?"

He laughed softly and shook his head. "Not usually, no."

She found this interesting, and she couldn't help wondering if he'd ever gone years without an answer.

Three years is a mighty long time. . . .

CHAPTER 32

THE HOURS TILL THURSDAY EVENING ticked by, and Lucy could find no reasonable excuse to stay home from the grief support group, especially when her father just assumed she was going again.

When the time came, Lettie asked why Lucy was tagging along, and Mamm said she was keeping their father company. The answer seemed to satisfy Faye, but Lettie still looked puzzled and studied Lucy hard.

Sooner or later, I might have to tell them something more, Lucy thought.

Lucy and Dat said little to each other in the carriage on the way to the community church. Her father parked the buggy near a large tree at the far end of the lot.

Lucy decided it was a good idea to sit with Sue Kaiser and Janey Marshall, her discussion partners. After all, it made sense to get better acquainted with them, and she felt bad about being rather withdrawn during her first meeting. This week, she was determined to be more receptive, if possible. *And going forward, too.* The latter thought nearly stopped her in her tracks. *Can I see this course through to the end?*

As she and her father entered the church, Dale Wyeth was not in his usual place as the greeter. Instead, an older man from the group shook her father's hand and smiled at Lucy, welcoming her back.

Isn't Dale here? she wondered, feeling a little disappointed.

Following the opening prayer, the leader began the lesson for the week, and Lucy braced herself—the loss of a child was painful territory to revisit. Right away, she could see that the theme was as difficult for Linden Hess as for some of the others present.

Linden talked about the stages of grief he and his wife had suffered following the death of their little girl. "At first we felt it was unfair that our daughter's life was cut short. Yes, we believed she was with the Lord, but we wished we'd had more time to make memories with her," he shared, tears welling up. "We had to remind ourselves that God understood—*understands*—our loss, and we tried our best to communicate this truth to our other children as often as possible. But I can tell you it wasn't easy." He paused to remove a white handkerchief from his pocket and wiped his eyes. "And it's still hard, every single day."

Linden went on to discuss how critical it was to have family support. "It's important to talk through your grief."

Lucy's stomach churned. Fighting the urge to bolt, she refused to so much as glance at her father, seated beside Dale, who'd arrived late.

Coming tonight was a mistake. Lucy folded her arms, hugging herself—the gathering room suddenly felt chilly. In all truth, she was even more uncomfortable than last week and beginning to feel mentally exhausted. *How will I manage?*

But she did her best to listen later when Janey, seated next to her, shared about the death of her four-month-old son to SIDS. Observing the woman's deep sadness, Lucy could no longer hold back her emotions, and tears slipped down her cheeks.

"Oh, Lucy . . . you have such a tender heart." Sue slipped an arm around her.

The gesture made Lucy all the sadder. In the midst of this pit of suffering, she'd lost track of where she was, and when she could finally speak, she said quietly, "I'm ever so sorry . . . I don't want to cause a scene."

"Sometimes it helps me to talk about what I'm feeling," Sue said. "Maybe it's the same for you."

Lucy shook her head. "I'm just not ready." Besides, she didn't feel right about airing her dirty laundry to *Englischers*, no matter how well intentioned they seemed.

Sue and Janey offered to pray for her right there, but as Lucy reached for her purse and pulled out a tissue, she shook her head. "I *do* need your prayers . . . just not here. Not out loud." She thanked them and excused herself, needing some cool air.

She headed toward the restroom and took a few sips at the drinking fountain, then stepped outside. There, she stood staring up at the starry sky. In the distance, near an old mill, grain dryers buzzed in the evening stillness.

What am I doing here? Lucy wondered, realizing she had come so close to spilling the full truth about herself.

She tried to calm down, but all she could think of was the horror she'd felt when Janey spoke of the death of her little one.

Walking now, Lucy paced off the perimeter of the parking lot several times, remembering that her father liked to stay and fellowship following the benediction. *He must not have seen me leave,* she thought as she walked to the horse and buggy. She would wait there.

Deep in thought, she caressed Caney's long, sleek nose, whispering to him, forcing her thoughts onto other matters. She couldn't deny how excited she was about the possibility of Gracie's rental house working out for Kiana. How very different her life could be. . . . *A whole new future.*

Lucy heard footsteps and turned to look—it was Dale coming toward her, taller in the mix of light from the parking lot and the shadow where she stood. "Hullo," she said.

"I saw you leave." He reached to pet the horse. Their hands brushed lightly, and she pulled back. "Are you okay?"

She nodded. "I'm impatient to see how Kiana reacts to the news of the rental," she said, diverting the conversation. Then, smiling, she said, "Really hope she comes to the food truck tomorrow."

"Please remember that I want to help, Lucy."

Thinking of their hands touching for that split second, she felt distracted.

Then Dale added, "Let me know when I can take Kiana and you to the car lot. Just call when you know for sure," he said, reciting his cell number.

"So kind of you. *Denki.*"

They said good-bye, and shortly afterward, Lucy's father came out of the church.

She moved to the carriage, sliding onto the front bench seat, glad for Dale's willingness to assist with getting Kiana on her feet. *He enjoys helping others. That's all it is.*

Lucy tensed as her father climbed in beside her and lifted the driving lines. She had felt this sort of stress around her father for years. *Jah, since returning home from Ohio.* Surely he was aware of it, too.

"You and Dale were alone in the parking lot," he remarked as the carriage pulled out onto the road. "And the two of yous were out together last evening, too."

"It's nothin', Dat," she replied, hoping to settle this quickly.

"Yesterday was about helpin' Kiana." She folded her hands in her lap, squeezing them tight.

"I'm responsible for the care of your soul, Lucy. And I can't help thinking 'bout your last experience with an outsider."

Dat needn't remind her of that.

He caught her eye. "Why *is* it that you gravitate toward men outside the church?"

She swallowed hard. "Dat, *you* brought Dale into our lives."

"'Tis true, but you're spendin' too much time together. I see this with my own two eyes."

Lucy bit her lip, resolutely determined not to clam up. *That's what I always do,* she thought. *And nothing ever gets solved.*

"If you hadn't sent me away, things would've turned out much differently."

"*Ach,* Lucy," her father muttered.

"And it was *your* idea to come to this grief group where people actually talk about their sorrow."

"Daughter . . ."

"I want ya to hear me out, Dat."

Her father hurried the horse. "We must trust such things to *Gott's* sovereign will . . . and daresn't question."

Daresn't question?

He continued. "I'm following *Gott* on this."

A cork popped inside of her. "But you're not God! Yet you destroyed my plans to marry my baby's father . . . and it's ruined everything since."

"What I did was best for all concerned, including you," Dat shot back, his shoulders rising as he drew a breath.

"*Nee,* it was so you could save face—not let it be known that your daughter had sinned with an *Englischer.*"

"Lucy, be thankful I spared ya from the *Bann.*"

"Maybe I'd be better off excommunicated."

"*Puh!* You can't mean that." He shook his head. "When will ya learn to think before ya speak or act? *When?*"

Seething, Lucy said what she'd held inside too long, what she truly believed. "It was *you*, Dat. You and God caused my baby to die." She took another breath, then let it out slowly. "My baby deserved the chance to be born."

Her father gripped the lines tighter, staring straight ahead.

Lucy was shaking, but she'd finally had her say. And yet she wasn't finished. "I've tried to get your approval, Dat—yours and God's. I've tried to find forgiveness somehow, find some kind of peace . . . but whatever I do is never enough."

Turning toward the window, she wanted to get out and walk home. The vast fields were dark as she looked out her side of the buggy, past the spot in the road where a single moment had nearly altered Abe Riehl's family forever.

Quietly, she spoke again. "I'm not givin' up my friendship with Dale just 'cause you made a mistake."

Then, lest she make any further hot-tempered remarks, Lucy clamped her lips shut. She heard her father sigh, but he said nothing more.

***

Back home, Lucy fell onto her bed, clinging to a pillow. She burrowed her face in its softness and relived the day she'd first told her parents of her pregnancy. Oddly, it was Dat who had taken the more gentle approach with her, at least at first, when Lucy began revealing her and Travis's elaborate wedding plans. Mamm, however, was full of questions, desperate to know more about the worldly young man Lucy had pledged to marry. Mamm's eyes had teared up. "But you'll be shunned!"

The mood in the house had fallen into one of concealed desperation. Lucy had felt so alone—and mortified—when her mother asked her to pack a few things a mere two days later.

"You're going to Ohio to help my cousin Sally for the time being," Mamm had announced. At the time, Lucy was six weeks along in her pregnancy. *I had no say in what was to happen to my wee babe.*

Lucy rolled over on the bed, staring at the dresser on the opposite side of the room. *I wanted to please Travis,* she thought now, knowing full well she would have left the People for him. Anything to make him happy. *Anything but end my pregnancy, that is. Oh, how I hoped he would warm up to the idea of being a father!*

Dat had demanded that Lucy return the engagement necklace when he'd caught her coming in late one night, wearing it and her fancy clothes. And she'd tried to return it, but Travis insisted she keep it and sell it for money to use for the baby, since Lucy was bound and determined *not* to terminate the pregnancy . . . against his wishes.

Kind as Travis usually was, she could not understand how he was able to reject the result of their love—the tiny life growing within her. *How?* To this day, it plagued her. "Like Dat's willingness to disown me if I didn't submit to his way," Lucy whispered, sitting up and going to the window.

She stared down onto the backyard, faint now in the golden light from the kitchen window. There, Travis had stood after dark, near the purple martin birdhouse. She had left her lantern on so he could see her waiting in the identical spot where she stood now. Travis had waved her down with his flashlight, much like an Amish beau attempting to get her attention by shining his light on her bedroom window. *Only there was nothing honorable about what we did that night, consummating our affection.*

She groaned at the thought of her disobedience, the wretched guilt she still carried like a never-ending weight. Lucy had made Travis the center of her life, yet she'd refused to abort their baby when he demanded it. How humiliating it had been to tell her appalled parents about her out-of-wedlock pregnancy.

We were going to be married, Lucy had told herself repeatedly after Dat put her on the bus. She had clenched her fists and jaw, watching for hours as the cities and the countryside rushed past in a blur. *I felt so abandoned and alone.*

At the time, she let her parents think she was in agreement with giving up the baby for adoption. But she harbored a secret in her heart and never told anyone but Martie the truth, only submitting in her initial actions as her father swept in and altered her future.

I had no intention of giving my baby away.

CHAPTER 33

HOURS LATER, LUCY WENT TO HER DESK and removed each of her journals—the ones where she'd recorded the good deeds and places where she'd given of her time and energy, noticing on every few pages the way she had expanded her volunteer work to include more and more.

More people to help . . . more to save. People like Kiana and little Van.

She fought back tears; she couldn't sustain the pace of her daily life. It wasn't as if God had called her to run herself into the ground. No, something else was driving her: Lucy wanted to crowd out the pain in her heart.

Drying her tears, she found little satisfaction in looking at the journals. Instead, there was a frantic sense of busyness, if not outright obligation. *Burning the candle at both ends isn't the answer,* she thought miserably.

Lucy removed her *Kapp*, took down her waist-length hair, and brushed it vigorously. She thought of Lettie and Faye taking turns brushing each other's hair and tried to be glad for their closeness. Who besides Martie could she confide in? Not Mamm, and certainly not Tobe, now that she'd pushed him away.

She outened the light and dressed for bed, then slipped under the covers, glad that tomorrow was a new day. Lucy pictured Kiana's face, beaming with happiness. To think that Gracie Friesen's comfortable little guesthouse could be hers for the taking! This, at least, was a small consolation as Lucy attempted to unwind. Too many emotions, too many hurts had been unearthed this evening.

"Something's happenin' with Lucy," Christian told Sarah as they retired for the night, the room devoid of lantern light.

"She's on edge all the time, ain't so?" Sarah moved closer to him.

"I'm afraid it's more than that." He explained what had transpired during the buggy ride home.

"The poor girl." Sarah rested her head on his shoulder. "She should've put this behind her already."

He reached for the second quilt, trying to find the words to admit a truth. "Well, she's right . . . I *did* push and push. Just when she needed us most, I pushed her right out the door." He coughed. "Things didn't start out that way, but my annoyance grew into something fierce and ugly, I admit that now. I poured my fury with Travis out onto Lucy."

"All of this is comin' to a head only now?"

"Seems so. I daresay Lucy's bitterness has blocked any hope of resolution . . . or forgiveness. Things have taken a step back between her and me, I'll say."

"No wonder she's been absent—visiting elsewhere or sick in bed—for every communion service since losin' her baby."

"Makes sense to Lucy, maybe, but it's playin' with fire," Christian whispered, pondering the weight of it. "And here we have another fasting day comin' up. Communion Sunday comes in a little over a week."

"I really need to talk to her." Sarah shifted slightly. "She can't keep pretending all's right with *Gott* and the church. Ain't *gut* for her or for building unity amongst us, neither one."

"But it's treacherous to partake of communion when there's unconfessed sin in one's heart." Christian knew well the New Testament verse about eating the bread and drinking the cup unworthily.

"A fearful thing," Sarah whispered. "Which must be why Lucy has purposely stayed away."

Christian was quiet.

"Should we both speak to her?" Sarah asked.

"Ain't wise, not after Lucy's outburst tonight." He paused, wishing what he was about to say were not so. "And now there's yet another *Englischer* lookin' her way."

"Your friend Dale?"

"It's my fault for bringin' him round in the first place." He sighed and turned toward Sarah. "I was beginning to think Dale looked up to me, like he would to a father figure—his own dad passed away so recently."

He hesitated to tell her more, then went ahead. "I caught them talkin' in the parking lot tonight. Well, I shouldn't say *caught*. They were quite open and unashamed 'bout it. Not like the other fella, who snuck around so."

"*Ach*, let's not jump to conclusions." Sarah placed her hand on his chest. "I believe Lucy's learned from her past mistakes. Truly, I do."

"I'm counting on it." Christian kissed Sarah's cheek and began his silent rote prayers before letting sleep take him over.

<hr />

Martie checked on Josh in his crib once more, having nursed him later than usual, trying to soothe him so Ray could sleep.

Walking the length of the hall, she stopped to peer out at the half-moon, then sat on the cane chair, the only piece of furniture in that corner. It had been another very busy day. *Exhausting, really.*

Slipping her hands around her middle, Martie caressed the tiny babies within her as she prayed.

She needed time to sit and relax before going to bed. She relived the events of the day, including the unexpected visit from Eppie, who'd fairly pranced into the house midafternoon, bringing her usual list of unsolicited ideas for Martie's weekly column. Martie had merely smiled when the woman mentioned having seen Lucy with a fancy young man. "She got into his pickup truck, and they drove away together," Eppie had said, shaking her head.

Martie had wondered aloud if perhaps Eppie had happened upon the buggy accident, when Lucy had gone with the Riehl children in Dale's pickup.

"*Nee*, 'twas just last evening," Eppie said, quite adamant that Lucy was the only one who could have possibly been sitting beside the outsider.

"Are ya sure you aren't mistaken?"

Eppie's crinkled cheeks turned pink. "I saw what I *saw*." She described the tall, blond *Englischer* who had opened the door for Lucy, quite "gentlemanly like," before they drove off toward the Old Philadelphia Pike. "I daresay it's that fella who's been spendin' time with your father."

"Have ya thought that maybe he was just giving Lucy a ride?" Martie hoped for an innocent explanation.

Eppie had looked at her like the idea was downright *lecherich*—laughable. "I think I know trouble when I see it."

But what Eppie didn't know was that Martie had already

written a column about an outsider's interest in learning the simple ways from the Amish round here. *The Amish just down the road, in fact,* Martie thought, wondering what Dat and others would think when they read about it tomorrow in *The Budget.*

CHAPTER 34

KIANA AND HER SON did not show up for Friday lunch, and Lucy stewed over this while cleaning up afterward.

How could I have missed them?

Then it hit her—of course they hadn't come! Kiana and Van were enrolled at a shelter that included meals and other programs.

I have to find a way to the Water Street Mission. Considering it was market day in several locations, including the Green Dragon in Ephrata, Lucy realized she would have quite a wait before one of the paid drivers arrived. She went around and asked a few volunteers if she might get a ride with them once they returned to the Salvation Army with the food truck. Ken and Jan said they were sorry but had appointments. "Next time?" Ken said with a grimace. "Really sorry, Lucy."

Thankfully, Laurita said she could drive Lucy there once they finished cleaning up.

Then Lucy remembered Dale's standing invitation to help. She deliberated that for a few moments, certain he would want to meet her at the mission, if possible, to be there when Lucy gave Kiana the latest news.

Mustering up the nerve, Lucy asked Laurita if she could make a call for her, and next thing, Lucy was staring at a smartphone, unsure how to use it.

"Here's what you do," Laurita said, taking time to demonstrate. "Got it?"

Somehow, Lucy managed to punch in the numbers, and when Dale answered, his voice sounded so clear, it surprised her. "Hullo?" she said. "It's Lucy Flaud. I'm calling from downtown Lancaster." She filled him in on her plan.

"I'm actually headed that way now—need to drop something off on the way. After that, I can meet you at the mission."

"That's great," she said. "I'll see you there."

She smiled as she clicked off and returned the phone, pleased by her decision to call. "*Denki* so much, Laurita." She felt her face flush.

"Whoa! Did I save your life or something?" Laurita pushed the phone into her jeans pocket.

"I just feel so happy for one of the homeless young women we used to serve food to. Do ya remember Kiana?"

Laurita said she did, still eyeing Lucy suspiciously.

"I've got the best news for her—an honest-to-goodness answer to prayer."

Turning to the cleanup at hand, Lucy could hardly stop smiling.

⁓⁓⁓

Kiana's face shone like a Christmas candle. "I can't believe this . . . I really can't." Pumping her fists, she looked from Lucy to Dale. "It's the best news I've had in, like, forever!"

Lucy gave her a hug, caught up in Kiana's enthusiasm.

The three of them made plans to visit the Friesens this coming Sunday afternoon. Kiana said she could get a ride there, if Dale could bring her and Van home, and Dale agreed to do that. "I'll meet you at Gracie's," Lucy offered.

After Kiana returned to the shelter, Lucy exclaimed to Dale that being able to help her friend was a reminder of just how much she herself took for granted.

"Don't we all?" Dale nodded as they stood near the entrance. "We appreciate the essentials most when we've lost them."

"I sometimes wonder what the Lord thinks when He looks down from on High and notices things like this."

"Notices?" Dale said as they began to walk. "He's *behind* it all, orchestrating these blessings."

She considered that, eager to be God's hands and feet here on earth. "Days like this make me want to be in many different places at once, ya know? But I can't do it all."

Dale added, "That's why we look to our Creator, who is everywhere present."

"Dawdi Flaud used to talk 'bout things like that." She paused. "He once told me, in the midst of a miserable day, that God knows the end from the beginning for each of us . . . and He knows the *middle*, too, when we're discouraged and can hardly keep our heads above water."

"Don't we all need someone to care enough to point us in the right direction sometimes?" Dale asked.

She walked farther with him, toward the parking lot. "It'll be *wunnerbaar-gut* to introduce Kiana and her son to my Mennonite friends."

"*Wunnerbaar-gut*, indeed."

This made her smile. "You speak *gut Deitsch*."

When she found herself standing in front of his pickup truck, she realized they had fallen into conversation without her really meaning to.

"I could drop by for you on Sunday, if you'd like," Dale suggested, putting his foot on the driver's-side running board.

Lucy thanked him for his courtesy. "I appreciate that, Dale, but I can easily meet you there."

She walked back toward the front door of the mission, where her regular driver was already awaiting her, thanks to the quick call she'd placed earlier.

On the ride back to East Lampeter, Lucy was quiet, not participating in the chatter of the other Amishwomen in the van. Instead, she thought of Tobe, wishing she might share the joy she felt for Kiana. Too soon Tobe would exit her life . . . for a new one in Colorado—or so she assumed.

What will my life be like without him? she wondered, wishing she didn't have to find out.

CHAPTER 35

THE ROOSTER'S CROWING penetrated the predawn silence as Lucy dressed quickly that Saturday. She brushed her hair and wound it into a neat, tight bun, securing it with bobby pins before tying a dark blue kerchief around her head.

She had a hankering to surprise Mammi Flaud. It wouldn't be the first time she'd gone over to cook breakfast next door before heading up the road to help Martie.

The gas lamp already lit the kitchen area with a warm glow as Lucy crept inside the small outer room and hung her jacket on the only empty peg. She heard talking, and going around the corner, she saw Lettie sitting with their grandmother at the table. It looked as though her sister was crying, her hair in a loose bun uncovered by either a scarf or *Kapp*. The pink candy dish, half full of sweets, was set within Lettie's close reach.

"*Ach*, I'll come back later," Lucy said when Mammi looked up and spotted her.

"Ain't necessary." Mammi waved her in. "Your sister could use some extra attention."

"I'll make some waffles, then," Lucy said, wondering why Lettie looked so glum. "Okay with you, sister?"

Lettie nodded her head.

"I'll cook the eggs," Mammi said, getting up.

Lucy stood next to Lettie and touched her shoulder. "Maybe some breakfast will make ya feel better." She said what their mother often suggested when one of them was down in the dumps.

Lettie moaned softly but didn't say what was troubling her.

Lucy slipped over to the counter to work alongside Mammi, gathering the ingredients for the waffles, then mixing the batter by hand. In just a few minutes, they moved to the stove, their movements as practiced as when Lucy helped her mother cook. All the while, Lucy was aware of Lettie's occasional sniffs and gloomy expression. *Poor thing.* And she could see that the candies in the beautiful dish were disappearing quickly.

"Oughta be a nice sunny day," Mammi said, turning down the gas under the scrambled eggs so they wouldn't stick.

Looking out the window and seeing the lights still on at the neighboring farmhouse across the field, Lucy agreed. "Daylight sure is scarce now that we're into October," she said.

"How quickly we forget from one year to the next." Mammi peppered the eggs and glanced over her shoulder at Lettie. "You all out of sweets, honey-girl?"

Lettie grinned and even giggled a little. "Too much sugar makes me a bit silly."

"Well, better'n crying, I daresay." Mammi laughed as she moved the eggs around in the frying pan. "How close are we, Lucy?"

"Just a few minutes more." She removed the second waffle and poured more batter on the waffle iron, then closed the lid.

When they were ready, Lucy and Mammi carried the food over and sat down with Lettie. Mammi bowed her head for the silent prayer, and Lucy and her sister followed her lead. Lucy thanked God for the delicious breakfast before them and prayed that all would go well tomorrow for Kiana at the Friesens'. And she tucked in a prayer for Lettie, too.

"Amen," Mammi said, lifting her head. "Now then, dig in, girls. There's a-plenty."

"Did ya tell Mamm you were comin' here?" Lettie asked, wiping her eyes with a paper napkin.

"*Nee*, did you?"

"*Ach*, she'll guess," Mammi said. "Where else would yous be this early?"

Lucy scanned the living area, her gaze lingering on Dawdi's old chair, which Mammi had brought with her when she'd moved there. "Remember how that itty-bitty dog you used to have would sit at Dawdi's knee and plead for a treat?"

"Oh, do I ever. Ruby could beg with her eyes like nobody's business. And, oh, that little head and ears . . . soft as silk," Mammi said. "Too bad I gave her away, after—"

"Ruby sure had a noisy bark for such a small pet," Lettie interrupted, perking up at the talk of the cute pup.

"Your Dawdi and Ruby were a jovial pair," added Mammi. "Not that Ruby didn't care for me, too."

Lettie smiled, her lips parting. "I still miss Dawdi's smile," she said, tears welling up again. "And the way he talked so gratefully 'bout the Lord."

Lucy caught herself nodding as her sister poured more syrup on her waffles.

"You'll have a sugar high for sure unless you eat more eggs to offset all that. Maybe I should fry up some bacon, too," Mammi suggested.

Lettie rose and poured milk for everyone, including a tall glass for herself. "Cryin' makes me hungry."

"You gonna be all right?" Lucy asked.

"Guess so. We all get over bein' jilted eventually, *jah*?" Lettie forced a smile. "Sorry for braggin' like I did last Sunday, comin' back from Ammon and Sylvia's. I spoke too soon about the Mast boys—must have had this comin'." She explained that Matthew had decided he didn't much like double-dating with twins. "Maybe we weren't acting mature enough . . . cutting up, ya know. Who knows?"

"Well, the two of yous together can be double trouble," Mammi teased. "And with twins bein' courted by brothers who could pass for twins . . . well, who's to say your Matthew ain't right?"

"He's not *my* Matthew anymore."

Mammi looked Lucy's way, her eyes concerned. "You know there are other fellas in the district who'll treat ya better," encouraged Mammi.

Lettie shrugged and cried some more. And Lucy reached across the table to squeeze her hand.

Christian sat on the church bench with all of his sons during Preaching. It wasn't hard to keep his mind on the first sermon, which lasted twenty-five minutes and introduced the theme of humility for the second sermon to come. The congregation of the People silently prayed the Lord's Prayer as they knelt at their benches following the first sermon. Then the second preacher stood before them and began to pace as he read James four, verse ten: "'Humble yourselves in the sight of the Lord, and he shall lift you up.'" After the squabble with Lucy on Thursday, Christian's heart was particularly attuned to the message therein.

During the testimonies afterward, Christian contemplated Lucy's startling admission. The fact that she still carried resentment toward him wasn't good for her, nor for him. *I never meant to banish her like she thinks.*

There had been much more behind the decision to send her so abruptly to Ohio. *Just till she gave up the baby for adoption,* he recalled. *Sarah's and my decision.* Yet who could have known that Lucy would lose her tiny babe at just nine weeks into the pregnancy?

Christian had never found any comfort in that. The miscarriage had ultimately spared Lucy from having to live life as a *Maidel*, yet his daughter had been no more inclined to date anyone in the years since her return than visit the man in the moon.

I must talk more candidly with her, he decided, hoping it might help clear things up between them.

❧

Together with the other menfolk, Christian helped to convert the wide-open gathering room into a temporary dining area. A third or so of the benches were altered to create tables while the rest were put into place for seating. There were chunks of cheese and peanut butter spread, and thick homemade bread—simple fare, to be sure, but it was what they were accustomed to. Bountiful bowls of pickles—sweet and dill—graced the ends of each table, and there was plentiful snitz pie.

Bishop came and sat next to him as Christian was thinking about pouring another cup of coffee. Bishop Smucker was eager to talk. "I made Jerry Glick an offer on his dairy farm. Want it for my eldest grandson," he said, reaching for a chocolate chip cookie.

Surprised, Christian said, "Didn't realize it was on the market just yet."

The bishop indicated that Jerry had hoped to avoid listing it with a real estate agent. "It's wise to keep our farms tied up with Amish, ya know."

"Agreed," Christian said, his mind stuck on the apparent fact that Tobe had decided to go west with his family.

"You and Sarah are stayin' put, *jah*?" Bishop looked him in the eye.

"I have no plans to move anywhere till the Lord calls me Home."

Bishop Smucker slapped him on the back. "*Gut* to hear, *Bruder*. And I don't say that lightly."

Later, on the way out to the stable with James and Solomon, Christian noticed Lucy standing near the potting shed with Lettie, their heads together. It was unusual to see them together without Faye.

Does Lucy know Tobe's decided to leave?

"I'm real sorry you're sad over Matthew Mast," Lucy told Lettie as they hung back away from the other young women waiting to go in for the shared meal.

"Not sure why I wept in front of Mammi Flaud yesterday." Lettie shook her head.

"She loves ya, Lettie. We all do."

Lettie looked at her suddenly. "You're ever so sisterly today. Yesterday too."

"Well, you're hurting."

Lettie was quiet for a moment. "Not to be rude, but it seems this is the only time you reach out, Lucy."

"What do ya mean?"

"Just that you seem to jump over hay bales to help people who are down and out." Lettie shook her head. "Do I have to be this needy for you to pay me any mind?"

Startled, Lucy wondered, *Is this true?*

"Oh, Lettie, I *do* care about you. And Faye, too. I'm sorry I don't show it more."

Lettie gave her a small smile. "Still, I worry 'bout ya, sister. Who do *you* run to when things are crumblin' round your feet?"

Lucy felt flustered by the question. "It's always been Martie for me . . . much like you go to Faye."

Shrugging, Lettie sighed. "Right now, Faye and I are on the outs—she thinks Matthew wouldn't have broken up with me if I hadn't said certain things."

"Well, what do you think 'bout that?" Lucy asked gently, not wanting to spoil this rare moment between them.

"*Ach*, Lucy, I don't know what got into me last night after *die Youngie* gathered over at the deacon's for apple dumplings." Lettie sniffled. "Am I really outspoken enough to run a fella off?"

Lucy bit her tongue. No need to add insult to injury. "Try to remember what Mamm says: There are plenty of nice Amish boys just waitin' for your perty smile to catch their eye."

Wrinkling her nose, Lettie reached for Lucy's hand. "You're kinder than me, Lucy, and always have been."

"Well, I wouldn't go that far."

"I'm sorry if I offended ya." Lettie leaned closer. "Forgive me?"

Lucy squeezed her hand. "I'm glad ya didn't mince words. Honest, I am."

CHAPTER 36

WHEN THE FAMILY HAD ARRIVED HOME from church, Mamm approached Lucy and asked if they might talk privately, so Lucy suggested they go upstairs to her room.

In the quiet of the sunny space, her mother sat on the rocking chair near the window, motioning for Lucy to sit nearby. Lucy could only imagine what was on her mind.

"Your father and I talked following your, uh, discussion after this past week's grief class," Mamm began. "We're both concerned that you haven't been attending communion Sundays since—"

"Mamm . . ."

Her mother's eyes were sad, not accusing. "My dear, it's one thing to hide your guilt from your family but quite another to hide from the ministerial brethren."

Lucy glanced about her, suddenly wishing the door was closed. No need for Lettie and Faye to overhear. She rose to shut the door soundly. "My heart's still in pieces, Mamm. I can't think of takin' communion and bringing more tribulation on myself."

Her mother fell silent and turned toward the windows. She sighed heavily, obviously at a loss for words.

"This is something I've pondered many times. I just don't know how to move past my sin."

Mamm gazed at her. "My dear, it's the Lord alone who forgives."

Lucy sighed. "I really don't see how I can find a way to make things right, though."

Mamm looked dejected. "It's not in your power to redeem yourself. Just ain't possible."

The comment hit home, crashing down on Lucy's head as her mother rose and left the room. *Dat . . . and now Mamm, too,* she thought, knowing it was wrong to go for communion, considering the state of her heart.

<hr />

Lucy felt uneasy as she got on her scooter and left the house for Bud and Gracie Friesens' later. The afternoon sun had burned the blue from the sky, and the neighbors' woodshed and the corncrib looked dark, even withered, beneath its intensity, despite a bank of dark clouds to the west. She noticed the field corn belonging to the neighboring English farmers had already been harvested, whereas many of the Amish farmers were still in the process. *Most will probably finish up this week.*

As she turned into the Friesens' long lane, she spotted Dale, who waved. He was standing outside with Kiana and Van, talking with Bud and Gracie. It delighted Lucy to see Gracie already so engaged with Kiana. She parked her scooter and hurried to join them near the cottage-like guesthouse.

Bud was doting on little Van, letting him pick up one of the barn kittens as the five of them walked over to the white guesthouse with dark green shutters. Kiana pointed out how pretty the golden mums were in pots along the small front porch. "This reminds me of my childhood home," she told Gracie, smiling over her shoulder at Lucy.

The lovely refuge might just be the salve Kiana's broken heart needs, Lucy thought. *And having Bud and Gracie nearby will be an added blessing. . . .*

———

After the short tour of the house, Kiana seemed ready to sign on the dotted line, but Bud said her word was her bond, and after she said yes to their conditions, they shook hands to agree. "You may move in whenever you're ready," Bud said, looking nearly Amish, minus a beard, in his Sunday clothing, including tan suspenders.

"I never dreamed my son and I would live in such a peaceful place," Kiana said, adding that she didn't have much to bring with her. "I'll need to get a part-time job to buy some furniture and things."

Gracie's face burst into a smile. "Say, our neighbors next farm over are looking for a babysitter three afternoons a week. I'm sure they wouldn't mind if your son tagged along."

"Oh, I'd be interested in doing something like that! Yes, that would really help," Kiana said, reaching down to hug Van. "This is the pot of gold at the end of our rainbow," she told him, and he clapped his hands. She quickly explained it was one of his favorite bedtime stories.

"No gold-filled pots round here," Bud said with a laugh. "But there's an unlimited supply of God's grace."

Kiana nodded, eyes glistening. "Even better."

A sudden wind blew up, and it began to rain. They moved onto the small porch, and Gracie and Kiana made arrangements for the move to take place tomorrow, with Bud's help.

Bud handed Kiana a key. "Though we never lock our own doors."

When Kiana was ready to go, Van dawdled, already attached to the gray barn kitty. Gracie assured him he'd have plenty of time to play outdoors. "Our farm is your home now, too," she said.

With a strong downpour settling over them, Dale asked Lucy

if she might like to ride with him to take Kiana and Van back to the shelter. "You'll stay dry," he said, eyeing the scooter.

Lucy agreed, hoping this wouldn't upset her mother, as last Sunday's ride with Dale certainly had. It wasn't her intention to defy the church ordinance or her parents' wishes.

Dale put the scooter in the bed of his truck, and the four of them climbed inside, Kiana and Van in the pull-down benches on either side behind the front seat.

As Dale drove toward Lancaster, Lucy brought up the fact that she and Dale had gone last week to look at used cars. "We wanted to find one that might work for you, Kiana."

Kiana frowned, obviously puzzled, and Lucy said she wanted to give her the money for a down payment.

"You've already done so much," Kiana protested.

"I insist." Lucy smiled and reached back to squeeze her hand. "It would mean so much to me."

Dale glanced at his rearview mirror. "Perhaps you could view this as sort of a heavenly gift."

Kiana relented and said she would only accept the money if she could write Lucy an IOU. "It may take a while, but I will pay you back."

Lucy stood her ground. "A gift is a gift."

Later, after they'd taken Kiana and Van back to the Water Street Mission for their last night, Lucy thanked Dale for intervening. "I honestly wasn't sure she'd accept."

The rain was still heavy as Dale pulled into a coffee shop and parked. "Hope you don't mind if we stop here for a quick caffeine fix." He grabbed an umbrella and hurried around to open her door, holding the umbrella to keep her from getting soaked. Inside the coffee shop, the aroma of espresso greeted them as they got in line.

Dale offered to pay for her beverage, and when they'd gotten their coffee, they found a table in the far corner. He guided her to a chair, his hand on her elbow, then pulled out the chair for her. Lucy was thankful for the semi-privacy, already sensing a few intense stares from other customers, some Plain, including Rhoda Blank and her husband.

Oil and water don't mix—neither do Amish and English," Mamm had said more than once.

Dale mentioned how very generous she was in offering to help Kiana get a car.

Lucy shrugged it off. "Well, the money came to me in a most unexpected way," she told him, reluctant to reveal too much. "It has to do with the time in my life when I was too interested in the outside world."

"When you considered learning to drive?" He smiled.

She nodded. "I wasn't a very devout church member, to put it mildly. And it's still hard for me to forgive myself for my disobedience."

Dale nodded, opening the top of his coffee to add some sugar. "Well, forgiving isn't something we do only for others. Oh boy, have I learned that. It's an essential step in bringing our hearts back to wholeness."

"Now ya sound like your minister."

Dale grinned. "Believe me, I'll never be as wise as Linden Hess, but I know I need someone to cover my flub-ups—past, present, and future. Someone who doesn't push me into admitting, 'Yes, here's this huge weight, and I'm tired of carrying it.' *Someone* who waits for *me* to lay it all down at His feet."

The Lord Jesus, Lucy thought, an aching lump growing in her throat.

○○○○○○

The rain had diminished somewhat as Dale parked his old pickup in her father's driveway. Gallantly, he walked Lucy to the back door, taking her by surprise yet again. She could hear rumbling coming from upstairs and assumed the twins had been gawking from the window, just as they had done the first time Dat invited Dale over.

Before he turned to leave, Lucy said, "*Denki* for the delicious coffee . . . and for helpin' Kiana and her little boy." She paused and looked into the face of her wise friend. "And for everything else, too."

Christian had been looking out the stable door every few minutes for Lucy's arrival, wondering if Dale might bring her home, since another rainstorm had blown through the area. So he hadn't been too surprised when the red pickup pulled into the drive.

He'd let Lucy get indoors first before heading to the house. Christian watched as Dale removed the scooter from the pickup bed and then accompanied her to the door.

Were Sarah and I wrong about Dale's intentions?

Christian observed his daughter and her friend say good-bye. He honestly didn't know what to think. Considering Dale's gentlemanly demeanor, it was altogether possible he was simply being as polite as he was friendly.

Two rabbits crossed the barnyard when Christian finally headed to the house to find Lucy. He felt it was time to share with her about his own difficult past . . . his frowned-upon courtship with Minerva Miller. It was only right for Lucy to know she wasn't the sole family member who'd struggled against the church.

He found her sitting out on the long side porch, a black woolen shawl wrapped around her. Inching the door open, Christian cleared his throat. "Want some company?" he asked.

"All right," she said, quickly diverting her gaze to the floor.

"Ya know, there are some ways in which we're a lot alike, Lucy," he began, taking a seat near her. "It's past time I told you 'bout my first courtship."

Lucy glanced at him.

"You see, I had my sights set on a girl, instead of on *Gott*," he confessed. "Wanted my own way more than anything the church had to offer me then. I was a foolish teenager, pushin' the boundaries."

Lucy raised her head a bit, listening.

"Thankfully, my father got me straightened out, put his foot down 'bout any ideas I had to marry Minnie. In fact, he demanded I break up with her . . . said I needed to get myself back on the straight and narrow."

"I don't understand." Lucy's frown was apparent. "The Millers are Amish."

"*Jah*, her family is steadfastly Amish, but at the time Minnie had begun to stray a bit, curious 'bout other churches. She wasn't sure she wanted to stay Plain. And we started attending a more progressive church for a while, which broke both our fathers' hearts." Christian inhaled deeply, hoping this was wise, sticking his neck out. "We even discussed running away to marry, planning to sort everything out later." He added that they hadn't thought much of anything through. "We believed we were in love. All we cared about was being together."

Lucy's eyes were wide now. "I never knew this, Dat."

"*Nee*, and I didn't think ya needed to, till now." Christian bowed his head for a moment, then continued, looking back at Lucy again. "Eventually, when I came to my senses, I forgave my father, grateful he'd stepped in when he did. And I forgave myself, which was the hardest part of all."

Lucy was blinking fast, and he wondered if she might cry.

"Ain't something I'm comfortable talking 'bout," he told her. "I guess some of us in this family are more open to correction—and molding—than others. 'Tis sad but true."

Sniffing, Lucy slowly nodded her head.

"Sometimes we hold our sin too close, making it harder to

relinquish it to God," he said quietly. "I know one thing for sure: The Lord's a mender of hearts . . . if we just ask for His forgiveness and turn from our sins."

"The Heart-mender," Lucy whispered, wiping her tears. "I think I needed to hear this, Dat." She sighed audibly. "Just think, you would've missed out on Mamm if you'd married Minnie."

Christian felt sincerely moved by Lucy's comment. "I'm thankful every day for your mother . . . such a caring and devout woman." He looked upon Lucy with such a strong feeling of parental affection. "I hope you won't deny yourself the possibility of such a special love someday, daughter."

Lucy rose quickly. And he did the same, meeting her halfway with a welcoming embrace.

CHAPTER 37

THE SKY'S AS GRAY AS A GOSLING, Martie mused as she washed her boys' faces and let Jesse be excused from the breakfast table, where she'd lingered with them, telling again the beloved Bible story of Jesus and the little children, one of Jesse's favorites.

She set about redding up the dishes, hoping it wouldn't rain till the clothes were dry. Thankfully, Lucy was due anytime now, and Martie could hardly wait to see her again. It wasn't just for the wonderful help but also for the female companionship. Sometimes, it felt like Martie was talking toddler-speak all day long. She looked forward to mealtime, as well, interested in Ray's leisurely talk about his work, though his recent mentions of the families moving west worried her, truth be told. He still hadn't said anything about whether he meant for them to go, too, and she hoped that Eppie had managed to get the facts wrong. *It wouldn't be the first time!*

Later, when Ray arrived in the kitchen, he gave her a smile, and she observed his gentle way with Jesse as he stooped to talk with him, asking in *Deitsch* if he'd like to go out and help sweep in the barn again.

Jesse was all for it, practically leaping into Ray's arms.

Dear, patient man, Martie thought, knowing well that having Jesse in the barn would surely slow her husband down.

Ray winked at her as he headed toward the back door, Jesse waving at her and little Josh. "I have something to tell you at the noon meal," he called over his shoulder.

She groaned inwardly. Could it be more news about Colorado? She'd heard for sure that James and Joanna were making plans for a move there, possibly when Glicks were leaving. Was Eppie right, and James's talk had influenced Ray, too?

Oh, she sincerely hoped not.

***

Lucy had opened her journal much earlier than usual that morning, rereading the words she was determined to remember: *"The Lord is a mender of hearts."* Her father had stated this with such assurance.

As she dressed and prepared for the day—helping to make breakfast and carrying down the family's washing—she pondered the things Dat had said, surprising as they were. To think her upstanding father had been tempted and gone astray, and yet found redemption.

Might there be hope for me?

This time of year, one really didn't have to keep track of the calendar, Lucy mused, already missing the long days of summer as she stayed around to help Lettie wash breakfast dishes while Faye and Mamm put another big load in the wringer washer.

When Mamm returned to the kitchen for another cup of coffee, Lucy remarked about the lack of sunshine.

"Be thankful for all things, Lucy," her mother promptly reminded her. "That includes whatever weather the Lord *Gott* bestows on us."

Her firm tone wasn't lost on Lucy. *She's still upset about communion Sunday,* Lucy thought, feeling guilty as usual, knowing she was letting her parents down once again. And because of this tension in the house, Lucy thought it was probably a good thing that nothing was planned with Dale for the week, although she'd likely encounter him on Thursday evening. *If I attend again.*

Lucy handed a freshly washed and dripping plate to Lettie to dry just as Faye came running indoors, waving a letter. "Look what I found in the mailbox," Faye said with a grin. "Our neighbor saw me out sweeping the driveway and mentioned she'd seen a young man put something in our box a couple hours ago."

"Who's it from?" Lettie wondered, trying her best to catch a glimpse as Faye handed it over to Lucy, who dried her hands on her apron right quick.

"No return address. Just says *To Lucy Flaud,*" Faye told Lettie as Lucy excused herself, and Faye took her spot washing dishes.

In the next room, Lucy sat and opened the note, which she saw was from Tobe. Surprised yet secretly pleased he'd bothered to write, she was glad he was still being friendly.

Dear Lucy,

Good (early) morning! I am writing this before the sun has risen, but I couldn't think of leaving with my family for our Colorado visit without telling you that we're going today. We plan to return in time for communion Sunday, so it's going to be a quick trip.

This will be an adventure, of sorts, as we scope out the possibilities for land to purchase. My father hopes to buy a large ranch and possibly split it up with several families—there'd be hundreds of acres to divide. He'd prefer one with an existing farmhouse and outbuildings, though naturally, Dat will want to build on some Dawdi Hauses, like we do here.

Also, if you hear that our bishop has made an offer on our farm, it's true. Dat has told us the bishop wants it for one of his grandsons. We're all relieved to know it will stay in the capable hands of the People once everything's settled for our move to Monte Vista.

I hope you have a wonderful day, Lucy!

Your friend,
Tobe Glick

He certainly didn't have to write, Lucy thought, folding the note and glancing toward the kitchen doorway. But going the second and third mile was something Tobe was known to do, and she couldn't help but smile.

———

As Lucy took her scooter up the road toward Martie's later that morning than usual, Dorothea Holtz came to mind. *Dear woman, how is she holding up?* Lucy wondered, waving to the neighbors out with their six-mule team, harvesting field corn.

She picked up the pace, anticipating seeing the sweet couple again once she was done at Martie's.

After much pleading on her part, Clinton had agreed to tell Lucy the story behind the footbridge that very afternoon.

———

Martie seemed especially talkative when Lucy arrived, asking what she knew about the Glicks' plans for their recent trip to Colorado. Lucy shared what she knew from Tobe's note. Martie was glad for that much but still seemed rather unsettled to think that people they'd grown up with were heading off to parts unknown. "It just doesn't make sense."

Lucy assumed her sister was having a difficult morning. Maybe she was experiencing morning sickness again . . . often worse with twins, Lucy had heard. She recalled having a rough time herself initially, but she couldn't allow herself to dwell on that. Oh, if only she'd carried her wee babe to term—what would it have been like to hold him? Lucy had always thought of her baby as a boy, though of course she didn't actually know, since she'd miscarried so early on. It sickened her that she would never be able to look down with tender love into his peachy little face.

But watching Martie, Lucy felt sure something more than just carrying twins was affecting her sister. *She seems almost agitated.*

"What's troublin' ya, sister?" Lucy asked.

Martie sighed. "You know all the rumors flyin' round 'bout one family, then another, itchin' to move out west. Well, turns out Ray's ponderin' making that move, too."

"Surely not," Lucy whispered.

Lucy considered this later while she rode her scooter to the hospice after the noon meal she'd cooked for Ray and Martie and the boys. *They would have good company out there, what with Tobe and his family going,* she thought, though sadly.

Halfway there, she realized how much she looked forward to running into Tobe while headed to the hospice and other places around the area. *I didn't foresee how much I would miss seeing and talking to him. . . .*

At the hospice, Lucy found Clinton at Dorothea's bedside, cradling her hand in his. She looked like a porcelain doll in her pink satin bed jacket. Clinton motioned for Lucy to enter, asking her to close the door behind her.

"Dottie's had a few days of severe pain," Clinton said quietly as Lucy pulled up a chair next to him. "She started a new medication yesterday morning, and it's eased her somewhat."

Lucy's heart ached for them both.

"The nurse says she'll be in and out of awareness as a result." Clinton sighed, dark circles under his eyes. "It's good you're here, Lucy. Dottie was asking for you."

Lucy said there was nowhere else she'd rather be just then, aware of not only the dim room, but the gray cloud cover outside the window. She inquired again about the significance of the little footbridge on Witmer Road.

"I'm certainly not going anywhere, so if you have the time . . ." Clinton said, his voice trailing off.

"I'll be here all afternoon." Lucy's throat constricted as she witnessed the struggle between life and death on Dorothea's petite face.

Slowly, Clinton began. "Have you ever felt instantly at home with someone?" he asked. "That was how I felt when I first met Dottie Kreider at a high school football rally not far from here. Seventy years ago nearly to the day," he said, his voice cracking.

––––––––––

Clint had sprained his ankle and was perturbed to be sitting out the first football game of the season, beating himself up for jumping down a flight of stairs to show off for the guys.

Dottie and two of her girlfriends came down from the bleachers after the game, encouraging him that in a few short weeks, he would be back on the field. Clint wasn't so sure, not as swollen as his ankle was. But he could see that Dottie's friends were eyeing the other players, while her attention was fully on him.

Dottie's thick brown shoulder-length hair and pretty face caught his eye, but she looked away, the shyest girl in their sophomore class. And as he got to know her better, it became clear that Dottie wasn't as pretty on the inside. When he invited her to a youth gathering at his church, she quickly refused, even though they'd gone to several activities at their school together, he on crutches, she helping him along.

By the time they were seniors, Dottie had fallen in with a

fast crowd. Clint, popular because of his status as a quarterback, continued to focus on his studies and help with the youth department at church, eager to attend college.

At the end of the first semester, Dottie dropped out of school. Clint worried she might never graduate and heard she was frequenting bars and spending time with older guys. Unknown to her, Clint had been thinking about her since tenth grade, asking God to watch over her.

Four years passed, and after college, Clint went on to graduate school, getting a degree in accounting. He landed a job working in a firm with other certified public accountants and bought a house near Amish farmland. In his free time, he served as the youth pastor for his church. Clint had a few dates with some young women from the church, but nothing came of them.

Then, one rainy springtime afternoon, he ran into Dottie at the Bird-in-Hand Bake Shop on Gibbons Road. She recognized him immediately, and he experienced the same joy at seeing her again. They talked in the checkout line, catching up on each other's lives, and Clint invited her for supper the next evening.

One conversation led to another, and they began seeing each other regularly, until he boldly invited her to attend church with him.

"Oh, Clint," she said, shaking her head. "I'm no church girl. Have you forgotten?"

But Clint didn't give up praying for her, and while they continued to occasionally see each other as friends, he couldn't get Dottie out of his mind.

Another year passed, and their coffees and dinners became less common as they grew apart once again. Clint would see her from time to time from afar in different places around Lancaster County. Eventually, he heard she'd moved back home to help her mom look after her ailing brother, so Clint decided to visit them one Sunday afternoon.

"Barry was the light of Dottie's life," Clinton told Lucy. "And when leukemia took him before his thirtieth birthday, Dottie was overcome with sadness."

Stirring just then, Dorothea's eyes fluttered open. "Barry?" she asked weakly. "I saw him last night . . . he came into this room." She struggled to speak. "Never said a word . . . but it was . . . so real."

Clinton frowned. "Barry's been gone for years, darling."

Dorothea nodded drowsily.

"Our friend Lucy's here now," Clinton told his wife, leaning near. "I've been telling her how you kept me at arm's length all those years."

Dorothea gave him a momentary smile and closed her eyes again, sighing deeply.

Clinton looked steadily at her, his gaze nearly reverent. He turned to Lucy before resuming his story. "It was after Barry's death that Dottie surprised me a week later by sitting in the row in front of me at church. As before, she warmed to my attention, and soon we were again seeing each other every weekend. Our dates consisted of lengthy discussions about life and the choices she'd made, many of them poor. Dottie was down on herself and realized we were polar opposites in temperament and ethics. 'You're nice and I'm naughty,' she would say."

Polar opposites. Lucy thought suddenly of Tobe.

Clinton stopped and inhaled slowly. "Just when I thought Dottie was going to surrender her past, her sadness . . . she broke up with me."

Lucy winced.

"Nearly every time we were together, Dottie said she didn't deserve someone as kind and good as me. Yet only after the breakup did I really begin to think there was no hope for us."

Another four seasons came and went, and Clint kept busy with his accounting work, especially at tax time, his client list growing as word spread of his integrity and competence.

One day, he picked up the society page in the newspaper and saw a picture of Dottie Kreider alongside an article. She was hosting a holiday house tour, and the man posing beside her was Phil Buchner, a linebacker from Clint's old high school team. He read the article, curious to know if she was married, and was tempted to look up Phil in the yearbook. That night, he hurried home to search his rec room bookshelves and found it. Holding the yearbook, Clint realized how futile this was. He and Dottie had no future together. That was apparent—God had not answered his prayers, at least not in the way Clint had desired. Why torture himself further?

Clint dropped to his knees, asking the Lord to come into Dottie and Phil's lives in a powerful way, to draw them tenderly to Him. "Bring godly people across their paths," he prayed whenever he thought of Dottie.

Then, late one night, he received a call from a gas station down near Quarryville. Phil had been drinking . . . Dottie's car was totaled . . . would Clint mind coming for her?

Without delay, he got out of bed, pulled on jeans and a shirt, and headed out, his heart in his throat. By the time Clint arrived, the police had filed the accident report, and Phil had been arrested, the car towed away.

When Dottie saw Clint, she threw her arms around him, sobbing. Clint wondered if she, too, had been drinking, but that was not the case. She was battered and bruised, but the paramedics determined there were no broken bones. Dottie wanted desperately to talk, which she and Clint did over coffee and brownies at a nearby twenty-four-hour coffee shop. Dottie had witnessed her life flash before her, and she'd despised what she'd seen. She pleaded with Clint to take her back, and he gently reminded her that she was the one who'd kept leaving. "I assumed you'd married Phil."

Shaking her head, she looked most serious. "I'm ready for your church, your kind of life . . . and your Jesus," she said sincerely. "I'm a mess, Clint, but if God's Son is anything like you . . . I want to know Him."

The following Sunday, Dottie went with Clint to his church. At the end of the sermon, she walked the aisle to the altar and never looked back on her old life.

"That day totally changed her self-worth . . . her sense of who she was," Clinton said, tears on his face.

"Your prayers were answered at last," Lucy said, her heart deeply moved. *He had such patience.*

Dorothea's eyes were half open now, her head nodding.

Clinton raised his wife's slender hand to his lips. "None of us deserves God's great love," he whispered. "That's why Christ came and bridged the gap. And that's where the footbridge comes in."

Dorothea looked at Clinton fondly. "Tell Lucy . . . darling."

The door opened, and the nurse entered to check Dorothea's vitals, then asked Lucy to leave so she could administer a shot.

Lucy stepped outside, leaving Clinton with his wife, trying to imagine what Clinton might tell her about the bridge.

CHAPTER 38

CHRISTIAN WAS FINISHING UP a few chores when one of Caleb's farmhands came by the house to say that Dale Wyeth had called. "He wondered if ya might come over at your convenience, sometime today or tomorrow."

Christian thanked him, then hitched up and headed over to Dale's place. There, he was warmly welcomed and ushered into Dale's kitchen, where the plans for a goat shelter were sketched out and laid on the table. Dale's work on the hen house seemed to be going well enough that Christian wasn't sure why he needed to sign off on Dale's next big project.

Yet Christian looked it over and agreed it was a well-thought plan. *Does he have something else on his mind?* He noticed the framed pastoral farm scene on the opposite side of the kitchen, featuring the Twenty-Third Psalm. *Like my Dat bought for Mamm's kitchen years ago.* He could not dismiss the coincidence.

Dale asked for the name of the feed salesman the Amish farmers preferred, then took Christian out to see his new genera-tor. "Little by little, I'm getting there," Dale said, smiling. Was it Christian's imagination, or was the young man more jovial than usual?

They walked off the perimeter of his plot, and Dale mentioned possibly thinning out some of his white and red pines in the woods near his field to let the hardwoods grow. "I've read oak and maple are best for heating the house . . . though I'll have to buy most of my wood."

Dale's certainly serious about all this.

Dale asked his opinion on what crops to plant come spring. "I'd like a much larger garden than I put in this year. I also need to have Lucy and her sisters come over sometime and show me how to preserve food."

"Honestly, my girls are busy enough as it is," Christian told him, making this very clear.

"There's always next year," Dale acknowledged as they turned back toward the house. "I still have much to learn."

About making friends with an Amishwoman? Christian wondered. *How much has Lucy told him about her past relationship with an outsider? Anything?*

<hr />

"Ah, yes . . . the footbridge." Clinton seemed to enjoy telling Lucy how fond he and Dottie had always been of the lovely setting, even during high school days. "I tried to be casual about it when I suggested Dottie meet me there at the bridge on September twelfth that year of her accident. I'd chosen the spot not only because she thought it was such a pretty area, but because of her rejection of Christ all those years. The bridge symbolized, at least in my mind, the all-encompassing love of our heavenly Father, connecting humankind to His grace and love."

Lucy pondered this, starting to understand.

"When Dottie arrived, I waited for her at one end of the bridge, slowly walking toward the center. As she met me there,

I knelt on one knee and opened a small ring box. 'Will you be my dearest love?' I asked."

"She didn't waver—it was as if Dottie had sensed what I'd planned." Clinton smiled, tears rolling down his weathered face.

Dorothea roused just then and lifted her head a bit, her eyes fixed on Clinton. "I said . . . yes . . . to my beloved," she whispered huskily from her now elevated bed. "And yes . . . to my Savior."

Lucy was captivated by Dorothea's radiance—like a bride on her wedding day. The sight was sweet, even sacred; Lucy almost looked away out of respect. But in spite of the intimacy of the moment, she could not take her eyes off the couple.

Dorothea struggled to breathe, and Clinton rang for the nurse.

Getting up with much effort, Clinton left his cane at his chair and stood over his wife, leaning against the bed rails. He bowed his head, one hand in hers and one raised toward heaven. "Be merciful, O Lord."

Dorothea gazed innocently into his eyes for a tender moment. Clinton leaned down to kiss her and placed his hand on her heart. Some time after the nurse arrived, Dorothea joined the church triumphant, as Clint described her heavenly homegoing.

Lucy brushed away her tears, yearning for such a precious love of her own. And for all the rest of the day, she basked in their story, having seen them year after year, commemorating their engagement at the little bridge. *The beginning of a love for a lifetime . . .*

 ⁓⁓⁓

Hesitant to return home just yet, Lucy slowed her scooter when she came to the footbridge. She pictured Clinton's marriage proposal there—the towering trees much smaller decades ago, swaying gently around the couple. Lucy wondered how many times the bridge had been repaired or replaced over the years since that momentous day.

Leaving her scooter on the roadside, she made her way down over the small embankment, planting herself on the sidewalk, gazing at the bridge ahead. *Divine grace bridged the gap for Dorothea,* she thought, recalling her father's recent talk with her, as well. The kind of enduring love Clinton and Dorothea had experienced could only have come from the Lord. He, alone, had been the most important key to their relationship from the start. *And despite all Dottie did wrong, Clinton was there for her. . . .*

When Lucy returned home, she went to the hen house, her mind occupied with thoughts of the upcoming grief class. Would Clinton feel up to attending the group so soon after Dorothea's passing? She'd already decided she wanted to go to the funeral. *Knowing Dale, he'll want to be there, too.* Clinton and Dorothea, like Kiana and Van, were another link between her and her newfound *Englischer* friend.

When Lucy brought in the basket of eggs, Mamm and the twins were chopping vegetables. Mamm was silent, but Lettie smiled and Faye looked glum—a complete switch for those two.

"Remember the older gentleman I told ya 'bout, Mamm? The one I saw at the footbridge, then at market, some time ago?" Lucy sighed deeply. "Well, his wife, Dorothea, passed away this afternoon while I was there with them at the hospice."

"Oh, my dear, I'm sorry," Mamm said, opening her arms to Lucy.

"I'm awful glad they were together at the end. Such a sweet couple." Lucy stepped away to check the eggs, handling them carefully to make sure they weren't broken.

"Oh, I almost forgot," Lettie told her. "Your friend Kiana called Uncle Caleb's barn phone and left a message for you."

"*Denki.* I'll do the rest of my chores first." Lucy hurried to her room, glad for this—something to brighten up a rather bittersweet afternoon.

After helping her sisters with the supper dishes, Lucy returned Kiana's call amidst the bellowing Holsteins at her uncle's farm.

"We're all moved in, thanks to you, Lucy." There was a lilt in Kiana's voice.

"I'm so happy for ya!" She offered to visit next week and take them for a ride in the family buggy. "Van might like that."

Kiana sounded thrilled at the prospect of not only seeing Lucy again but of some additional fun for her son.

"*Denki* for callin', Kiana. I'll see ya once you're settled in, and bring the promised check, too. All right?"

So it was agreed that Lucy would come by with the horse and carriage next Monday.

Christian was out in the stable after supper that evening when Deacon Miller came rushing in, *The Budget* all rolled up in his hand like he was looking for flies to swat. "Have ya seen what your daughter wrote?" He slapped it against the wooden post.

"*Jah*, read it last Friday, when it was delivered." Christian wondered why Edward was frowning so.

"There are rumors 'bout you takin' an English fellow under your wing—showin' him what to do in case the lights go out. And this confirms it."

"I have nothin' to hide, Deacon."

"Well, then, I advise you to reconsider helpin' this young man. I've heard from more than one person that Lucy's taken a real shine to him. James and Rhoda Blank saw this outsider and your previously *rappelkeppi* daughter at a coffee shop in Bird-in-Hand. What's worse, Lucy rode away with him in his truck—on the Lord's Day, no less!"

"I have a world of respect for ya, Deacon, but whatever Lucy was doin' with Dale, I doubt they were on a date." Christian wasn't sure who to be more put out with—Dale Wyeth or the deacon. As for himself, he had never been one to spread gossip, nor pay it any mind. "It's an odd time for this discussion, Deacon."

"The way I see it, it's the *bescht* time, considering our fasting day comin' up. Sweep out all the sin in the camp."

He must think Lucy's at risk.

"Listen, Christian: If this young man might lead your daughter astray, why not cut ties? Or at least let him know not to seek her out."

Christian could not deny the wisdom of that. Nodding, he agreed, "Since ya put it that way. . . ."

CHAPTER 39

EARLY WEDNESDAY MORNING, Lucy went to the outer room between the kitchen and the back porch and slipped on her black coat, thinking she ought to help Martie more frequently this week. *She'll be relieved to see me.*

Stepping outside, Lucy watched a flock of geese fly like miniature arrows over the barnyard in a perfect V formation, their wings beating rhythmically.

Lettie scurried out of the house and onto the porch steps just behind her. "*Ach*, so glad I caught ya, Lucy. Would ya mind if I walk over to Martie's with you? Maybe I'll stay an' help with Jesse and Josh while you clean or cook or whatever."

"I'd like your company, sure." Lucy was curious; Lettie had never sought her out like this before. "Is Faye comin', too?"

"She wants to go with Mamm over to Glicks' while they're gone to look over some items set aside for the big sale next month. I guess there will be a few others there, too. The Glicks want to move things quickly, in preparation for the bigger move early next spring—might even be March, I heard."

Ah, so she's dying to talk more about Tobe, thought Lucy, not sure she was up for it.

"By the way, Mammi Flaud said something 'bout all of us help-ing her with some piecework for one of her quilts sometime after communion Sunday," Lettie said with a glance at the *Dawdi Haus.*

At the mention of communion, Lucy felt tense.

"Fasting day is this Friday, don't forget." Lettie looked at Lucy. "And I hope ya feel well enough to attend on Sunday."

So, Lettie *had* noticed. Most likely everyone else had, too. "Bein' healthy's a *gut* thing, 'specially for Holy Communion." Lucy meant it in more than one way, but let it be. *Nourishing a healthy body . . . and soul.*

They headed up to Witmer Road at a brisk pace, staying on the shoulder, off the pavement. The morning haze had begun to lift as the sun shone across the fields.

"Listen, Lettie," said Lucy, "I'm real sorry for not being very sisterly. I just always assumed Faye was the sister you most cared 'bout."

Lettie dipped her head. "It's obvious why you might think that."

"Ain't a *gut* excuse, though."

They walked in unison, their shoes scuffing against the pebbles along the roadside. Several carriages passed by, and she and Lettie waved at Aunt Edna Lapp in the first one, followed later by the Millers. Lucy thought of Dat's sharing about Minnie and was glad to be on much better footing with him now.

"If ya wanna know the whole truth of what happened between Matthew Mast and me," Lettie said as they took the bend in the road, "I was flippant, even suggested he might find someone in Colorado who wasn't nearly as much fun as me."

"You said that?" Lucy was surprised. "Wait . . . the Masts are leavin', too?"

"Didn't ya know?"

Lucy shook her head.

"Well, the way things are goin' with Mark and Faye, I wouldn't be surprised if Faye ends up out there, too," Lettie revealed. "They'll be married eventually."

Lucy gasped. "You two are like sugar peas in a pod, though! Faye'd actually leave ya behind?"

"That's another reason why I've struggled lately."

"Oh, Lettie." Lucy stopped walking and reached for her hand. "I had no idea."

When Lettie settled a bit, she dried her eyes. "I can't imagine Faye goin' away. It'll feel like my right arm is missin'."

Lucy agreed. "And I can't figure out why this notion of joinin' another settlement so far away is catchin' on with our church members." She thought of Martie's concerns again.

"Ya surely know that Tobe's decided to go with his family, too. They've got a good offer from Bishop Smucker—I s'pose their place is as good as sold."

"*Jah*, Tobe told me this himself."

Talking about this with Lettie brought it all back—Tobe's courtship proposal, the pleasant night she'd walked with him nearly to the Lincoln Highway, and Tobe's friendship all these years.

"You're upset, ain't ya?" Lettie blew her nose.

"Just wonderin' how much this will affect our community."

Lettie nodded. "Faye argues that it's not anything that comes as a surprise, though, 'cause Plain families have been doin' this sort of thing for years."

"Do Dat and Mamm know Faye might be followin' the Masts out there?"

"Not yet."

Lucy breathed a grateful sigh as Ray and Martie's house came into view. She didn't feel like mentioning that their brother James was also headed that direction, nor Martie's worry that Ray was considering this, as well.

Lettie can hear this directly from Martie, Lucy thought sadly. *If it comes to that.*

⌘

Thursday morning, the day of Dorothea's funeral, Lucy got up in time to bathe and dress, then left with one of their paid drivers in the passenger van. Several other Amish folk from her district were headed for the same church gathering, including Rhoda Blank and her husband from Bird-in-Hand.

When she entered the church, Lucy noticed Dale standing off to the side, wearing a black suit, white shirt, and subdued black-and-gray-striped tie. When he spotted her, Dale walked her way, his smile bright. "Would you like to sit together?" he asked, mentioning that his mother was under the weather and unable to make it.

Lucy realized the Amish folk from the van had already gotten in line to sign the guest book, so she and Dale did, too. Secretly, she was glad Dale had singled her out.

"Is your father coming?" Dale asked, handing her an order of service with a picture of a younger Dorothea on the cover.

"His work has him tied up." She was surprised Dale would even expect him to attend.

Following his lead into the church sanctuary, Lucy noticed many sprays of flowers along the front, as well as the pure white casket adorned with a mass of peach-colored roses on top. Everything about this funeral was completely foreign, but she smiled, remembering Dorothea's penchant for peaches.

The first two hymns were unfamiliar to Lucy, but she followed along in the songbook, and after hearing the first verse and chorus, tried to sing along, though softly. Dale's deep voice was reassuring.

Before the sermon, four of Clinton and Dorothea's grown children and two of their grandchildren stood before the packed church and spoke of their mother and grandmother's virtues, as well as sharing favorite memories. Dorothea's eldest daughter, Elaina, talked about the simple joy of just being with her, sitting and talking over warm tea. "That alone was my greatest delight."

When Clinton slowly rose to his feet, Lucy was surprised he had the strength to get up and speak. The place was hushed as he walked with his cane and some assistance from one of his grandsons to a podium set up near the closed casket. The dear man looked ever so feeble and pale.

"It may have seemed to anyone who knew me back then that I had somehow rescued Dorothea," he began. "Nevertheless, while I was attempting to live a pleasing life before the Lord, I was also terribly lonely, missing the young woman who had come in and out of my life . . . the girl who one day would become my wife."

He removed his white handkerchief and wiped his eyes. "It was around that time that I purchased an embroidered bookmark to give to Dottie and tucked it into the New Testament.

"That day, I learned something about Dorothea's name. It means God's gift." A sigh rippled through the crowd as he looked fondly at the casket, then moved to take a single peach-colored rose from the massive bouquet. "And quite truly, in every way, Dottie was God's gift to me."

Lucy pressed her hand over her mouth, fighting tears, and for just an instant, Dale reached over and covered her free hand with his. Startled, she was glad her father had not come today.

CHAPTER 40

CHRISTIAN WAS GRATEFUL when Sarah brought some hot coffee out to the barn midafternoon, taking a moment to mention the community was all abuzz about the homeless young woman Lucy and her *Englischer* friend had helped. "Have ya heard they're stayin' over at Bud Friesen's?"

"*Jah*." Christian nodded. "Lucy told me. James and Solomon and their wives donated some canned goods when they heard," Christian said, stopping to wipe his brow with his blue paisley handkerchief.

Sarah smiled and said that was awfully nice. "Lucy's generosity must be catching."

"I can't agree more, though I'm hopin' this isn't just an excuse to spend time with Dale," he said, which made Sarah shake her head. Then she scurried back toward the house. *No doubt she's worried, too, after reading* The Budget.

Christian hadn't been able to locate their copy of the periodical since he and Sarah had read it last Friday. It seemed odd for it to walk off like that, and he wondered if Lucy had even seen it yet, since she hadn't said a word about it.

Maybe she's been too busy.

From the high vantage point of her room, Lucy watched her father ride out of the lane. She was under the weather, and after this morning's funeral, she didn't have the strength to be around other grieving people . . . nor Dale Wyeth. *Have I spent too much time with him lately?*

On the heels of the passings of Wendell and Dorothea, hearing that Faye was most likely leaving for Colorado, too, and possibly Martie and Ray, was too much for Lucy to contemplate.

And Tobe.

Moving to her desk, Lucy reached for the curriculum and read through the information for the class she was missing—"Where is God in Our Grief?" Her gaze fell on the pretty quilted coverlet Martie had made for Lucy's baby after Lucy left for Ohio. It was lying on the armrest of the settee.

Have I held God at a distance? Is that why He feels so far away?

She picked up the small quilt and smoothed it, then folded it and placed it in her hope chest before she slipped over to the sunroom area. There, she sat, bowing her head, the space dimly lit by a small lantern. *I didn't even have the courtesy to tell Dat I wasn't going tonight.*

Tomorrow, they would fast during the breakfast hour. Most families skipped just that meal prior to communion Sunday. "I have lots to pray about," she murmured, recalling Clinton's talking about how Dorothea had long struggled: her will versus God's.

Closing her eyes, Lucy prayed silently, getting a head start on tomorrow.

~ ◦ ~

After the support group adjourned, Dale sought out Christian to ask how Lucy was faring. Christian said he had been glad she could attend Dorothea's funeral today, close as Lucy had been to the woman.

"I had expected she might be here tonight," Dale commented, looking around. "Is she okay?"

Christian didn't know for sure and didn't care to let on. "It's possible she'll return next week."

"Please let her know I asked about her," Dale said politely.

And while Christian tried to read Dale's demeanor, he couldn't decipher whether or not the man had romantic intentions. He remembered Deacon Ed's visit earlier this week, *The Budget* in hand. No, as much as Christian liked Dale, he would *not* relay his message to Lucy . . . adding coal to an already simmering fire.

Jesse and Josh were sleeping soundly upstairs when Ray came in from outdoors. He pulled his chair out and sat down at the head of the table, asking for some coffee.

"So late?" Martie asked.

Ray nodded and pulled on his beard. He seemed fidgety, which wasn't like him. "*Kumme*, sit with me, *mei Lieb*."

With the pregnancy, Martie didn't dare drink coffee at all, particularly at this hour, so she got herself some cold water from the faucet and brought her tumbler over and sat down, waiting for the water to boil.

"As I told you Monday, I've been mullin' things over with James, taking time to decide whether a move to Colorado might be a *gut* thing for our family, too."

Martie set her water down, a sick feeling in the pit of her stomach.

"I've come to the conclusion that movin' west to join with the other families could be a wise thing. But we won't leave when all the others do . . . not with the twins coming. It makes better sense for us to stay put for the immediate future," he said, reaching for her hand and holding it on the table.

So he does want to go, but not right away, she thought, wanting to be brave. Even so, it was hard.

"I should have told ya before now what I was thinking . . . didn't wanna put added stress on you. Your happiness and the health of the babies is uppermost," Ray said.

"I'd heard some things, and I must admit I was frettin' more than I should have." She smiled a little. "But I do trust ya, Ray. You know what's best for us."

He leaned near, searching her eyes. "This is the chance of a lifetime. We can purchase many more acres there, and for so much less than here. We'll have more land to pass on to our children someday."

"What 'bout our families?" she had to ask. "We'll be leavin' them behind. After all, your parents are getting up in years, ya know."

"Our relatives can visit. The trains and vans go both ways." He kissed her hand.

She nodded, and when the water came to a boil, she asked if decaf was all right, hoping that way he could sleep more soundly. "Have ya told your father any of this yet?" she asked as she stirred in the instant coffee.

He nodded. "Daed's real curious what we'll discover out there— sounds like he and Mamm might even want to join us, once we're settled."

"Now, that'd be all right with me." *More hands to help with four little ones!*

"But no sense worryin' *your* parents just yet," Ray said, blowing on his coffee. "Seems they've got enough to handle with Lucy."

"What now?" she asked.

He hesitated, as if thinking how to say it. "Well, seems the Blanks saw Lucy with an *Englischer* at a coffee shop on Sunday afternoon. Seemed to be awful cozy . . . like they were on a date. She even left there in his pickup truck."

"*Nee,* I can't believe this!" And lest she spoil their time together, Martie rose right quick and went to the cookie jar.

After she'd had a nibble or two, she returned to the table and offered some to Ray. They discussed his fasting for breakfast tomorrow, in keeping with their tradition, though due to her pregnancy, she wouldn't be joining in.

"Better safe than sorry," Ray agreed.

Later, after they'd outened the lights, Martie wondered how many others had seen Lucy with Dale Wyeth over the past couple of weeks. *Cozying up, for goodness' sake!*

If it was true that Lucy was entertaining romantic notions toward yet another outsider, Martie worried her sister would not partake in the fasting and prayer tomorrow—let alone communion.

CHAPTER 41

THE FIRST THING LUCY DID early the next morning was run up to Uncle Caleb's barn and call the woman in charge of organizing the food truck crew. Lucy indicated that today was a day of religious observance and apologized for the late notice.

"I completely understand," the supervisor said kindly.

Uncle Caleb's watchdog barked loudly at a bird that had flown down from the barn rafters, and Lucy covered her ear, thanking the supervisor and promising to be there next Friday.

When she returned home, Dat and Mamm were kneeling reverently in the front room with bowed heads and folded hands. Mammi Flaud had joined in, as well, bless her heart. Upstairs, Lettie and Faye were praying silently on either side of their bed.

Seeing her family united in this way, Lucy felt all the more convicted. And when she'd reached the third floor, she went to her sunroom area and knelt beside the settee, folding her hands. "O Lord God, please wash my heart clean. 'I acknowledge my transgressions: and my sin is ever before me,'" she prayed, quoting the anguished cry of King David of old.

"My burden of sin is too heavy to carry," she whispered between sobs. "I beg Thee for relief . . . for peace. I yearn for Thy forgiveness—I need it more than food. I need to find the strength to forgive myself, too."

She went on to pour out all of her misery, her sin and her deceit, praying through a veil of tears. "I no longer blame Thee, O Lord, for letting my baby die." She paused, then added, "I ask Thy forgiveness for this in the name of Thy Son, Jesus Christ . . . the great Heart-mender, who surely wept alongside me."

There was no feeling of warmth like some folk said they experienced following such an entreaty. What Lucy did feel was a great sense of relief, and she longed to fully open her heart to God and to obey His commands. She was free of the weight of her sin and her sorrow, willing to forgive herself at long last.

All during family worship, while her father read the Bible, Lucy struggled to keep back tears. She had never been so tenderhearted while listening to God's Word. Mamm looked over at her a couple of times when Lucy sniffled, yet Lucy did not feel ashamed. *I've bottled up so many tears. . . .*

Later, Lettie was the one who came privately to her, in Lucy's bedroom, and asked if she was all right.

"*Denki* for caring," Lucy said. "It's sweet of you, Lettie." The lightness in her spirit was undeniable now, and she wanted to bask in it before going down to help Mamm get the noon meal on the table.

Lettie hugged her, then tiptoed out of the room, her footsteps soft on the stairs.

<hr />

The peaceful atmosphere of the house prevailed even after the noon meal, although there was plenty to do to get ready for the Lord's Day.

Lucy made fast work of dusting and sweeping, surprising even Mamm. *Next thing she'll want me home every Friday,* Lucy thought, not entirely opposed to the idea. When she was finished and her sisters started wet mopping the floors, Lucy hurried over to Mammi Flaud's to clean her smaller house, too.

"Awful nice seein' you round here today," Mammi remarked.

Lucy felt different somehow, less inclined to rush off. "Feels real *gut* to be home for a change."

"There's a certain harmony when we all work together," Mammi said, a twinkle in her eye. "We feel rooted and grounded, ya know?"

Lucy understood.

While mopping the floor later, she was surprised to find last week's copy of *The Budget* lodged under Mammi's settee. Curious, she looked at the mailing address and realized someone had carried her parents' paper over to Mammi's. But why?

Lucy was a bit hesitant to bother with reading the newspaper on this day of reflection, yet once she had wrapped up her chores, she decided it wouldn't hurt to take time to read only Martie's column. She slipped out to the porch, where she looked up the page number, then flipped to the column.

The month is nearly gone. We've had some heavy soakers lately, making it difficult for farmers to harvest their corn.

There's a new baby boy at the home of Jim and Mary Blank, James and Rhoda's son and daughter-in-law. Father and mother are happy for a son after four daughters.

We've had a frequent visitor in our area recently—a Good Samaritan who continues to show up in various places, even helped Abe Riehl right his overturned buggy and got his children home safely following a terrible accident on a rainy Saturday afternoon recently. This very Englischer has been spending a lot of time at my father's house, gathering tips on woodburning stoves, going green, and building a chicken coop. Seems like he's fast becoming one of the family!

"Wha-at?" Lucy cried. "Martie wrote about *Dale?*" She closed the newspaper and sat there, stunned. What could have persuaded her to share such a thing?

She groaned at the thought of the entire Plain population of the country reading this. Not to mention the local ministerial brethren!

Getting up, she walked around the house to the back door, knowing there was no way to shield her family from reading Martie's account. *Likely they've already seen it.*

Yet if so, why hadn't her parents, at least—or the twins—said anything about this? Surely even Mammi had read it.

Nonetheless, Lucy knew precisely where she was going to take herself off to, and right this minute!

When Lucy neared Ray and Martie's, her sister was outside pushing the stroller down the lane, coming this way. She looked downright sad.

"What's a-matter?" Lucy called.

"Ray talked frankly with me yesterday 'bout Colorado. He definitely wants to move, but not till the twins are at least toddlers." Martie seemed to need to pour out her heart. "So it won't be for a few years yet. Says he wants me close to family while the twins are babies."

"What a huge relief for you." Lucy hated the thought of Martie leaving, even if it was a couple of years from now. She fell into step with her sister, wondering how far down the uphill lane she would go with little Josh babbling in the stroller and Jesse walking alongside.

How many more people must I say good-bye to?

"I'm surprised to see ya." Martie smiled momentarily. "Did I schedule you to work today?"

Lucy shook her head. "I just needed to know somethin', sister, if ya don't mind. Why'd ya write what you did in your recent column? The brethren will be all over Dat, for certain.".

"That wasn't my intention, but . . ." Martie stopped walking and turned the stroller around so they could head back toward the house. "I'm worried 'bout you, Lucy . . . others are, too."

"I've really enjoyed Dale's company. He's helped me in more ways than anyone can possibly know . . . or understand."

"But close friendship often leads in a different direction, remember?"

"Still, I'm not a child anymore." Lucy didn't mean to sound indignant.

"Honestly, I never dreamed that little snippet I wrote would trouble ya," Martie said more gently now, her eyes serious. "I should've taken you into consideration."

Lucy couldn't imagine bearing a grudge toward sweet Martie. "I forgive ya, sister. I do."

Martie motioned for her to join in pushing the stroller, hands nearly overlapped as they walked to the house.

I wonder how long before one of the preachers talks to Dat about this . . . if someone hasn't already, Lucy wondered.

───────

The minute Lucy had left for Martie's, Christian felt in his bones that it was time to hitch up the old buckboard and head to Dale Wyeth's hardware store in town. After exchanging a casual greeting, he put it right out there. "The church brethren fear you'll get our Lucy shunned."

Dale's eyes widened. "I wouldn't think of jeopardizing your daughter's standing."

"Well, you two *have* been quite friendly."

Dale nodded. "Yes, I'm fond of your daughter."

Christian set the record straight. "Then, you must surely know that Lucy has been baptized. She cannot marry an *Englischer* without dire consequences."

"I see," Dale said, his expression solemn.

Christian studied the man, this most gentle and thoughtful soul. A thought came to him. "May I ask—are ya thinking of goin' Plain, then?"

Glancing over toward the register, where several customers were waiting in line for the clerk, Dale folded his arms. "Hadn't considered that."

Christian pondered this frank exchange and wondered if he ought to say what he was thinking about Jerry Glick's boy. It couldn't hurt, not if it caused Dale to think twice when it came to pursuing Lucy.

"Since you've spent some time with my daughter, maybe she's mentioned her longtime friend Tobe Glick."

Dale shook his head. "She hasn't, no."

"Well, if you ever run into her again, you might ask 'bout him." He threw it out to Dale, hoping he might say something to Lucy. If Lucy was honest about Tobe, maybe then Dale would skedaddle out of her life without need for further confrontation.

All the same, Christian felt downright *ferhoodled* during the drive home. Just when he'd started to consider Dale a fine friend, the tables had been turned. *On Lucy, too.* Was God putting her to the test with yet another outsider? At the thought, Christian fidgeted with the driving lines. Was God testing *him?*

He directed Sunshine to move to a trot, unable to interpret Dale's baffling response to his visit. The young man definitely hadn't denied any romantic leanings toward Lucy. Christian could only hope their man-to-man talk didn't make Dale all the more determined.

Have mercy, O Lord!

CHAPTER 42

LUCY WAS SURPRISED to see Deacon Miller's eyes light up when she arrived at his farmhouse in the pony wagon the next afternoon. His wife, Annie, smiled warmly, inviting her inside. She led Lucy to sit at the kitchen table with the deacon before returning to rolling out piecrusts for the meal to follow tomorrow's communion and foot-washing service, which would last nearly all day.

"There are things I've needed to tell ya, Deacon . . . things I held back," Lucy said, beginning her freewill confession. "I'm sorry it's taken me this long to be ready." She was astonished at how much easier this was than the last time. Coming clean was required in order to partake of communion, and having finally asked God's forgiveness with a contrite heart, Lucy felt free now to reveal her past misdeeds to Deacon Edward.

The deacon was sympathetic yet firm when he posed his question. "Why did ya withhold a full confession back then?"

Lucy hung her head for a moment, breathing a prayer for divine help. "I was too embarrassed to tell all, and angry at my father for forcing me and my *Englischer* husband-to-be apart—and for makin' me leave to live faraway with a relative I didn't know. But I realize that's a poor excuse, and I ask your forgiveness. My relationship with Travis Goodwin was something I chose, and I don't blame anyone else for the consequences. You see, Travis was not only my fiancé . . . he was also the father of the baby I lost to miscarriage." As she said the words, a sense of relief—and peace—washed over her.

Deacon nodded his head slowly, eyes moist. "Lucy, the fact that you have come to confess on your own, without persuasion, indicates you are sincere in your repentance."

Lucy bit her lip. "I surely am." She expected he might put her off church for several months or longer, which she certainly deserved.

He paused. "Have you forgiven your father for the past?" His eyes pierced her. "Because as I see it, that may well be the very next place to start."

Lucy bowed her head, acknowledging his wisdom. She waited for his pronouncement of punishment.

But none came. Instead, Deacon Miller encouraged her to join the membership for communion and foot washing tomorrow, if her heart was ready. "Will you be amongst us?"

"It's a kindness I certainly wasn't expecting, Deacon," she said gratefully. "I prayed the prayer of King David yesterday, and I trust my heavenly Father to forgive me."

The deacon smiled. "He alone is faithful to cover our sins."

Later, when she said good-bye to Annie, Lucy was amazed that the deacon had said nothing about her friendship with Dale Wyeth. *He didn't even hint at it.*

<hr />

Feeling nearly weightless, Lucy was tempted to skip to the pony cart. She was deeply affected by the acceptance and compassion Deacon Edward had so kindly demonstrated. Now she wished she'd had the courage to do this years ago.

Back at home, Lucy washed her hands and helped Mamm with supper preparations while the twins worked with Dat in the barn. Her heart warm, Lucy even asked if they might include Mammi tonight for the meal. "I think she'd really like that," Lucy said, eager to hurry next door right away with the news.

"By the looks of ya, dear, I think *you'd* enjoy it most," Mamm said, grinning. "You're all aglow."

"Confession's *gut* for the soul, Mamm. I never knew what that meant till now." She sighed, wondering how her mother would respond to what else she had to share. "And that's not all: I also talked to the deacon today—made things right at last."

Mamm's eyes filled with tears. "Then I 'spect you'll be present tomorrow?"

Nodding, Lucy said, "Our family is united in preparation for the remembrance of the Lord's Supper."

Mamm moved to embrace her. "Oh, my dear girl, *Gott* has truly answered my prayers."

⁓

Twilight would be falling soon, but Lucy waited till after supper that night to talk to her father, knowing he would go out to check on the livestock one last time before family worship.

A scrap of the setting sun was still visible over the distant ridge—a brilliant benediction to the day. Chipmunks and birds would soon have a heyday in the clearing behind the woodshed, looking for the bits of nuts Faye regularly spread out at dusk.

Thinking of the deacon's kindly reminder, Lucy made her way to the stable, where she found Dat grooming Sunshine, humming a hymn like Jerry Glick often did, only more softly.

Her father looked up, eyes registering happiness.

"I've come to apologize," she said, going to the gate and leaning on it as he had done another evening. "I know this is rather late, but I'm sorry I brought shame on you and Mamm . . . and disgrace to our family."

"Oh, Lucy. Of course I forgive you." He put down his curry brush and went to her, standing on the other side of the gate. "Pushing you away was the worst thing I could've done. It caused further pain for you . . . for both of us." His look was supportive, the light from the large barn lantern creating a golden sheen around him. "I've earnestly prayed that you'd forgive *me* one day, as well."

She saw the fervor on his face. "I do forgive you, Dat. And now I realize why I waited so long. I was tryin' to pay penance for my disobedience." Lucy touched the back of his hand, and he placed his on top of hers and clasped it there. "It means so much that you loved my poor baby enough to attend the grief classes, Dat. I've never told ya, but it truly does."

He shook his head. "Losin' your little one thataway was mighty distressing, and I grieved sorely." He paused, patting her hand, then reached to open the gate to the next stall. "But that's not why I started goin' to the Thursday night meetings."

Lucy absorbed this. "Was it Dawdi's passing, then?"

Her father's chin trembled. "As difficult as losin' my lifelong best friend was . . . *nee*."

She was puzzled. What other reason was there?

Dat turned to pick up the lantern, moving to Caney's stall now.

"Why *are* ya goin', Dat?" she asked, gathering up the grooming items from Sunshine's stall and carrying them over.

He stroked the horse's mane. Then, looking her way, Dat said softly, as if struggling to contain his emotion, "Because I'd lost *you*, daughter."

Lucy let out a little gasp, and seeing him stricken there, she ran to his side.

Slipping his arm around her shoulders, her father whispered, "'Tis all right now. Everything's gonna be fine."

CHAPTER 43

YEARNING TO GO OUT WALKING, as she often did at dusk, Lucy wanted to process all that had taken place these past days . . . especially the cherished moments between her and Dat.

She turned south past Uncle Caleb's farm and beyond, recalling the evening Tobe and his dog, Spotty, had come this way . . . and their difficult conversation. Seeing carriage lights, she moved farther off the roadside, carrying Dat's flashlight directed at traffic for good measure.

The moon was on the wane, which made it easier to see the stars—luminous dots of light against the ever-darkening sky. She swung her arms as she went, hankering to see the Glicks' big farm, recalling the fun she'd had there as a child—playing in the vast haymow, flying through the barn with Tobe on the rope swing.

"What can it hurt just to wander over there?" she murmured, supposing the Glicks might be gone yet.

Crickets still chirped in the ditch along the road, since there had been no frost. High overhead, an airplane rumbled past, drowning out the pastoral symphony. The familiar narrow lane appeared, and she turned in, noticing the glow of gas lamps in the front room and the kitchen behind. She thought of turning back, but seeing the Glicks were home, Lucy decided she might better explain her reasoning to Tobe—why she hadn't accepted his courting invitation.

A raccoon scuttled across the driveway as she strained to see past the barnyard. Picking up her pace, she spotted Tobe in the stable door, reaching high for the hayfork.

She hurried toward him, unsure what she might say if his father or his older brothers were also present.

But it was only Tobe who turned and saw her coming, his eyes wide as he motioned her inside.

"*Denki* for your note," she said first off. "It was nice to know what you'd be doin' out in Colorado."

His brown eyes shone in the lantern's light. "Mighty nice seein' ya, Lucy."

"How was your trip?"

He laughed a little. "It was a long time getting there and back, and not as much time in Colorado as I would have liked." He reached up to remove his straw hat and rubbed his neck. "Monte Vista is like a whole different country, really. Mighty dry . . . no humidity to speak of. And the altitude is higher than here—makes your skin prickle. The town is in the shadow of two narrow, jagged mountain ranges. *Ach*, I wish I had some pictures to show." He pointed in the direction of their eastern hills. "There's no comparison to those."

"Plenty of land, too?"

He nodded. "I wish you could see those wide, open spaces . . . even the sky looks bigger there." Tobe paused thoughtfully before he continued. "Dat had all his options lined up before we ever arrived . . . had a clear idea of what he wanted. He made an offer on nearly a thousand affordable acres, which we'll split with several families. The seller accepted right away."

So this seals it, she thought. *Tobe's really leaving.*

"Lucy? You look sad."

She made herself smile. After all, this was to be a happy time for his family. Quickly, she mentioned that Faye was also planning to go to Colorado with the Masts, at Mark's request. "Quite honestly, I dread bein' separated from her," Lucy said, heavyhearted.

"Mark and Faye must be real serious."

"*Jah*, and it's no secret now. But what a *wunnerbaar* new beginning for her . . . and for all of you." Forgiveness was like that, too—a clean slate, she thought.

"I heard that Ray and Martie and their family will likely join us, maybe in a couple of years." Tobe leaned on the hayfork.

Lucy grimaced. "You'll get to see little Jesse and Josh grow up." *And the twins yet to be born*, she thought with envy.

"Maybe your family will go out sometime to visit them." He sounded surprisingly hopeful.

She smiled. "I'd like that. Just glad the big move's not happening for a while yet."

Tobe shifted his weight and glanced toward the house. "Guess I'm fortunate my family can stay intact."

I'm happy for them. . . . She wished Tobe all the best in his new life, wanting it to be everything he hoped for.

Unexpectedly, he picked up the lantern and rested the hayfork against the wall, then waved for her to depart the stable with him. Lucy followed as they walked west, along the field lanes, out past the cornfield, to the large pond. They strolled along its border, Tobe caught up in telling about the ten-year-old Amish settlement in Monte Vista, about the initial challenge the Old Order community had had in creating a new church district. Most Plain families there were making a living raising hay and sheep, or building log cabins or storage sheds, and the women created home arts—crafts and food items—to sell. "There's a smidgen of tourism, but nothin' like here. Plenty of privacy."

As always, Tobe's optimism was appealing, and she lost herself in the rhythm of his words.

As they approached the opposite side of the pond, he brought up the large turnout expected for the church service tomorrow at the bishop's house. "My parents were worried we wouldn't get back in time for communion tomorrow." Tobe looked fondly at her. "Our last one here . . ."

The lantern's light dipped and danced across the grass ahead of them. Oh, she wanted to open her heart to him. Didn't he deserve as much?

Even so, the old arguments sprang to mind as she looked into his dear face. *Nee,* she thought. *Better that he remembers me like this.*

They made their way clear around the pond; then, still sharing about his Colorado adventure, Tobe insisted on seeing her safely home. And Lucy was more than content to accept.

Christian read beyond the usual number of chapters from the old *Biewel* that evening, taking his time. Now and then, he glanced at Lucy, grateful for their renewed father-daughter relationship, mended over the course of a few days.

When they knelt for prayer, he used the *Prayer Book for Earnest Christians,* choosing a prayer of gratitude to read aloud before they silently said their rote prayers.

And long after the family had retired for the night, when the hush fell over the house, the verses Christian had read aloud from Ephesians lingered in his heart: *But God, who is rich in mercy, for his great love wherewith he loved us, even when we were dead in sins, hath quickened us together with Christ, (by grace ye are saved). . . .*

A chill was in the air early Lord's Day morning as Martie made her way across the bishop's walkway, toward the line of women waiting to go into the temporary house of worship. Colorful leaves floated down as she spotted Ray carrying little Josh and holding Jesse's hand, and her heart swelled with thankfulness for her husband.

Bishop Smucker and his wife were the hosts for the autumn *Gross Gmay*—"big church"—a solemn yet joyous gathering commemorating their agreement of unity and peace. And most of all, a time for renewing their dedication to God and to one another as a people set apart.

In all the years of her church membership, Martie had gladly embraced the spiritual journey that took place prior to the spring and fall communion services, and the time of reflection and recommitment to God and the church. This particular assemblage of the People would span morning and afternoon until close to four o'clock, when dairy farmers would return home for milking.

It did her heart good to see Lucy in attendance. *Blessed be the Lord*, Martie offered up as airy sunbeams poured through the windows.

A sacred time followed the singing when first the bishop, and then each of the ministerial brethren, reconfirmed his harmony with God and the congregation—the *Gmay*. Then, one by one, the rest of the membership declared peace with their heavenly Father.

After the two sermons, which centered on Christ's crucifixion, each member partook of the bread and the wine representing the Lord's body and shed blood.

Martie was heartened when Lucy went out of her way to choose Lettie as her partner for the foot-washing ritual. Martie well knew that Lucy had struggled with that sister's pointed remarks, especially the past few years, and since this was Lucy's first communion service since her return from Ohio, broken and despairing, Martie believed the choice was significant.

The People sang a hymn from the *Ausbund* as the members tenderly washed and dried one another's feet, the men and women separately. Martie could see Lucy's tears from where she sat as Lucy humbly stooped to wash Lettie's bare feet in the small tub of warm water, demonstrating more humility than had she knelt.

Mamm washed and dried Martie's feet, and when Martie had done the same for her, they each offered the other a holy kiss. Mamm's face was solemn as she said to Martie, "May the Lord God be with us," and Martie replied, "I say amen to peace."

Later, when it came time to reverently depart the house, checks and cash were placed in the alms box, a twice yearly collection taken up for the needs of the community.

Martie was delighted when, out of the corner of her eye, she saw Lucy open her purse and slip something in the box. It was one more indication that her once wayward sister had returned safely to the fold.

Yet what will Lucy do about her English friend?

Martie could only wonder.

CHAPTER 44

SEVERAL NEW HOSPICE PATIENTS had arrived since last Monday afternoon, the day of Dorothea Holtz's passing. Lucy missed seeing her pretty name posted on the door—*gift of God*, she remembered.

She also remembered how Dorothea loved hearing God's Word read aloud, so today Lucy had brought her own King James Bible, choosing several uplifting psalms to share with her assigned patients. *Life-giving words.*

Whenever she relived yesterday's celebration of unity with the People, Lucy felt peaceful, and she did her best to spread the same soothing balm to everyone she encountered today.

At the end of her shift, on the way through the soaring atrium, Lucy stopped suddenly at the sight of Dale. She smiled as she greeted him. "Are ya signin' up to volunteer, maybe?"

He chuckled. "I stopped by to see you, Lucy." They walked to the front entrance, where he held the door for her. "Do you have time for ice cream?"

"Sounds *wunnerbaar-gut*, 'cept I rode my push scooter."

He grinned. "One of the benefits of owning a pickup is being able to transport a pretty girl and her scooter."

Blushing, she wondered why he'd really come.

"We missed seeing you at grief group." Dale opened the passenger door and waited until she was settled inside.

Lucy waited for him to load her scooter in back, then watched him hasten to the driver's side and slide behind the steering wheel.

"I took time to read the study pages for that lesson," she said, without explaining her absence. "The theme grabbed my attention. That and some specific things you said last week, Dale."

"Well, I hope whatever it was made sense." They moved out of the parking spot and onto the road.

"*Jah*, things about faith which really got me thinkin'."

They drove through Bird-in-Hand and farther east to the Kitchen Kettle Village, Dale suggesting a stop at the Lapp Valley Farm Dairy and Ice Cream Stand. The day was perfect, the afternoon temperature still warm despite the position of the sun.

There, Lucy ordered peach ice cream; Dale chose pistachio. The quaint shops and cobblestone walkways were appealing, and she hoped they might stroll about for a while. Almost immediately, Dale proposed doing so.

The bold-colored foliage and eye-catching window displays made her look twice. Dale pointed out the fake black crows scattered around the area, some perched on baled hay. Lucy liked the harvest-themed decorations on store stoops—large block candles, gourds and pumpkins, and cute jack-o'-lanterns.

"I realize we haven't known each other very long," Dale said as he finished his ice cream cone. "But now that we're past the initial sizing-up stage, we've really clicked . . . become friends."

Lucy was quick to agree. "Your attention to Kiana and her son was a big part of it, ain't so?"

He shrugged, as if assuming anyone would have cared enough

to help. "And you, Lucy . . . what a caring young woman you are." He smiled at her.

She shrugged, feeling a bit timid.

They spotted a scarecrow wearing an Amish hat, and Lucy went over to look at it more closely. "You dressed like this once for a few hours, remember?"

Dale chuckled. "But I never wore the hat." He went on to recount how kind her Amish neighbors had been that terrible day, and how calm Lucy had seemed following the accident.

Calmer than I feel now, she thought. "You should try on the hat." She forced a smile. "See if it fits."

So he did, tilting his head comically. "What do you think?"

Their eyes met, and that quick, Dale was grinning. He looked out of place, and they both knew it.

He removed the hat. "I'm afraid this is the closest I'll ever get to being Amish." Placing it back on the scarecrow, he adjusted the hat carefully.

She was glad when they resumed their stroll. Goodness, but they'd gotten nearly too close to something, talking all around it.

"I wanted to see you today, Lucy . . . because I wish things could have been different for us." He paused. "You see, I would have liked to move past our friendship to dating and really get to know you. But I would never tamper with your church membership." Somehow, he knew about her baptism and their strict *Ordnung.*

Dale's words played over in her mind. *He's saying good-bye....*

They walked without speaking for a time, heading toward the exit and seeing a young Amish couple laughing and talking, apparently in love.

"Tell me about Tobe," Dale said unexpectedly.

She wondered how he knew, then quickly put it together. *Dear Dat, looking out for me.* Lucy smiled and began to tell about her childhood friend, sharing happy memories of school days and of having grown up with Tobe. She also mentioned his fine reputation amongst the People. "He wanted to court me, but his family's movin' out west."

"Tobe's leaving, too?"

She nodded.

"So you aren't interested—"

"It's hard to explain, really."

Dale stopped walking. "I wish you could see your face."

"Why?"

"Well, your eyes light up when you say his name."

"It doesn't matter." She shook her head sadly. "Not anymore."

"Listen, maybe it's not my place to say this, but we've shared some things. Mostly spiritual."

Nodding, she wondered what was coming.

"You once admitted to keeping God at a distance." His voice grew softer. "Like we all do at times."

She lowered her head. "I haven't given Him a chance. I know that."

Dale was slow to continue. "I guess I'm wondering if you've given *Tobe* a chance."

Lucy felt immediately annoyed. It wasn't his place to pry, to peel away at her private life.

And Dale seemed to realize that, too, his gaze turning apologetic. He raised his hands as if conceding. "Okay, okay. None of my business, right?"

She smiled. "It's *gut* we're heading home, *jah?*"

They walked toward the parking lot in silence, and in her heart, Lucy knew this was the last she and Dale would spend any time together. It was for the best, too, especially after coming so close to abandoning her Plain life to marry a worldly *Englischer*. Her parents were right; she really ought to be more careful.

Above all—and Lucy felt this strongly as she picked up her pace toward Dale's truck—she was actually fine with being single, if that was God's will. Even so, getting acquainted with Dale Wyeth had been an added surprise. *And a blessing.*

"Thanks for your helpful tips on simple living," he said as they drove back toward East Lampeter. "I'm ready to install my wood-burning stove next week."

"Congratulations," Lucy said, happy to hear it. "And thank you for helpin' me find my way back to grace."

He frowned slightly, but there was no need for her to explain. To think the Lord had used an outsider to point her in the right direction.

Her visit to see Kiana and Van was enjoyable, and Van made a point of telling her that all the barn kitties were coming to their back door, meowing and wanting more treats.

"Bud and Gracie warned us about that," Kiana said, referring to their sudden congregation of cats. "And also that the mice population will explode in their barn if we make a habit of feeding the cats."

"Well, I guess spoilin' the kitties for a little while won't hurt," Lucy said, ruffling Van's hair.

"Van is learning so much about nature . . . and God," Kiana told her during the horse-and-buggy ride as Van sat on Lucy's lap. She let him put his hands over hers while she held the driving lines.

Kiana looked rested, the dark circles under her eyes already scarcely visible. There was a new peachy hue to her cheeks. "Things are working out for me here." She told about neighbors donating small pieces of furniture, including a chest of drawers and table and chairs. And Bud had brought down the double bed from their guest room for Kiana to borrow, for the time being.

Later, after returning to the farm, Kiana invited Lucy inside to sit at the table, where she had sugar cookies on a plate and brought out some fresh milk. Lucy joked that she was fitting right in, showing such Plain hospitality. She asked what type of used car Kiana was considering and learned that Bud and Gracie had taken her over to the car lot to decide.

After the treat, Lucy wrote out a check in Kiana's name for a generous down payment, and Kiana wept at the amount. She got up right quick and opened a drawer near the sink and produced a homemade card. "Van liked the idea of red and pink hearts all along the border, so we alternated making them."

Van came over and pointed out the hearts he'd drawn and colored in. "Miss Lucy, Mommy's bestest friend."

"That's so dear," Lucy said. "And you must call me Aendi Lucy, like my nieces and nephews do."

"What's *Aendi*?" Van asked, his head tilted to one side.

"It means Auntie Lucy, sweetie," Kiana told him.

Lucy smiled as the little fellow ran back to his toys. "Is there anything else yous need?" Lucy asked.

"A hug before you leave would be nice," Kiana said. "I get at least two a day from Gracie, and, oh, the family devotional times Bud and Gracie have invited us to are just what my heart has been longing for." She lowered her eyes for a moment. "I've started drafting a letter to my father, by the way, hoping to share some of the things I've learned lately from the Bible." Here, Kiana paused, her lower lip trembling. Then, struggling with emotion, she continued, "Gracie tells me nearly every day, 'If it matters to you, Kiana, it matters to the Lord Jesus.'"

Lucy nodded. This sounded like something Dawdi Flaud used to say. *Or Clinton Holtz.*

"When ya get your car, bring Van over, and I'll introduce ya to my twin sisters and show you around our big farm," Lucy offered. "Maybe we'll take the pony wagon out on the field lanes, too. How's that?"

Van enthusiastically bobbed his head.

Before she left, Lucy opened her arms to Kiana, and Van squeezed in, too. The laughter in the little guesthouse brought grateful tears to her eyes, and a thrill of joy rippled all the way down to Lucy's toes.

CHAPTER 45

FOR THE NEXT FEW DAYS, Lucy felt remarkably satisfied staying home and helping Mamm and Mammi Flaud with fall housecleaning, as well as cooking and baking, leaving only to continue her work for Martie. She and a few other women, including her twin sisters and Mamm, as well as Cora and Emma Sue, pieced together a quilt over at Mammi Flaud's. Lucy realized she'd missed working alongside the womenfolk and delighted in seeing Mammi's quilt come together so quickly. They talked congenially together, eventually discussing Faye's plans to go west. Mamm wore a happy face, but Lucy knew it would be hard on her to have Faye so far away.

"Let's all go out there and visit her," Lettie suggested. "At least for the wedding!"

Mammi Flaud looked sad momentarily, and Lucy guessed she might not feel up to making the very long trip. Lucy's heart went out to her, and for the time being, she decided to slow her pace of volunteering, possibly including Lettie or Faye, or even Mamm herself from time to time.

On Thursday morning, before Lettie and Faye came downstairs for breakfast, Dat asked Lucy if she wouldn't mind skipping the grief support group to play Dutch Blitz with the family that evening. However, being a conscientious man, he encouraged her to read through the rest of the curriculum at a later date, which Lucy readily agreed to do. Neither of them brought up Dale Wyeth, but Mamm indicated that Dat planned to check in with him sporadically to see how he was managing the changes he'd made in his lifestyle. "Especially once winter's blast comes."

Each night, in the privacy of her room, Lucy included Tobe and his family in her prayers, asking God for wisdom for the families relocating to Monte Vista. She prayed for Faye and her beau, too . . . and for Ray and Martie. Going to a drought-ridden area would definitely be a test of endurance, a challenge she could not imagine. It was a relief to her, and to Mamm, that Ray had taken Martie and their unborn babies into consideration, deciding to wait before making the taxing move.

That Saturday, after reading to a new hospice patient, Lucy slowed her scooter and stopped at the footbridge on the way home. Warm memories of Clinton and Dorothea Holtz filled her heart, a testament to God's faithfulness.

Breathing in the crisp air, she wandered over the hilly area to the paved pathway toward the bridge. The peace she felt was almost tangible, and she was thankful beyond measure for her and Dat's reconciliation, as well as her reconciliation to the People as a whole. This included her growing relationship with Lettie, who admitted to hiding Martie's column under the settee at Mammi Flaud's in an attempt to prevent sisterly strife.

Daily, Lucy purposely embraced the blessing of forgiveness.

"My future is bright . . . even without a love like Clinton and Dorothea's," she whispered as she came to the bridge.

She walked right up to it and stood there, trying for a moment to put herself in youthful Dottie's shoes. Then, leaning on the railing to watch Mill Creek rippling past, she marveled at the tranquil, gurgling sound and the current carrying with it deep red and gold leaves, twigs, and seeds.

Losing track of time, Lucy reflected on her renewed faith and her precious family.

She heard a dog's playful yapping, then the jingle of its tags, and straightened as the dog came bounding over the rise toward her. "Well, hullo, Spotty," she said, bending low to pet him. "Where's your dutiful master?"

There was much panting and several foiled attempts to lick her face. Unable to resist his exuberance, she knelt to play with the dog, jokingly warning him not to fall into the creek. "You could end up clear down at Lancaster County Central Park and the roaring Conestoga," she said, thinking she ought to take the spaniel home. Would he follow her scooter, perhaps?

She picked up Spotty and cuddled him, then heard her name carried on the breeze.

Tobe was coming down the hill, grinning, the dog's leash in his hand. "Lucy," he called to her. "I see Spotty has tracked you down."

While Lucy held on to Spotty, Tobe snapped on the leash before setting him down. "This pup wants his freedom, and then when he's off the leash, he takes off runnin'. Honestly, I thought I'd lost him this time."

"I guess you just need my help keepin' track of him."

Tobe laughed, meeting her eyes. "Actually, I was hoping to run into you today."

"Me too," she murmured.

Spotty played in the grass while they enjoyed the sunshine,

talking over the past week since communion. It was Tobe who mentioned the foot-washing ceremony. "It was *gut* seein' you there again, Lucy. Really *gut*."

"I don't know when it's felt so *wunnerbaar* celebrating the Lord's Supper."

Tobe nodded, eyes serious. "I was prayin' for ya."

This was so like him—not mentioning the years of absences, supporting her with silent encouragement and prayers, giving her the courage to finally say what she knew she must. "I went to see Deacon Miller and his wife the Saturday before communion," she said timidly, finding her way. "There are some things I've been holdin' back . . . things I needed to own up to."

His expression softened, yet for a moment, she worried, *Will he reject me?*

Struggling with the likely consequences, she pressed on. "It's only fair that you know the reason I turned down your courtship offer," she said, tears threatening.

Tobe drew near. "You don't have to—"

"I want you to know everything," she said, continuing with her revelation to the deacon three years ago, and what she'd recently confessed. "You have no idea . . . such a mess I've made of my life."

"Lucy," he stated, "don't ya know . . . I've *always* loved you? Nothing in your past can change that."

She sniffled, brushing away tears. "But I didn't . . ."

"*Ach,*" he whispered, eyes bright. "Who amongst us is perfect, *jah*?"

She found only acceptance in his adoring gaze and could scarcely believe it. Spelling things out in prudent terms, she lowered her voice. "I would not be a lily-white bride. . . ."

Tobe touched her elbow, a tender gesture that soothed her soul. "You've been runnin' helter-skelter all this time, showing kindness and love to everyone else."

She nodded despite her tears. "S'pose I have."

"My dearest Lucy . . . isn't it time ya let someone love *you?*"

The past three years flashed before her—all the striving to be *good* enough, rushing about and filling up her hours, pushing God out of her life, and holding her family and Tobe at a distance.

He's right, she realized, overwhelmed by Tobe's affection.

He reached for her hand, and together they watched the water wend its way beneath the bridge. "I've prayed for this moment," he said, turning to face her. "I've had ya picked out for a long time."

She leaned into him, smiling. Oh, to be as composed as Tobe seemed! "I never imagined such a sweet acceptance, let alone redemption," she said, suddenly understanding that the love she was feeling for him must be, in some cautious way, an acceptance of herself. "I love you, too," she whispered. "Ever so much."

Just then, they heard loud honking and tires squealing.

"Spotty!" Tobe dashed away toward the road.

Lucy's heart was in her throat. She hurried to see if the dog was all right, and here he came scampering down the slope into Tobe's arms, his leash trailing behind him.

"Is he safe?" the driver called through his open window, his voice shaky.

"He's fine," Tobe assured him. "You stopped in the nick of time."

The elderly man nodded, then waved and headed slowly onward.

Well, for goodness' sake . . .

"Did ya recognize him?" Tobe asked, gripping the leash.

"Remember the gentleman here, on this footbridge?"

Tobe accompanied her to the parked scooter. She got on and pushed forward while Tobe and Spotty walked alongside.

"Was that the man?" Tobe asked.

She couldn't help grinning. "I'll tell you all 'bout it . . . while we're courting."

"We'll have plenty of time for that and many other stories during the long Colorado winters," Tobe said.

When we're wed, she thought, heart dancing.

"Together," he said. "Like we're s'posed to be."

She glanced back at the bridge and had a sudden burst of energy.

And Tobe ran to keep up with her.

Epilogue

"SLEEP, SLEEP, MY LITTLE ONE," I sang, rocking my firstborn—
the dearest infant boy I'd ever laid eyes on, all wrapped in the
quilted coverlet Martie had made years ago. *Baby Jerry . . .*

I walked to the window, not far from the cradle Tobe had built,
and watched the sky dimming, twinkling stars appearing. The
Sangre de Cristo and San Juan Mountains looked even more
majestic in the twilight, rock-solid reminders of God's blessing—
of getting us here safely five years ago, helping us learn to pipe
water in to irrigate crops, and helping us to blend our lives with
Amish of like faith and tradition already here.

It's a joy that Ray and Martie and their family—Jesse, Josh, and
their twin girls, Mary and Martha—live within walking distance
of us, and not far from Tobe's father and mother, too. We are a
small yet growing family and circle of friends . . . old and new.

I'd missed Martie terribly those first two and a half years as
I endured the wailing of springtime winds and snuggled near
the coal heater stove with my very caring husband, holding my
breath for each letter from home. I was skipping-happy when we
heard the news that Ray was finally heading to Monte Vista with

Martie and the children, ready to make the long, long journey to join us in this dusty, challenging world of vast cattle ranches and sheep farms, where jagged Blanca Peak rises high above the flat terrain.

Dat, Mamm, Lettie, and Mammi Flaud all came for sweet Faye's wedding to Mark Mast the year after Tobe and I moved here. They stayed with us for ten blessed days, marveling at the growing Plain community here, till Dat got restless and decided it was time to get Mammi home again, none of them the worse for wear.

Lettie is also married now with a baby of her own, having wed the bishop's eldest grandson. They are the busy beneficiaries of Jerry Glick's former dairy farm. Tobe and I delighted in being able to revisit his childhood home when we returned home for a visit prior to our own little one's birth six months ago. We spent hours walking all over the land, reliving our childhood fun. And we stopped by our footbridge, too, recalling Clint and Dottie's love story, amazed and grateful for the way the Lord brings couples together.

Faye and I have become much closer since coming here. What a surprise it was when we discovered we were both expecting our babies around the same time! Her son, Mark David, is going to be a hefty boy, that's for sure, having weighed in at nine pounds at birth.

As for my charity work, I still do occasional volunteering from time to time, though my reasons have surely changed, and I suspect as our baby son grows, I'll cut back even more. No longer do I strive to fill an empty heart, or to earn favor—favor already so generously given. These days, I give of my time to share the gracious love of the Savior, who was patiently waiting for me all along. Tobe and I have even found a few things we can do side by side!

The peace of twilight folded over my precious baby and me.

Turning, I placed him in his cozy cradle and stood there for a moment to make sure he was soundly sleeping.

As I walked toward the doorway, I spotted Tobe near. "I thank *Gott* for you every day, Mrs. Glick." He moved toward me, then took my hand in his. "My forever love . . . and the *wunnerbaar* mother of our baby." His eyes searched mine.

"I still cannot imagine havin' missed out on this life with you," I said in between his kisses.

Tobe chuckled as he put his arm around me and gently led me down the hall. "Did ya really think I was gonna let ya?"

Author's Note

IT HAS BEEN DECADES since Dave proposed to me at a redwood bridge amidst the shining green mountains of Colorado. That bridge has since faded but continues to stand as a symbol of that memorable anniversary, just as the footbridge in this story does for Clinton and Dorothea, though for a myriad of unique reasons.

A number of years ago, I began writing a novel titled *Beyond the Bridge*, which fictionalized Dave's and my love story, anchored in part by what we have always referred to as "our" bridge. And while that manuscript was eventually set aside for *The Shunning* and its sequels, I replanted a few of those original story kernels into this manuscript.

The idea of helping others as an attempt to atone for past mistakes was one I wanted to develop years ago but shelved. Then, more recently, Dave's and my cousin Kirsten documented on Facebook her selfless acts of compassion via numerous charitable organizations during "100 Helpful Days." Her lovely journey reminded me of that forgotten premise, and I adopted it for my character Lucy Flaud. Thanks, Kiri, for jiggling my memory!

Over the years, numerous people have encouraged me on

this writing path strewn with sleepless nights, joy, and tears. My insightful line editor of more than twenty years, Rochelle Glöege, has not only helped sort through scene sequencing, character arcs, and everything in between, but proficiently manages to bring out the best in my writing ability, something for which I'm ever appreciative.

No one can fathom the fun I have talking through title options or book synopses with my longtime acquisitions editor, David Horton, who cheerfully reads through each final draft prior to my novel's journey to the printer . . . and always catches the mistakes I strangely miss.

My gratitude also goes to my husband for sharing his experiences with the Salvation Army's soup truck and distributing food to the homeless—and making breakfast and lunch for *me* when I'm on a crazy-tight deadline. I also wish to thank Aleta Hirschberg for her account of reselling fine jewelry to a local establishment, Barbara Birch for proofing the final galleys, Hank and Ruth Hershberger for expert research assistance, and Beverly Fry for her help with information about hospice care. Elizabeth Birch was my junior grammatical assistant—thanks, Lizzie!

One of Mennonite Central Committee's faithful volunteers who wishes to remain anonymous shared with me essential input for scenes relating to Lucy Flaud's work in this book at MCC. So helpful!

With sincere appreciation, I acknowledge the distinguished Amish-related writings of Donald Kraybill, as well as the inspiration I gleaned years ago from the *GriefShare* curriculum and classes, which were a source of true comfort and healing after my mother passed away.

For the purpose of this particular novel, I have fictionalized the lead time for *The Budget* scribes (columnists), as well as shortened the time it would take to travel to and from Monte Vista from Lancaster County via train and van. (Not a round trip Amish would likely make within the space of a week!) Also, the hospice in this story is purely fictional, and Clint and Dottie Holtz could not have visited the Bird-in-Hand Bake Shop when they were courting, as it was founded in 1972. However, I am very fond of the place, so I included it.

To the diligent and remarkable Bethany House marketing team headed up by Steve Oates—also my tour manager since 1998—I offer my thanks for this incredible journey. Each of you has supported my work in ways too plentiful to recite here.

My prayer partners are a constant source of support, absolutely essential for each new story waiting to be birthed, as well as the latest releases wending their way to readers to inspire, heal, offer peace, and increase faith. I am grateful for all of you!

Finally, to my children—Julie, Janie, and Jonathan—and granddaughter, Ariel, your dear love, interest, and prayers (and cheering me onward!) mean more than you can ever know.

Soli Deo Gloria!

Beverly Lewis, born in the heart of Pennsylvania Dutch country, is the *New York Times* bestselling author of more than ninety books. Her stories have been published in eleven languages worldwide. A keen interest in her mother's Plain heritage has inspired Beverly to write many Amish-related novels, beginning with *The Shunning*, which has sold more than one million copies and is an Original Hallmark Channel movie. In 2007 *The Brethren* was honored with a Christy Award.

Beverly has been interviewed by both national and international media, including *Time* magazine, the Associated Press, and the BBC. She lives with her husband, David, in Colorado.

Visit her website at www.beverlylewis.com or www.facebook .com/officialbeverlylewis for more information.

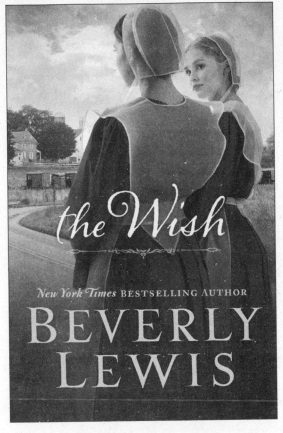

The Wish

The Next Novel From Beverly Lewis

AVAILABLE FALL 2016

More From
BEVERLY LEWIS!

Visit beverlylewis.com for a full list of her books.

Old Order Amishwoman Eva Esch feels powerfully drawn to the charming stranger from Ohio. Will the forbidden photograph he carries lead to love or heartache?

The Photograph

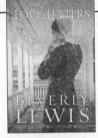

When Marlena Wenger is faced with a difficult decision—raising her sister's baby or marrying her longtime beau—what will she choose?

The Love Letters

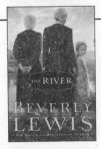

When two formerly Amish sisters return home for their parents' landmark anniversary, both are troubled by the past and the unresolved relationships they left behind.

The River

Also From
BEVERLY LEWIS

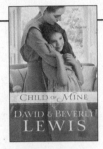

Kelly Maines has never stopped searching for the daughter who was taken from her. Eight years later, will she find her at last?

Child of Mine (with David Lewis)

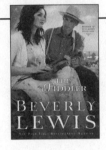

Journey home to Hickory Hollow, the setting where Beverly's celebrated Amish novels began in *The Shunning*! With her trademark style, this series of independent books features unforgettable heroines and the gentle romances her readers have come to love.

HOME TO HICKORY HOLLOW: *The Fiddler, The Bridesmaid, The Guardian, The Secret Keeper, The Last Bride*

BETHANYHOUSE